Ujjal Dosanjh was born in the Jalandhar district of Punjab in 1946. He emigrated to the UK in 1964 and from there to Canada in 1968. He was Premier of British Columbia from 2000 to 2001 and a Liberal Party of Canada Member of Parliament from 2004 to 2011, including a period as Minister of Health and Minister Responsible for Multiculturalism, Human Rights and Immigration. In 2003 he was awarded the Pravasi Bharatiya Samman, the highest honour conferred by the Government of India on overseas Indians.

The Past Is Never Dead

A Novel

UJJAL DOSANJH

SPEAKING TIGER

SPEAKING TIGER BOOKS LLP
125A, Ground Floor, Shahpur Jat, near Asiad Village,
New Delhi 110049

First published by Speaking Tiger Books 2023

ISBN: 978-93-5447-495-8
eISBN: 978-93-5447-493-4

10 9 8 7 6 5 4 3 2 1

Typeset in EB Garamond by SŪRYA, New Delhi

Printed at Shree Maitrey Printech Pvt. Ltd., Noida

The past is never dead. It is not even past.

—William Faulkner

Prologue

'Our ancestors would slaughter you people at the altar... Our orders were to kill you...remember that,' said the voice, as if they'd done him a favour by letting him live.

That voice—the only voice that had spoken to, or rather at, him—had constantly hurled obscenities for what seemed like two days now. The vehicle in which they travelled sounded and felt like a small delivery van. It eventually dumped him on a gravel road—as the voice had instructed its companions.

After a few minutes of lying inert, counting to two hundred and not to a thousand as he had been told, he removed his blindfold and opened his eyes and realized he was several miles away from home. In the dark and cold winter night he walked through the fields, bushes and across short-cuts. His limbs were near frozen. He found the pay phone he had remembered seeing earlier once by the road he was on now and called a taxi which took him home to 2 St Leonard's Ave, Bedford.

Once in his room, he wrapped himself in blankets, sat on his bed and looked out. Across the street, beyond the four-foot-tall brick wall, stood the deserted St John's Railway Station and a red telephone booth near its entrance. He had used the telephone there scores of times. His ears remembered the clanking of the coins falling through the slot. The steadily falling snow appeared less than white, discoloured. The station lampposts shone dim, much dimmer than usual. He prayed for a storm—a rainstorm, typhoon, earthquake, snowstorm, any storm. Anything! Something to wash everything away.

After a mysterious disappearance of over twenty-four hours, he had just returned home.

'Everything all right, son? Can I come in?' said Udho after knocking on his bedroom door, his voice muffled. Kalu heard the lump in Udho's throat. He jumped out of bed and locked the door.

'No, Bhapa. I'll see you in the morning. I've already told you, everything's all right,' he said, clutching the doorknob tightly in his right hand. His head touched one of his turbans hanging by the hook on the door. His body trembled as he turned to look at the mirror on the dresser. He thrust his clenched fist into it. The mirror cracked, but no shards fell off.

'Son, what was that noise? Everything all right?'

Kalu put his hands on his heart, afraid his father would hear its agitated pounding. He knew his father hadn't believed a word he had said. The countless fragments of the fractured mirror reflected his naked body, dissected by the cracks. His hands moved from his heart to his head. The touch felt odd to his hands. He looked into the mirror again. It showed no hair on the face, the head and the rest of the body, except at the crotch and some by the armpits. His legs wobbled under him. His hands moved to feel his neck and its hairless small. He noticed the marks of the turban on his forehead. His facial skin that normally hid under his turban was lighter compared to the darker brown on the rest of his face. The black birth mark on the left side of his forehead stared at him; without the Sikh turban, the hair on his head and beard, the birth mark was visible, and his Chamarhood felt exposed. In the corner of his eye, he could see the solitary bulb hanging from the wire on the ceiling.

He thrust his fists into his eyes and turned away from the mirror. When he dropped his fists, his eyes opened to a portion of the wall above the headboard. Framed portraits of Ravidas and Ambedkar, deemed deities for the *untouchables*, looked down at him. In the dim light of the ceiling bulb, they looked anything but godlike. The garlands around their necks reeked of mortality; like nooses, they screamed death.

Kalu's eyes turned to the small framed black-and-white photo of Udho on the bedside table. He seemed to jump out of the frame, dressed as Kalu remembered him in 1942.

1

From the huddarory—literally a pile of bones outside the village, a carcass pit—Udho used to walk barefoot, carrying on his head the skins of dead cattle for leather, and meat for the night's meal. Banjhan had reduced Udham Singh to Udho: How dare the skinner of dead cattle expect to be addressed by a full name? Five-foot-seven, of light build, the light-skinned Udho worked the lands of zamindars and skinned their dead cattle for a puny share of the seasonal produce, the occasional used clothing and carrion.

Even as a child he saw how zamindars were always dressed in laundered, clean clothes, a symbol of their power and the fact that they owned the land and didn't work it themselves. One day, with his soft baby hands, Kalu felt Udho's bare callused ones, and his feet and their ruptured, dry soles, overgrown nails filled with earth and traces of dead cattle.

'Son, I don't want you to grow up a Chamar. You will never do what made my hands and feet like this,' Udho had said to Kalu.

After the hard and dirty work, in his spare time, Udho, like the zamindars, dressed in washed and clean clothes. 'The bastard thinks himself a zamindar,' Kalu had heard young and old zamindars say of his father. As far as Banjhan was concerned, Udho had no claim to clean clothes or to his humanity. He was a mere beast born to beasts, to serve the upper castes. He couldn't ever be allowed the right to even assert a right.

One night, a zamindar found one of his oxen stolen. He hired cattle theft-tracers, men who claimed to be specialize in determining who had done it. After a quick investigation, they fingered Udho.

'Why not? The man wears clean clothes. He has to have money!' the zamindar said when Udho was brought to him.

Standing nearby, Kalu picked up a broken piece of brick. His body tensed, the top half and head leaned right to swing back and hurl the brick at the zamindar.

'Kalu, no,' Udho yelled and held him back just in time.

The police came to Banjhan. Udho was summoned to the Dewankhana. He told Banti to keep Kalu at home as he set out from the Chamarli—the Chamar quarter of the village. But Banti was busy cooking in the rasoi, and the boy scampered off after Udho to the Dewankhana, where he hid behind a pillar.

'No, sarkar, I didn't steal the ox,' Udho pleaded with the policeman. He sat on the ground while the zamindar and three policemen sat on chairs.

'Look at this bloody Chamar's audacity to deny the crime! You know, right, how we'll get a confession out of you?' shouted the policeman in his khaki uniform and striped red and blue turban. Kalu's heart pounding, from running all the way from home, raced at the insult.

'Sarkar, please don't talk like that. I'm an honest man. I do an honest day's work seven days of the week.'

'A Chamar, not confessing to the crime...and he has the temerity to demand I treat him fairly!' said the cop.

'Sarkar, put me on trial if you want. But please don't abuse me like that...' Udho said. 'And please don't hurt me,' he said, bending his head. His body was his only possession, if that.

At that, the other two policemen rose from their chairs and kicked Udho with their shiny leather boots.

'Bastards! You can't do that to my father,' shouted Kalu, revealing himself from his secret perch behind a pillar. The turbaned cop rose from his chair and ran towards Kalu who dodged him around the pillars of the Dewankhana. The other two now pushed Udho's face down on the ground and beat him with their police issue steel-tipped bamboo lathis like they would beat maize to separate corn from cobs.

'Stop, please stop. You broke my bone,' cried Udho.

The lathis continued raining. Kalu picked up a broken brick and hurled it at the cop pursuing him. It hit the mark, throwing his turban off and opening up a bloody gash on his forehead. The zamindar sat him on the chair and tied a piece of his turban around the wound. The other two cops now abandoned Udho and took off after Kalu. In a few minutes, they returned without him, only to find a dozen men from the Chamarli carrying lathis, shouting obscenities at the wounded cop and the zamindar.

'We're only letting you go because Kalu asked us to save his father without hurting anyone,' said one of them.

The police made a hasty retreat. The men lifted and carried a writhing and moaning Udho. One of them thrust the red and blue turban of the wounded cop into his hands.

'Kalu got him good,' smiled Udho, lifting his head and grinding his teeth.

'Wish I'd stolen the bloody ox. At least I could go to a proper city doctor to fix my legs. The bloody things are taking forever to heal... I can't even work. We'll die hungry,' he said to no one in particular after the village hakim had massaged and splinted his legs for the umpteenth time in several weeks in their courtyard the size of the dining room in the house of the zamindar whose ox had been stolen.

'I'll go to more zamindar households to make cow dung

pathiyan. We'll get their leftover food in the evenings,' said Banti, feeding Kalu the leftovers from the night.

The hakim's treatment went on for another few weeks. Udho could walk around now.

'No pain now, hakimji. But the limp in the left leg... what about this?'

'Can't do anything about it. You should feel lucky you're not dead,' said the hakim after the last massage. He then turned to Kalu and said, 'And well done, son, for splitting the bloody cop's head open.'

Realizing that the cops had given him a limp for life, Udho turned to Banti and said, 'From today, you will not make any more pathiyan for those zamindar dogs...I wish I could skin those cops alive,' as his eyes surveyed the knives and cleavers he had used all his life on the dead animals.

A few weeks after he resumed his deboning and skinning work, Udho heard from Bali the cobbler that Gandhi had launched the Quit India Movement. The year was 1942 and Gandhi was asking the British to leave the country. The village organized a demonstration in support of Gandhi's call. Udho, Kalu holding his finger, walked from the Chamarli to the Dewankhana. Half of Banjhan's men stood around the spot where the cops had broken Udho's leg; there were none from the Chamarli. As Udho and Kalu stood at the periphery and waited for the march to begin, a voice yelled from the chattering crowd, 'No untouchable allowed. Get lost, you Chamars.' The chattering turned to silence. Reluctantly, the limping Udho allowed Kalu's tiny hand to pull him away.

Within days, Udho borrowed money from a kind merchant, bribed the officials and got a passport. In a twisted irony of fate, a man who had wished to participate in the Quit India movement to rid the country of the British, left for Britain. After working a range of low-paying jobs, from janitor to watchman, in different towns, he settled in Bedford, at the Britannia Iron and Steel works on Kempston Road. As a precondition to being hired to do the heavy manual labour he had to remove his turban, trim his hair and shave his beard. Having been a turban-wearing Sikh in Banjhan hadn't brought him freedom from caste or hunger; working in the Britannia foundry perhaps would, he believed.

His strong and large bare hands, which once skinned and deboned Banjhan's dead cattle, were grateful for the foundry issue gloves. The work was exhausting, the pay good. He lived less than a hundred yards from the St John's train station and about a fifteen-minute walk to the town centre with several other tenants, all Punjabis.

'I'm not living in the same house as Udho Chamar,' Mulakh Raj had yelled, pulling out his janeu, the sacred thread the Brahmins wear.

'Raju is also a Chamar. You eat what he cooks,' said the landlord.

'Why didn't you tell me?'

'You know now. Why don't you leave? Udho's and Raju's pounds are the same colour as yours.'

Mulakh Raj, also from Banjhan but a graduate of the Punjab University, worked at the Stewartsby Brickyards. The tenants all took turns cooking and cleaning. Though he initially balked at the prospect of Udho the Chamar touching his dishes, let alone cooking for him, Udho soon became the favourite of the household. Mulakh would often joke how they ought to band together to start an Indian restaurant.

'Only the goras would eat food touched by me,' Udho would say, but in his heart he was delighted that the Brahmin Mulakh, who had never even sat next to him in Banjhan, was now his friend. He also helped Udho learn English, the inherent urge for acceptance helping to rationalize his actions.

The heavy work of lifting and pouring molten ore into moulds fetched a heavy pay packet. Soon, Udho bought a home on St Leonard's Avenue overlooking the St John's station and the red telephone booth, a few yards away from the home in which he had been a tenant. He urged Mulakh to move in as a tenant into his home but Mulakh declined. On weekends Udho would go to his home. The two would together walk into town over the River Ouse bridge to buy groceries. While Mulakh would return home, Udho would go to the library and try to make out the news in the newspapers at the County Library Reading Room. Before long his English was good enough to do the daily household chores—buying, selling and bargaining—by himself. His life in Britain had found its groove. It was finally comfortable but not yet complete.

'I miss you and your mother,' he would write to Kalu in every letter home.

2

A scrawny seven- or eight-year-old—no one in Banjhan's Chamarli kept a written record of births or deaths—when Udho left for Britain, Kalu grew up in Banjhan. He attended the non-profit Banjhan High School. He and Udho corresponded regularly. Banti was illiterate. Kalu was her window to Udho and the world, and Udho's to Banti and Banjhan. Despite now being richer than many zamindars in the village, he was constantly belittled and reminded of his place in the huddarory.

'Skinning dead cattle, eating carrion and working the zamindars' lands is both your job and destiny. God made it so,' his Brahmin classmate Subhash had said to him once. Kalu clenched his fists and lunged towards him. Were it not for his friend Boota—also a Brahmin—telling Subhash off and holding Kalu back, one or both might have given the other a bloody nose.

The boy was the last of the three children Banti gave birth to and the only one to survive exiting her womb. She had named him Kahla—the Punjabi word for hasty, or in a hurry. Aptly named, for she was in a hurry for him to grow up, so he would take care of her and Udho. Kahla, for his part, was in a hurry to become educated, in order to prove he was as good as anyone else. He was in a hurry to be considered a human being.

Everyone in Banjhan Kalan called him Kalu—blackie. He wasn't black. Like the other children in Banjhan Kalan, he was brown, but they felt entitled to call him Kalu Chamar. 'You don't deserve any different,' they'd tell him if he objected. Even in school, he was branded. The school had very few students from the *lower* castes, and no one other than him in Kahla's class. Banjhan had willed Chamar to be part of his name and being. And the school was but a part of Banjhan.

Years passed. Kalu grew taller. But at five-foot-two, weighing a measly forty-five kilos at the age of fifteen, he was no match for his better-fed classmates. He was lucky to be studying in a school that provided students benches to sit on. The school had been established by a couple of rich landlords. They had donated the land and the money to build it, not wishing village boys to be corrupted by the liberalizing influences of the city. Education to protect and perpetuate privilege had, perhaps unwittingly, opened doors to change.

One day, he found a spot next to the Brahmin boy Rajinder Kumar. There were no fixed seats for the children to sit in their classrooms. But caste dictated a protocol they were far from oblivious to. As Kalu advanced towards the vacant seat, Rajinder, a tall and muscular Brahmin with short but healthy, black, oiled hair, moved over to claim the entire bench.

'Move over,' said Kalu.

'Oye, Chamar! Go sit on the ground where you belong,' answered Rajinder.

'You Bahman bastard,' shouted Kalu as he swung his right fist at Rajinder's nose. Rajinder fell down. The blood from his nose splattered, dirtying his clothes and the floor. The teacher yelled at Kalu before taking him to the headmaster.

'I won't have a Chamar beat up Brahmins in my school... Get lost for the rest of the week. And bring your guardian with you when you come back,' his headmaster told him.

It wasn't unusual for Kalu to get into fisticuffs with upper-caste students who, like Rajinder, were in the habit of insulting him for being a Chamar. Unless the scuffles gave him something like a swollen eyebrow which was impossible to hide, he kept his bruises and bumps concealed from his mother. With an absent Udho, he didn't want to cause Banti any further distress. Out of the class of thirty, only his friend Boota, a son of one of the teachers, called him Kalu without suffixing it with the customary 'Chamar'. Boota would come to his home, sit near the chullah and devour the food made by Banti. But Boota's mother wouldn't let Kalu near her home let alone the chullah. She would pour water over Boota to cleanse him if he ever admitted to touching Kalu or sharing his food. In the processions in the village commemorating the birth anniversaries of Sikh and Hindu deities, the Chamars and Chuhras—those traditionally confined to the 'menial' task of sweeping—walked at a distance from the rest, behind the procession. While Boota was his chum, he could never help Kalu gain entry to the temples or the front line of the processions.

The only place that fully accepted Kalu was the Chamarli. Though he was much younger than most of them, the group of men that celebrated Ravidas's birth anniversary each year at the samadhi, or shrine, were among his best friends. Kalu appreciated the message of equality in Nanak's '*Manas ki jat sabeh ek he pehchan bo*'—humanity is one—but he liked even better the Chamar Ravidas's promise included in the Sikh Granth: '*Aisa basaoon sehar main Jahan milay sab ko unn, chhote baro sab sum basain Ravidas rahey persun*'—an aspiration for a city where everyone had shelter and food and all were equal. Ravidas stirred something in him.

3

The statuette of the deity Kali Ma and her trident stared at Kalu from inside Banjhan's shivala every time he passed it by, reminding him of his exclusion from it. Goddess Kali's protruding, long and bloodied tongue seemed eager to devour him. In her several hands the blood-dripping sword, the severed head of a man, the spear drenched in blood, all seemed to spew menace. The evening conch felt like Kali's call to arms and the bells the awakening and summoning of Kali to slay, or at least to keep away, the likes of lowly Banti, Udho and him. At the mere sight of this Hindu place of worship, Kalu's body would stiffen even as his insides shook.

There was little difference in how he was treated at the Sikh gurdwara. After the evening prayers, the one-room gurdwara was usually locked up. Only the Khanda, the sword, and the Nishan Sahib, the religious flag, stood exposed like sentries protecting the place from unwanted intruders like him. When none could see, he would throw small pieces of broken bricks at the Khanda to knock it off its pole. It stubbornly survived.

The shivala on the other hand was open at all hours. In the dark of night he would slip in and ring the bell or blow into the conch. The ringing of the bell invited God to accept the devotee's worship, and Om, the sound of the conch, signified purity and brilliance. Having thus polluted the mandir with his untouchable-ness, like a robber defying the gods to steal godliness, he would slither into the winding alleys and streets of Banjhan. There was enough darkness in them to hide him and his offences against the gods and the men who held themselves to the former and occupy that place on earth. Of his nocturnal defiance of Banjhan's creeds he never breathed a word to anyone.

It was Mahashivaratri, 'the great night of Shiva', at the shivala.

'I'm going to wear my colourful clothes like every year,' Boota said to Kalu and Banti while sharing pranthas at their home in Banjhan's Chamarli.

'Can I come too?' asked Kalu.

Boota kept up his chatter, complimenting the pranthas he was eating each time he got one fresh off the tawa. But, pranthas finished, he left without answering Kalu's question about Mahashivaratri. Kalu had only ever witnessed the celebrations at the shivala and the gurdwara from the far edges. He mentioned Mahashivaratri to his friends from the Ravidas Brigade, his name for the men who celebrated Ravidas's birth. None showed any interest except Jeeta, who said, 'They'd consign you to the periphery anyway.'

The incessant ringing of the bells and blowing of

conches filled the air that night. Dressed in blue turban, blue shirt and white pyjamas, Kalu joined the chanting throngs surging towards the shivala. To some eyes he appeared a stranger they had never seen before, but then he could have been a Jat Sikh. Many of them wore turbans. As the shivala drew nearer, the chants became louder. He could see the bell over the heads of the men as he jumped up and down. The force of the crowd pushing to ring the bell carried Kalu along until he was a mere arm's length away, his arm raised in the longing to touch the bell. The priest screamed. The bell fell silent but not before Kalu had swung it. He saw blood in the priest's eyes; death flashed before his. He could imagine Kali's bloodied tongue hanging out of the priest's mouth. The crowd kicked and punched him, dragged him out past the edge of the temple, and pushed him to the ground, kicking and punching some more. He lost his turban, baring the birth mark on his forehead. It was as visible as his caste to the priest and the crowd. In the melee, he spotted Boota and his teacher father. Their eyes met his before they looked away. His friends from the Ravidas Brigade had to help his battered and bruised body home.

'What have you done to yourself?' asked Banti.

A slender woman of medium height, she kissed her son's forehead, placing her lips on his birth mark as if to say, 'Be content to be who you are. I want you alive.'

'How could they do this to you?' she yelled, examining his body and limbs. Of course, she hadn't forgotten what they had done to Udho's legs. Kalu was silent.

'Chachi, he polluted the shivala. They had to do something,' said Jeeta of the Ravidas Brigade who had stuck around.

'The mandir is meant for everyone. What right did they have...?' yelled Kalu's spirit from his pummelled body. If he had bombs, Kalu would have thrown them at the shivala and the gurdwara.

'Have you heard of Ambedkar?' Kalu asked Jeeta.

Jeeta shook his head sideways. He didn't entertain subversion against Banjhan. He liked Kalu but couldn't imagine the established order disturbed. He worked a zamindar's land and skinned dead cattle when needed.

Banti cleansed Kalu and nursed him. He rested inside the only room in the house other than the kitchen. The windowless room felt both like a fortress and a prison. He had dared to step out of it and over Banjhan's barricades. Banjhan had thrust him back into his place.

A few feet from him on the wall was the only photograph of Udho taken in Bedford. He had mailed it to them, his beard and turban still intact before he had had his haircut to work in the foundry. Kalu had read 'St John's Photo Studio, Bedford' stamped on it at the back. He wanted to be like his father. Udho's beard and turban seemed like a rebellion against Banjhan's segregation of the Chamars. While the turban didn't help in Banjhan, away from the village, it could give the impression, however mistaken, of sameness. There was hope, faint though it was, that Sikhism's tenet of equality may yet make its followers meaningfully embrace the anti-caste creed, he thought.

Banti was little help. 'I don't know. It's always been like this, son. Your father knew. But we got to survive, didn't we? Can't fight the whole village!' she'd say, readjusting her chunni as if to protect herself from Banjhan whenever Kalu asked her how she and Udho coped with its insults.

Several days after Kalu's lynching at the shivala, Boota came to his home.

'Where were you when they beat up your friend?' Banti asked Boota as she swept the kitchen, focusing her large eyes on him.

'Ma, he wasn't there,' shouted Kalu from inside.

Boota remained silent. Kalu squinted at him. Boota looked at him, then down, and said, 'Who told you to go there? You know the rules.'

'They didn't ask the Chamars when they made the rules. You want me there but you're afraid of them. You have to make up your mind whether you're my friend or not. You won't even tell your mother about visiting my home,' said Kalu.

Kalu knew Boota was a coward. But he couldn't hate him; only his cowardice. In silence, Boota sat on Kalu's cot, wanting to be forgiven by his friend. Kalu remained unforgiving. But after Boota left, he wondered why he shouldn't let go of his anger. Banjhan didn't impinge on Boota's freedom to be considered an equal. It might have been unfair of him but why would he want to disturb the balance? How could anyone blame him for wanting to preserve his privilege?

4

Kalu and Boota were walking back to the village, enjoying the freedom, kicking up dust. They had just taken the last examination for matriculating from the Banjhan High School. The leafy stalks and spikes of the wheat crop fluttered in the breeze. The Punjab prairie seemed a wavy green carpet verging on yellow. But they were temporarily blinded by the plume of dust left in its wake as a van drove by.

'Must be some rich bastard! Why can't he slow down?' yelled Kalu, shaking the dust off his shirt and pyjama before wiping it away from his face with his palms.

'*Haan.* Some city bastard showing off,' said Boota, rubbing his eyes.

Of Banjhan yet consigned to otherness in its Chamarli, to Kalu, the van seemed from a world entirely beyond his own and even his imagination. Unable to comprehend the van's presence on dirt roads amid mud houses, the momentary lack of vision induced by the dust felt in sync with his mind rendered impotent by the shiny chrome of the vehicle. He had never seen such a van even in the nearest city of Hoshiarpur.

The dust kicked up by the van settled. He and Boota continued towards the village, separating at the trisection, Boota turning towards Banjhan and Kalu towards its Chamarli. Kalu was alone on the quarter-mile stretch that separated his world from that of Banjhan. This separation was a stark reminder, if one was needed, of how he belonged to Banjhan though was not of it. Banjhan depended on its Chamarli, yet oppressed it. Banjhan needed it, yet abused it. In its continuing exploitation of the Chamarli lay Banjhan's survival. Kalu wondered how many more centuries Chamarlis like his would live in bondage to their Banjhans. He thrust his right foot into the dusty road and kicked it up, as if the plume of dust mirrored the rancour in his chest.

As he turned off the road towards his home he noticed the beige and brown van, absent the dusty plumes that had set his skull aflame with fury. It stood in front of his two-room home. He scratched his temple to stem the riot of thoughts that gripped his brain. It could be someone with a message from Udho or some bad news. But what? His mind raced, and his heart raced faster. The door of the two-room hut was wide open. On the cot a few feet away from the chullah, a man in a Western suit sat sipping chai. Two neighbourhood men chatted with him while Banti worked at the chullah. The man glanced at him in the doorway, walked over.

'Oh, Kalu, my son, you've grown up,' he said, and embraced him.

Seeing Kalu's body twitch in the man's embrace Banti shouted, 'Kalu, it's your Bhapa.'

Kalu dropped his satchel to the ground and began jumping up and down, eyes wide in disbelief. They jumped, yelled and danced in each other's embrace until Udho said, 'I love you, son, but can't dance any more. I'll have a heart attack.'

One of the two men with his father left. Binda, the man still there, grated on Kalu. Binda had no business sitting with Udho. He had been the bane of Kalu's short life. He would often find Binda with Banti when he returned from school unexpected. That he was part of Udho's family, though from a distant genealogical branch, gave him an excuse to hang around. Banti was about seven years younger than Udho, who had been away for over ten years now. Kalu hadn't thought much of Binda's presence early on. But as he became curious in his teens about things sexual, he understood what kept Binda around Banti. A young man now, at seventeen years old, he reasoned that the unmarried Binda and husbandless Banti probably needed each other. But it did little to relieve his long simmering resentment. Kalu wanted to kill him for sleeping with his mother. But that would have only brought more disrepute to the family. All that was hush-hush would then be talked about openly.

Right now, Kalu was still taking in the fact that he had just hugged his father for the first time in years.

'Bhapa, I missed you. Ma did too,' he said. He wanted to reassure Udho she was still his. Turning to Binda he said, 'Chacha, your nephew was looking for you.'

'Oh, really?' asked Binda, getting up.

'Yes, not lying,' said Kalu as Binda left.

'Bhapa, I want to enrol in college. School is finished,' said Kalu with a smile, reminding him of the final matriculation exam he just took.

'Yes, son. You'll go to college but not here...in Bedford. English education for my son!'

Kalu's mind turned to the beige and brown Volkswagen Westfalia camper beside his hovel. It had lashed him with dust. It was Udho's—theirs. He had called Udho Chamar, gone across the seas to earn a living, a rich bastard; to make it worse, Boota had heard him. He regretted that as he shook his head and looked down at the dirt floor of the yard. His hovel, his world, was the colour of the earth's dust. The brown van suddenly seemed at home.

'Bhapa, you brought this from Dilli?'

In Kalu's world, Delhi was the ultimate destination. It was everything. It *had* everything.

'From Germany, son. Mulakh and I drove it to Banjhan.'

'Mulakh, the Bahman Mulakh, Bhapa?' asked Kalu, his voice louder than before.

Mulakh's family had led the assault on him for entering the shivala and ringing its bell. He wondered if he ought to tell Udho. If he did it might wreck their relationship, he thought, and desisted.

'Kalu's Bhapa, Mulakh's family beat up our Kalu at the mandir. See how he left from the outside? The kutta Bahman...the idiot didn't even come in,' said Banti, freeing Kalu of the burden of deciding whether to tell Udho or not. 'Idiot' was Banti's name for anyone she didn't know or didn't like. Her use of 'kutta'—dog—meant she had nothing but hatred for Mulakh's family for beating Kalu up.

Father, mother and son sat, talked, ate and drank chai all day as the neighbours kept dropping in to meet Udho, to see what the country of goras had done to and for him in addition to the Westfalia, a sure symbol of wealth.

'Son, come with me,' said Udho next morning after breakfast. He walked to the Westfalia. Kalu followed. A huge smile on her face, Banti watched them get into it and drive away. Kalu's chest puffed out in the front passenger seat when the camper was on the road from the Chamarli to Banjhan. Kalu heard noises. He looked back. The children of the rich and the poor alike were running behind the camper in the dust, screaming with the joy of a newfound toy. The men and women watched. Neither a bus nor a car, and a Chamar driving it! The incongruity gripped Kalu's mind.

The vehicle stopped in front of Mulakh's home. For the first time, Kalu wondered why a Brahmin would want to name a child Mulakh—country.

The cheers of children of the neighbourhood and the sound of the van brought Mulakh out to the veranda fronting the large brick and concrete home. If the Westfalia had a mind and an eye for fitting in, it would have been comfortable there. The home and the van standing in front of it didn't seem to belong to different worlds. Udho took out Mulakh's baggage from the Westfalia. Kalu helped him. Mulakh and his son Deepak carried it inside, the same Deepak who with many others had attacked Kalu. Kalu looked him in the eye as the baggage exchanged hands. Deepak looked away.

'How about some chai together before we leave?' Udho asked.

Mulakh went inside.

'I'm not making chai for the Chamars. And I'm sure they didn't bring their own bhaanday...they aren't touching mine, not even for water,' said a female voice which could be heard in the veranda. It was followed by a further exchange in hushed tones.

Mulakh returned, sat on the only cot in the veranda, and said that the tea was coming. He then asked father and son to sit down, his right hand pointing to the concrete floor.

The Westfalia took the road to Hoshiarpur. In his navy blue suit, red tie, white shirt and polished black leather laced shoes, Udho bellowed in anger, 'Kutta Bahman. When I lived with him and others I cooked for all. I went to the market with him. He taught me English. We slept, ate and drove together all the way from Germany...' as he drove with one hand, the other's index finger piercing the air and the silence in the van.

'Bhapa, don't say kutta Bahman; dogs are loyal.'

They crossed several dry, sandy beds of the choes, seasonal rivulets carved by monsoon water gushing down the outer Himalayas, the Sivalak Hills—tresses of Shiva. Kalu had traversed many of them brimming with fast-flowing, waist-high water on his way to Hoshiarpur and Mahilpur on foot and by bus. Crossing them in the Westfalia was the stuff of dreams.

The camper stopped in front of a teashop with a hay roof.

'Let's have something to eat and drink. That kuttay Bahman's wife...he wasn't even man enough to shut the bitch up,' Udho said as they got out. The son felt the father's humiliation.

The chai was on the boil. Seeing them, the Brahmin owner doubling as the cook said, 'Panditji, take the seats over here,' and gestured for them to sit at the benches close to where he was. The irony of being addressed as 'Panditji' prompted father and son to glance at each other and smile. Kalu looked around. On a couple of benches at the back, separated from the others, sat two men in scruffy clothes, their spades resting beside them, eating their packed meals with chai from the shop. Chuhra and Chamar road workers of some contractor for the Punjab Works Department, he thought. He saw people from the nearby shops gather around the Westfalia. It made him feel a little less foolish about his own first impression of it. Udho ordered burfi and boiled milk.

'Bhapa, I want chai.'

'What? When I was your age, no one wanted chai if he could get milk.'

'The youngsters today don't know the value of milk,' chimed in the owner.

The camper, the people that stood by admiring it, him sitting on a bench where Brahmins would sit, swishing chai past his lips to down the bits of burfi, his father in a three-piece suit next to him—it all seemed rather unreal. The bench he sat on was of the same wood, of a similar design to the two at the back. But it felt different, better. He looked away from the Brahmin cook. He was troubled by his own silence enabling the false pretence of being Brahmin. He was unnecessarily pained, he felt on reflection, because what the country did to him and his ancestors was far worse.

But the incongruity of it all lingered in his mind until the van reached the travel agent's office. Across the table at his office in the trendy Sessions Chowk of Hoshiarpur sat the Jat owner of Sondh Travels, the short, rotund, turbaned and bearded Jagjit Singh Sondh. Next to the black rotary telephone on the table stood a fair-sized globe with a British Overseas Airways Corporation plane perched atop—'BOAC' blazoned in blue on it and a miniature Union Jack at its nose—dominating the room. Kalu vaguely remembered the mini demonstration in Banjhan during the Quit India Movement of 1942. Not allowed to participate, Udho and he had had to leave. But walking away they could hear the chants of 'Union Jack, down, down!' There was no

Tricolour in sight in this office. His and Udho's fate was tied to the Union Jack.

Jagjit smiled, shook their hands and asked them to take seats opposite him before shouting an order for three cups of chai to the tea stall next door. Udho handed Jagjit the documents required for passports for Kalu and Banti. The tea arrived. Passing a cup to Udho, Jagjit said, 'It's nice to see some Jats come to the office; usually only Chamars come. Hoshiarpur district is full of them.'

Kalu looked at Udho and Udho at Kalu, in silence. With the price for the passports and air fare for three to England settled, an advance given, they were back in the Westfalia and free—only Kalu couldn't decide whether to laugh or to cry. He had felt a similar ambivalence at the chai shop too. In Mulakh's veranda, of course, he knew exactly what he wanted. He wanted to kill. Udho had signalled for calm.

5

Kalu led his parents to Mahilpur's Dalip Studio, named after the heart throb film star. The family needed passport photos and police clearance for Kalu and Banti. Udho had asked his foreman for a leave of six months as passports often took a long time to be made even when bribes were paid. The foreman had granted him only three. Dilip Kumar's photo adorned the studio's main wall, one of the zillion reprints and part of the owner's 'I took it' sales pitch. Kalu remembered it from his previous visits to Mahilpur. He would walk by the studio admiring Dilip's portrait. When he had first cast his eyes on Udho's shaven face, he had thought he saw a bit of Dilip in it.

Born Yusuf, a Muslim, the film industry had branded

him Dilip to make him more acceptable to the Hindus. This evoked a kinship with him in Kalu's mind. As a Ravidasia Sikh he wore a turban and had a Sikh name, but none of it could erase his birth as a Chamar. Like the birth mark on his forehead, it was permanent. His future had been preordained several millennia ago. He often hummed a song from Dilip Kumar's *Andaz*: '*Uthaye ja unke sitam aur jiye ja / Yoonhi muskuraye ja, aansoo piye ja*'. Bear their abuse and endure; gulp back your tears and smile as you always do. But despite his predilection for the poetry of those words, he couldn't abide bowing willingly to so-called fate.

The passport photos shot, Kalu insisted on a family portrait of the three of them. It used to make him angry that poverty had forced separation upon them. Afraid of it recurring, he wanted to capture the moment in the studio. Banti did not want to sit as an equal next to Udho on the chair. The marriage ordained sleeping with him. Sitting next to him for all to see—no woman in Banjhan did that! She was the remotest thing from being a rebel and she relented. The photographer asked her to smile, which she did, but not before hiding her left index finger under her chunni.

The petite Banti with high cheekbones had the long-fingered hands of an artist one could be proud to exhibit. But she had severed the tip of the left index finger chopping vegetables shortly after she arrived in Banjhan as a new bride. Udho had rushed her to the small Mahilpur hospital on the carrier of a borrowed bike. Everyone who knew her knew about her nail-less finger but she didn't want it memorialized in their first ever family photo.

At the thana for police clearance, Kalu saw Udho squirm as he bought the 'free' forms before paying a professional application writer to fill them in. The writer informed them that the papers had to be greased all the way to the passport office. Udho recoiled at that.

'Bhapa, how could you forget...bribery...? It's even worse now.'

'It's not like this in England. I never had to pay even a penny in bribes there.'

With the Mahilpur police station fully 'greased', the next stop for their papers was the district police headquarters in Hoshiarpur a few days later. Kalu waited impatiently. The sunrises and sunsets didn't feel or look the same as before. They were symbols of movement, yes, but the sun was not moving nearly as fast as Kalu wanted it to. Udho tried to keep Kalu occupied by preparing him for the trip, sharing his own story and what Kalu could expect in his new life in England. Kalu didn't enrol in college. Instead, he travelled with Udho all over the district in the camper. Wherever they went, they and the camper were received and revered as royalty. It obfuscated caste. But they found that the Chamarli travelled with them even though the camper momentarily blinded everyone to it. So on short errands in Banjhan or its vicinity, Kalu would persuade him to avoid taking the vehicle.

'No need to deceive ourselves, Bhapa. Not so often,' he would say.

On one of those outings without the van, Kalu silently walked half a mile with his father on the dusty road to the khooh, or well, where Master Hazara Singh lived alone. Kalu had seen his father this quiet and reticent only when they had walked to the small place where the Chamarli worshipped Ravidas.

'Why are we going to see the Jat Master? He's a rapist,' asked Kalu, puncturing the silence just before they reached the khooh.

'Kalu, he's a good soul. He's redeemed himself.'

'Good soul? He raped a Chuhri—a cleaner, not a Jatti, his own kind.'

As a young elementary school teacher, Hazara had raped the young Chuhri sweeper at school. Saving his victim from having to testify, he pled guilty, going to prison for several years. Drowned in remorse, he returned to Banjhan in the late 1930s. The victim still unmarried, since none would marry a raped woman, her father offered and Hazara accepted her hand in marriage. He had recently lost her to old age.

Though Gandhi had only reluctantly allowed the former rape convict to join the Congress, he soon became the face of the Quit India Movement in Hoshiarpur. During the bloody Partition, he risked death to save Muslims going across the border from Hindu and Sikh marauders seeking vengeance, money or the depraved pleasures of the flesh.

To buttress his point, Udho reminded Kalu of an incident Banti had informed him about. 'Just before you came, Chamari Meeto was gang raped at Daulat's khooh. Hazara was the only one to raise his voice,' Banti had said.

'He's always been there for the untouchables,' Udho said to Kalu.

The wrinkled Master Hazara sat on a cot close to the solitary buffalo tied to the only manger. There were no oxen any more, but tall grass marked the circle described by the Persian wheel which oxen must have once worked. The khooh's kutta—the piece of metal bolted to the ground round which the wheel moved—battered and worn for the years of clanging on the rotating axle, stood rusted; the tinds that once brought water up from the depths of the khooh hung waterless. Udho bent down and touched Hazara's feet. Kalu folded his hands in a silent 'Sat Sri Akaal'.

'Udham Singh, I didn't think you'd come see an oldie...a convicted rapist at that,' Master said, the smile making the wrinkles on his cheeks all the more prominent.

'No, Chacha, I got busy with Kalu and his mother's

passports. I often thought of you even in England...your courage to challenge the British...and also yourself.'

'Nothing special about it. One just needs to feel guilty enough. And what do I have if not guilt! Every day Sidhi lived with me I begged forgiveness. I don't have too many days on this earth now.'

'Chacha, you look good for another ten years at least.'

'A white lie... By the way, Kalu, our Kahla Singh...this young man is the lion of Banjhan.'

'Not even of the Chamarli,' said Kalu.

'No, Kalu, I heard of you ringing the bell at the shivala. In Banjhan, even the gods are deaf!'

'Chacha, as soon as I get the passports I'll leave. You're alone now. Anything I can do to make your life easy before I go?'

'It's all good but come and see me once before you leave. We'll talk about this piece of land,' said Master pointing towards the grass in the tracks of the silent Persian wheel.

Kalu's feet wanted to linger. Promising to return, they walked back as silently as they had come.

Once at home, Udho took out the only bottle of Johnnie Walker he had brought. He had intended to use it as an incentive for some official to hurry Kalu and Banti's passports up. But he had used rupees for bribes, sparing the Scotch for himself. An occasional beer at the nearby High Street King's Arms with Mulakh was the only drink he allowed himself. After what Mulakh did in Banjhan, though, even that routine was set to be abandoned. Since the visit the morning after his arrival in Banjhan, Udho had not looked in the direction of Mulakh's home. His estrangement from Mulakh made him sad but the fact that his friend had turned out to be a two-faced Pecksniffian made him sadder still.

Banti could smell the drinks he poured for Kalu and himself from the kitchen.

'You're going to make my son an alcoholic... You never used to drink?'

'Kalu has to know what it's like. He might as well learn it at home.'

They held their noses as they quickly emptied the brass glasses into their mouths followed by sliced onion and a pinch of salt. Kalu's curled-up nose, bared teeth and loud breathing made the angry Banti laugh. As his first ever gulp of Scotch took effect, Kalu wondered what about that piece of land Hazara had wanted to discuss before they left for England.

6

Udho wanted Kalu to get new shoes. He thought of his own calloused feet which once had dirt and carrion stuck in their overgrown nails. He couldn't afford shoes for Banti or Kalu then, let alone himself. He remembered how Kalu had eluded the police after stoning a cop whose companions were breaking his bones to extract a confession about an ox he hadn't stolen. A smile planted itself on his lips as he imagined the barefoot Kalu outrunning and outsmarting the cops with polished leather shoes. Having spent his early childhood without them, Kalu didn't mind still occasionally walking barefoot even though he didn't have to.

Banti used to take Kalu to cobblers near Mahilpur, two brothers, who hailed from her village, Nangal, a mile away. Each time they went there, whether to repair, order or pick up the shoes, she would leave Kalu at the shop and walk away into Mahilpur. Soon, one of the cobbler brothers too would leave. She would return several hours later carrying a small amount of something she said she needed for the household. Too young to argue with his mother, Kalu would keep it all to himself. Two years ago, he had disrupted the routine and gone to Mahilpur by himself for new shoes, but to a different cobbler this time. He had told her he didn't need her to come along.

On Udho's orders, the son now found himself going to Baali, the cobbler in the Chamarli, to have his footprint drawn on a piece of leather from Banjhan's cattle, skinned and dyed by a Banjhan Chamar, for a fresh pair. Kalu would have ended up at Baali's with or without Udho. He had already been to his one-room shop. Its cosiness appealed to him, even though he found the smell of semi-raw leather hung outside repelling. But it was local and he didn't want to be reminded of Banti's escapades into Mahilpur. Udho knew Baali. They were contemporaries. For Udho, the closeness lingered.

'Come, come, Udho's son, let's measure you,' said Baali as Kalu bent to sit down on the elevated door sill. A piece of leather soon lay under his right foot. With a fat lead pencil, Baali drew a line around one grimy foot, then around the equally dirty other, and asked, 'Binda's been to your home to see your Bhapa? And you? Not going to Mahilpur with Banti this year...?'

Suddenly, the stench inside the shop was more putrid than that of the leather hung outside. Kalu lunged at Baali, pushing him to the ground and punching his nose, causing it to bleed.

'You bastard... As if it's some secret!' screamed Baali, wiping the blood off his nose.

'Shut your mouth! Or I'll break all your teeth,' Kalu said before leaving. He'd have willingly been devoured by the earth below if only he could will it to part.

The clouds hung lower than normal. The evening's darkness

couldn't descend fast enough. Kalu wanted to go to sleep under a quilt in the dark two-room home and wouldn't have minded never waking up again. Walking home he cursed the kerosene lamp Udho had bought from Hoshiarpur. It lit up their home. He wanted the dark to envelope him and hide him in itself. He wanted the household to return to the cotton-wicked, mustard-oil clay deeva. Not much light ever emanated from it.

Udho had gone to the Ravidas samadhi in the Chamarli. He talked to the men gathered there every evening before returning home for the evening meal. Tonight, Binda was at the samadhi too. Everyone talked, but he was quiet.

'I bet you don't go see Udho every day!' someone blurted at him.

The insult about Banti's philandering in his absence was meant for Udho. He briskly delivered several punches to the man's face even as the victim kept saying, 'It's the truth.' Udho turned from him and landed an unprovoked few on Binda's head, knocking his turban off. Binda remained silent, using his elbows to parry the blows to his head. Fists still clenched, Udho left, walking briskly, not looking back. He passed by his home. He kept walking without even a glance at it. He had blood on his mind. But it was getting dark, and further down was Banjhan—Mulakh's world. He turned back.

Their silence greeted each other as father and son met at the door. The burning itch to bloody their hands had sent them into a stupor, each suppressing his pain, hiding it from the other. For an instant the light of the new lamp blinded them. Once able to see, they looked at each other and then at Banti, who, having just finished making the daal, was kneading the wheat aatta. The distinct squish of her fists pressing into the dough seemed to calm Kalu a bit.

'Bhapa, let's have some Scotch.'

He was dying for something, anything that would numb him comatose. Unlike the first time he had had it, tonight Kalu craved the drink. He saw Udho turn to the silent Banti before taking out the bottle from its hiding place.

'Give us onion and salt,' he asked her.

'Here...for your poison,' she said handing them a leftover peeled onion along with bits of rock salt. Kalu looked the other way.

The brass glasses to their lips, Udho and Kalu didn't wait before downing the Scotch. They took turns biting into the onion and taking pinches of salt, Kalu the contortioner going first. Banti served them their dinner and sat watching. They ate quietly, without a word about it being tasty, or the obligatory contented burp from either of them. Kalu placed the lamp in the kitchen to ensure its light didn't escape into the bedroom. Banti ate, cleaned the dishes and made sure the fire in the chullah was out before walking into the dark bedroom. Not a word was spoken in that room that night.

The silence was disturbed by the crowing of a rooster next morning. It was still dark as Kalu stepped out. A cool breeze heralding the monsoons greeted him. He stood wondering whether to go get a kikar branch for cleaning his teeth or make do by rubbing salt on them and gargling it out. He was about to go back into the house when Udho came to the door.

'Son, let's go get a kikar twig. I'm tired of the plastic tube-wala Colgate. It'll get us to walk a little too.'

A short katar in hand, they walked out to the road linking the Chamarli to Banjhan.

'Bhapa, the passports should be ready, no? The choes may start flowing again with the rain. If it doesn't stop we won't be able to go to Hoshiarpur.'

They had found a kikar by the roadside, a hundred yards away from Mulakh's home. Udho cast a momentary glance in its direction before chopping a twig and then another. Chewing the twigs and spitting out the tiny, ground fibres, the duo returned home.

Banti had fired up the chullah. The syrupy shuckered chai was ready. Already agitated by the silence in the household, she had just heard from her neighbour about what had happened at the cobbler's and the Samadhi. Her knees wobbled and temples pounded as if someone was striking them. Regret in her heart was no help to others but begging forgiveness meant confessing her sin. She heard footsteps enter the home. She poured tea and handed Udho the glass.

'I'm dying with shame, forgive me,' she said, almost in a whisper.

A few feet away, Kalu heard her words.

'Bibi, where is my tea?' he yelled before Udho could say anything. Udho's silence had to suffice by way of forgiveness.

The father and son were off to Sondh Travels. The old mango trees formed a canopy over the road between Mahilpur and Hoshiarpur interrupted only by the choes. The large raindrops falling on the moving camper made loud noises. Kalu lowered the passenger window a bit to let in fresh air. It allowed in the even louder noise of the rain falling on the sturdy mango leaves. But the din drowned the sense of unease in the van, and their stories of shame and pain tumbled forth, falling on solicitous ears unlike the rain on the windshield, which was constantly cleared away by the wipers. Sharing the Scotch had made them equals. Udho filled Kalu in on the as yet unshared parts of his life in Britain as they crossed the choes still awaiting their first flush.

Jagjit was on the phone. Kalu and Udho seated themselves.

'*O beta*, bring three chais,' he shouted through the open

window at the stall next door and extended a brown envelope towards Udho, saying, 'Two passports, three tickets.'

Udho pulled out Banti's passport and opened it. He kept looking at it.

'Bhapa, Bibi is still beautiful, give me the passport,' Kalu said, picking up the envelope.

Udho handed Kalu the passport. The apparent closeness between the two further endeared the 'Jat' father and son to Jagjit.

'At your named price, the camper is mine. I'll drop you at the Delhi airport and return with it,' he said, happy to be of help.

'Wonderful. Pukka ho gaya!' said Udho.

The two then drove away in the camper, relieved it would be off their hands. But there was no cacophony of raindrops this time to drown out the discomfort of the secrets exchanged.

'Bhapa, Bibi's photo... The red light district in Bedford you were telling me about. The white prostitutes...they didn't want to sleep with a "brown bastard"...'

Udho said nothing, unsure what Kalu was getting at.

'Bibi didn't sleep with the Jat rapists or some Chuhra and she didn't allow herself to be raped. That does happen in Banjhan.'

Udho silently drove on, through the choes, past small villages and towns. Kalu wanted to fly away to England that very minute if he could. So would the silent Udho, Kalu believed.

Mahilpur was about a mile away.

'Bhapa, how about mutton with some whisky tonight, to celebrate the passports and the camper deal?' asked Kalu. Udho was happy to oblige.

The ground was red with blood. The knives and the rope on which hung the freshly slaughtered and skinned goat—everything was red. The flies were lapping it all up. Kalu watched as the butcher weighed and wrapped the meat in old newspapers. Udho returned with two bottles of whisky from the 'Wine and Beer' shop next door. Smiles on their faces, they walked to the camper.

The van lit up the dark dirt road before it came to a stop at its usual spot in Banjhan. The deeva burnt in the kitchen. The aroma of the boiled and spiced daal filled Kalu's nostrils. Banti was about to pour water into the aatta to knead it when Kalu, carrying the meat and whisky, beat Udho past the door into the house and said, 'Bibi...mutton for tonight!' He saw her glance at him. He opened his arms, whisky and mutton still in his hands, and hugged her. Tears welled up in her eyes. He tried to say something, but despite the silence because of the lump in his throat the mother understood. He lit the kerosene lamp. It lit up the home.

It was moist and chilly in the yard. So they sat around the burning chullah in the rasoi as the meat simmered on the fire. The unique aroma of the meat and spices mingled with that of the spicy daal tingled his senses. It transported Kalu to an imagined world where Banti's hand with the tip-less index finger could conjure up a storm of culinary fragrances.

Udho poured water from the clay pitcher into a jug which he placed, along with two glasses and a bottle of whisky, on a small stool.

'Bibi, onion and salt... You know what goes with whisky!'

'Give me a minute. Let me finish the dough first.'

Kalu put the lid back on the bottle, got up and brought the onion and salt himself. Then he picked up another empty glass and placed it next to the other two. Udho shot a curious glance at the third glass but said nothing.

'Bibi, we'll wait for you to finish making the rotis. Then we'll eat,' Kalu said, helping with the fire in the chullah as Banti made the rotis.

'No, son, you eat. I'll manage.'

But Kalu kept tending the chullah, his mind going over the last ten years spent without Udho. Rotis blown oval now began coming off the tawa on the chullah.

Kalu poured whisky in one of the glasses and extended it towards Banti.

'Bibi, drink it. It'll kill your fatigue...and pain.'

Udho looked at Kalu and then at the glass, his eyes open, wider than Kalu had ever seen them.

'No, son. I'm a woman. Women don't drink in Banjhan or the Chamarli. We don't get relief from pain.'

Kalu saw her steal a glance at Udho's eyes. He poured the whisky in the other two glasses, handing one to Udho and raising the other himself. Within seconds, he banged his empty glass back on the stool, his face contorted beyond recognition until the salted onion went into his mouth. Udho emptied his glass too.

'Bibi, yours,' said Kalu pointing to her glass, the Scotch still in it, un-drunk.

She looked at Udho, picked up and downed her glass. In the bright light of the kerosene lamp, they sat around the chullah and ate. Udho regaled the kitchen with stories of his adventures and misadventures in Bedford. He didn't mention Mulakh, half a mile away in Banjhan, nor Bedford's red-light district.

7

Kalu put on his worn-out pair of shoes, the only pair he had. They were too tight for him. But he would not ask nor wait for Baali to make the new pair he had gone to him for. And he despised even more the thought of going to the cobbler brothers at Mahilpur. His parents may have been unfaithful to each other but it was no one else's business. Ten years were a lifetime to test one's sexual fidelity, and who said sexual fidelity equalled marital loyalty, thought Kalu as he walked beside Udho to Master Hazara's khooh.

As he had promised he would before returning to England, Udho planned to see him in the evening, but Master had sent an urgent message for both of them to come early. The clouds above seemed ready to unleash torrents of water upon the earth. Kalu took some deep breaths. He could feel the weight of the moist air. Despite the rains the mulberries around the well's circle didn't look monsoon green. Facing the narrow dirt road sat Master, across from two men in khaki police uniform with their backs to it. As Kalu and Udho came closer, Master said, 'I knew the police would come. I asked them not to show up. I told them I'd resolve all the problems. But they insisted on coming. I invited them here to ensure you do not lose face in the Chamarli.'

Binda and Baali had contacted the Mahilpur Police Thana. Udho was worried now. The cops could confiscate the passports which would take a long time and a lot of money to get back.

'Baali and Binda...you beat them up. We had to follow up. It's our duty,' said one of the cops.

'Our motorcycles will need to be greased to go back,' said the other.

The duo had the act worked out down to the finest detail. Little effort was wasted in delivering a clear message. The former freedom fighter and widower of Sidhi had had a standing in the Chamarli. He was one of them, at least through Sidhi. Most of Chamarli's disputes, and quite a few of Banjhan's, came to him before going to the police or the courts. Binda and Baali had come to see him too.

He dissuaded them from pressing for the attempted murder charge the cops wanted to frame. It would have meant a bigger bribe.

Udho handed fifty rupees to the policemen, enough to buy a new cycle or, alternatively, lots of grease. They had no reason to linger.

Hazara asked his domestic cum khooh helper, Piara Ram, to make chai and handed Udho some documents to sign. Hazara was transferring all his land to Kalu in return for a promise from both father and son that they would use the land to improve the lives of people in the Chamarli.

'I want to do this. Kalu is brave and just. You were always honest...now you're rich also. Hopefully, you won't keep the land all for yourself.'

'We'll be too far away to manage this, Baba,' said Kalu.

Kalu knew his father could not take on the responsibility. He was of England now and would be leaving for good in a few days. Udho didn't quite understand how a trust worked. But he knew that people often set up trusts with their ancestral property, and that these trusts managed public works, scholarships and the like. Such things could certainly be handled much better that way than by an uneducated man thousands of miles away, he argued. Kalu even suggested setting up a community centre on part of the land.

'You were always stubborn...' Hazara said. He knew they were not to be persuaded and thought it futile to insist beyond a point. 'Listen carefully now. Go back quickly. There could be others who'll try and frame you on some criminal charge or the other. Everyone knows you're planning to return to England. They will try and stop you. The police will be only too happy to help them,' he advised Udho before turning to Kalu. 'Take your father away from this hell,' he said.

When they finished their chai, Master handed Udho a gun and a few bullets, relics of the treacherous days of Partition. It had come in handy ferrying Muslim refugees to secure camps for crossing into Pakistan. As they left, Kalu stole a glance at Master's moistened eyes, imagining all the events they had witnessed, historic and barbaric.

The sky was overcast. The darkness of night was about an hour away. The camper, loaded with the baggage, stood ready inside the neighbour's yard. The three of them sat around the warm chullah eating their last meal in Banjhan. They planned to leave early in the morning and have breakfast on the road to Hoshiarpur. Passports, tickets, bankbook sat near the chullah, packed with other documents in the small hand purse Kalu had bought for the trip in Hoshiarpur. Kalu was feeling quite overwhelmed. He was no doubt sad about leaving. But the excitement of travelling across the oceans mingled with fright of the strangeness of it all. He wanted to calm his nerves and thought of the left over Scotch that Udho had handed to the neighbour. But he cooled himself down. He didn't want to be an alcoholic; and took comfort in Master's judgement of him as a brave boy.

So close to his departure, Kalu realized he hadn't seen Boota for many weeks. Ever since Udho's return, Boota had become somewhat distant. Mulakh and Boota's father were first cousins. All manner of thoughts about his friend were grating on his mind when he heard someone scream outside.

'Udhooo...motherfucker! I want to fuck Banti. She needs someone like me... You're useless.'

Kalu jumped out of bed, grabbed a steel-tipped bamboo lathi from the corner and ran out. Others must have heard him but none stepped out of their homes. Kalu recognized the voice. It was Karam Singh, Daulat Singh's nephew, the one who had raped Chamarli's Meeto just days before

Udho's return. Kalu was a few feet from him when Karam made the ultimate provocation. He said he wished to do to Banti what he had done to Meeto. Kalu heard a bullet fly skyward, followed by another obscenity from the cocksure rapist standing before him. He swung the lathi at Karam's turban. And then there was silence.

Karam lay face down in the dirt, not a sound coming from him.

Within minutes the Westfalia camper was heading to Banti's village.

'But we won't be able to hide there,' Udho said. Probably the only one of its kind in Punjab at the time, the camper would've easily been spotted by the police.

They reached Hoshiarpur overnight and hid behind the tea stall next to Sondh Travels. Kalu kept an eye out from the passenger seat while Banti and Udho rested.

The sun had begun to peek at him from behind the horizon when Kalu was alerted by the clanging of a lock just as he found himself slipping into sleep. The owner of the tea stall had just opened his shop. From him Kalu found out that Jagjit Singh lived just next door, in the building behind his office.

Jagjit Singh's barefoot servant Sadhu opened the gate. The camper was brought inside Jagjit's kothi. They waited in the veranda along with Sadhu, the latter's eyes fixed on his bare, calloused feet. On previous occasions at the office he had been quite talkative. Jagjit Singh came out several minutes later, his eyes dilated and turbanless hair tied in a gutta above his head.

'You bloody Chamars, why didn't you tell me what you were? Thank God for Mulakh Raj... Oye Sadhu, empty the camper. Throw the bags and these Chamars out. I'm not driving them to Delhi,' he barked, adding under his breath how the camper would now have to be cleansed and purified. The look of his beard, fastened with a strip of cloth tied at the head to press it in place for the day, not an unusual practice by any means, strangely made him look more menacing and the insults more threatening. Kalu, his bamboo lathi in hand, rushed towards Jagjit who ran in and locked the door. After breaking its large leaded glass panes, Kalu turned around and smashed the front and rear windshields of the camper. Part of him wanted to drive it away but it had already been registered in Jagjit's name. It comforted him that Jagjit couldn't drive it either, at least for a while. He'd have to spend a fair amount and wait for several months to get the windshields replaced, if that could be done at all.

Outside the kothi, Kalu, having vented himself, stood with his parents on the concrete floor near the gate post. He surveyed the old vine that covered much of it as they waited, contemplating what to do next. There was not a single green leaf on it. Kalu overheard Sadhu telling Jagjit's wife he had dysentery and needed to relieve himself. As an untouchable servant he was barred from doing so in the toilet at the kothi. He closed the gate behind him as he stepped out and gestured to Kalu to keep quiet. He picked up one of their bags and asked them to follow.

'The bastard was calling the police,' he mumbled as they walked.

Soon, they were in a taxi. Kalu said goodbye to Sadhu, thrusting a five rupee note into his pocket.

'*Main vi Chamara hi haan*,' Sadhu said as he pushed the money back into Kalu's hand. He, too, was a Chamar!

He looked away, waving an arm while wiping his eyes with the other hand. Kalu too looked the other way, his fists in his eyes. The taxi rolled on, the lathi sticking out of the passenger window.

8

Kalu rubbed his eyes and bent forward to look ahead as the taxi raced on. None of the passengers on board were eager to talk, and the taxi's rattling windows and glass filled the void. For over an hour, the car whizzed past oncoming traffic. Kalu watched every tree, every jeep and every motorcycle, looking out for the police khaki. Everything looked khaki. Even the slight fog appeared khaki. He'd been so focused on what was outside, he hadn't noticed that even Kirti the taxi driver was wearing his company issue khaki. The man had a big scar at his right wrist, near the Sikh kada, the bracelet that he wore. A sign of a life lived, thought Kalu.

They entered Phillaur. The roadside tea stalls spiked the aching hunger in Kalu's stomach.

'Don't stop,' he said, spooked when he noticed the police station on his left and sentry in khaki at its gate.

Kirti nodded.

As the taxi passed the Phillaur Fort, Kalu could see the bridge on the Satlej River. The choes of Hoshiarpur and now Satlej, unless quickly crossed, loomed like walls threatening to block his journey. The sound of rotary phones being dialled reverberated in his head as if every police station in Punjab had received Jagjit's call. Past the bridge was Malwa, a foreign country to Kalu. He had not been beyond Mahilpur and Hoshiarpur. If he succeeded in getting to Delhi and flying out across the oceans, he would be like a coward running away. Could this craven escape be a foundation for life in the Midlands of England? His hands and their wet palms ached clutching the steel-tipped lathi and the black purse containing the tickets and passports.

Midway over the Satlej Bridge, 'Kirti, stop the taxi for a minute,' shouted Kalu. Leaving the purse on the seat, he got out. At the back of the taxi, lathi raised in his hands as if to strike the bridge to break it, Kalu stood watching the waters of the Satlej below. If only the span behind the taxi could collapse, or if he could breach it, the khaki wouldn't be able to pursue them! But reality dawned just as soon. The steel-tipped bamboo had felled the rapist Karam in Banjhan. A murder weapon, he needed to get rid of it. He lowered it. It rested on the rusted rail for a moment, the steel tip shining under the sun. Then he let go. It fell into the water. No khaki would ever know whose it was, where it came from and why it entered the muddy waters of the Satlej.

'Let's go, Kirti, straight to Delhi.'

Freed of the lathi's burden the taxi crossed the bridge into Malwa.

'How about some chai? I'll get some petrol too?' said Kirti.

'Get enough. We're going straight to Delhi.'

'Not spending the night at Ambala?' asked Kirti.

Kalu pretended not to hear the question. Kirti stopped at a petrol pump. Soon, they were at a chai stall. Kalu ordered pranthas and chai for all.

'Kahla Singh, why did you throw the lathi into the river? It looked like a solid stick?' asked Kirti.

'It had tasted blood,' replied Udho who hadn't said a word since they left Hoshiarpur.

Udho had been thinking about Kalu's temper. In his time in Banjhan, he had only ever seen the untouchables, the Chamars and Chuhras in particular, absorbing all insults, never reacting. Their anger never boiled over. He massaged his forehead with both his hands before rubbing his temples and jaws. He bent to rub his lower left leg, the one that limped.

'Still hurts?' asked Banti.

Udho just nodded.

'It'll always hurt,' thought Kalu.

As Udho had bathed the other day, Kalu had caught a glimpse of his calves. The injured legs showed no scars any more other than the limp of course. He was curious. His father had never talked about the day Banjhan broke his legs.

Back on the road, Kalu's eyes focused once again on the long scar on Kirti's hand as it rested on the steering wheel.

'Kirti, the scar on your wrist...how did it happen?'

'Oh, I worked for a zamindar... I was tired one day. It was harvest season. We were cutting dry stalks all morning. I got up to straighten my legs and back and I was about to squat again when the zamindar assaulted me...took his sickle and slashed my wrist. "Bastard! We don't pay you to stand and gaze at the fields," he said. I ran away. I was scared. I wish I hadn't. I should've slit his bloody throat. But then the police would've caught me and tortured me. I started working for this taxi company as a cleaner. Then I became a driver.'

'Where are you from? Where did this...happen?' asked Kalu.

'Talwara village. Near Jalandhar.'

'Are you a Chamar?'

'Chuhra.'

'And you didn't tell us. We sat and ate with you,' yelled Banti.

Kalu turned to her, 'Bibi, do you want to walk to Delhi?'

'How long will it take to get to the airport?' asked Kalu.

'About five hours. But what's the hurry? You told Sadhu you'll spend a night at Ambala,' said Kirti, probing why Kalu had changed his mind.

'Bhapa's foreman threatened to fire him if he didn't return soon.'

The thought of khaki had frightened him so much that

he had lied to Sadhu of all people, who was helping them. He did not trust anyone. He cursed himself for it but he needed to keep his itinerary to himself. They stopped for chai at another roadside dhaba about an hour from the airport. Standing together, Kalu and Kirti chatted and drank their beverage. Udho and Banti sat at a table, Udho's forearms touching and at places glued to its grime. As they walked back to the taxi, Udho took out the gun from his jacket pocket and handed it to Kalu. After a brief conversation in hushed voices, Kalu said aloud, 'Do you know some good, cheap hotel here? Let's go there.'

Kirti did as he was told. But as they neared a hotel and he swerved towards it, Kalu said, 'Keep going, Kirti.'

'You said to go to a hotel...?'

'I know. Keep going.'

Udho didn't say a word. Kalu had been to school, Udho hadn't. The son had been in India for the ten years the father hadn't. As they were parting at the airport, Kalu handed Kirti the gun and said, 'Sadhu and you...it's yours.' The scarred hand grabbed it with a smile and drove away.

A policeman in khaki greeted them at the entrance to the single-storey airport, built on an area that seemed scarcely bigger than Jagjit's office and mansion taken together. Kalu examined the face in khaki. Leaving the baggage in a corner with Banti and Udho, he said, 'We can't wait for tomorrow's flight,' and walked over to the man piling the baggage onto a cart to take to the plane stationed on the tarmac. Udho saw them speak to each other. Kalu pulled his right hand out of his trouser pocket and appeared to shake the man's hand. The baggage handler promptly walked over to the BOAC check-in counter.

Soon it was Kalu, Banti and Udho's turn at the check-in desk. The man at the counter finished dealing with the passenger ahead of them and said, 'Your flight goes tomorrow but there's space in tonight's flight.' Udho smiled at Kalu, who placed the baggage on the rollers without much ado to be pushed towards the man with the cart.

Kalu was morose as they walked onto the tarmac, not lifting his head up. He couldn't even bear to look at the plane. He had just bribed his way onto an earlier flight because he needed to get away before Jagjit, a propertied travel agent likely with powerful connections, could create obstacles in his path. But all that he thought now was that he was fleeing like a coward.

Kalu's actions, particularly his attack on Karam, had been reckless. But the fact that he had shown resolve and street smarts in a completely unfamiliar situation—from Hoshiarpur to the airport—was lost on him. As was the fact that it was his very audacity that had saved them, for it hadn't occurred once to Jagjit to cancel their tickets. He couldn't imagine them bold enough to actually flee the country.

The interior of the plane stunned him. The lights, rows of seats, the orderliness and the light blue and white colours. After the disorder of the last two days, they had entered a new universe.

'We forgot to keep our bhaanday with us. Can I drink directly from the glass?' asked Banti staring at the orange juice and water the stewardess had brought once they took their seats.

'You had tea twice on the way. We didn't have our own glasses. Why can't you use this gori's glasses?' Kalu asked, not hesitating to pick the juice off the tray and handing it to her.

She grabbed it with her left hand with the missing fingertip and chugged it in one go. Udho instructed them about the knives and forks and the seated toilets of the plane.

The flight ready for take-off, the stewardess stood at the front delivering safety instructions. Kalu hadn't seen a woman with such authority. Banti couldn't ever be like her, he thought. For a Chamar, knowledge of English could never be enough!

The plane hadn't taxied to the runway yet. He needed to go to the washroom. Behind the door there was a light. The cleanliness was better than he had imagined it from Udho's description. He unbuttoned the pants but his Indian shorts underneath didn't have an opening. So he dropped the pants down, untied the string that held his underpants in place, sat down and relieved himself. Using toilet paper for the first time in his life messed up his hands and the gushing water at the basin splashed water all over. In the confusion, he forgot what he had to do to flush the toilet. Half wet, he walked over to his seat. Udho noticed and ran back before the stewardesses could see it and curse the bloody emigrants.

After the meal, with a cup of the fine BOAC china full of tea in hand, the embarrassment of the washroom mess behind him, seated between Bibi and Bhapa, Kalu could finally let his guard down. He thought how there would be no Chuhray if what he had seen in the plane's toilet could be recreated in Banjhan. It could end caste. A smile came over his face.

'What are you so happy about?' asked Udho.

Kalu smiled some more but said nothing. He didn't get out at the Karachi stop. Udho told him it would be the same as Delhi, the same people, cultural habits and history. He did step off the plane at the Paris airport though. The languages, sounds, sights and smells thrust his senses into overdrive. The aroma of chocolate and coffee was different from any he had ever encountered. Brought up on the myth of Jawaharlal Nehru's clothes being sent to Paris to be dry cleaned, Kalu floated about the airport. He wasn't a Nehru.

Nor were his clothes being washed there. But he was on his way to England, where he could live with dignity, without the inhumanity of caste. He bought a small chocolate to share with Bibi. He was sure Bhapa would have eaten lots of them in England. But as he unwrapped the chocolate, he noticed Udho didn't take his eyes off it. So he gave Banti half and shared the other half with Udho.

'Never had this in ten years,' Udho said. He had saved every penny to get his family over to England.

At London's Heathrow Airport, the immigration officer stamping entry on his passport smiled at Kalu. No one other than the stewardess had smiled at him at Delhi's Palam Airport—not the police officer, not the check-in man. The baggage handler had, but that was for the money he got.

9

On the train from London's King's Cross station, Kalu's eyes observed men, women, the roads, the trees, the bogeys, the seats, the difference, the sameness. He read every English word on anything, from billboards to train tickets. In his excitement to come to Britain he had ignored the possibility of there being a chasm between his and the new world. That speaking and understanding English with the accent was going to be difficult he had understood while listening to the stewardess' safety instructions on the tarmac in Delhi. His realization had only sharpened when, at the airport, Udho had asked him to enquire about buses and trains to King's Cross station. None had understood his questions and he hadn't got a word of their answers.

'Did you really matriculate?' the scene had prompted Udho to ask.

What he had seen, heard and read from Heathrow Airport to the Bedford rail station had thrust into him a dread of the days ahead and the tests and tribulations they would bring. Though no fault of his own, Kalu was completely ignorant of the world he was now to be a part of.

It was close to midnight as they walked home from the station. Udho and Banti carried the suitcases in hand while Kalu had the leather purse slung on his shoulder and the bundled bedding on his head.

'This is where you're coming soon,' said Udho to Kalu, pointing to Mander College a few yards to their left.

Kalu turned his head, the bedding on his head turning with him, to look at it. It was many times the size of Banjhan High School. An occasional car, bike or pedestrian passed them by. From Heathrow to Bedford, he hadn't come across any black or brown faces. Unlike the range of Indian faces from almost white to black and everything in between, the white faces all looked the same. Past the college, he stopped watching. He just wanted to be home, which Udho kept saying was 'just there'. It was taking aeons to get to. Kalu's mind had had little respite since the steel-tipped lathi had felled Karam and smashed the Westfalia camper's windshields. He didn't want to think any more. As he walked, he could barely feel his hands and feet. The cold had numbed them even though the bus from Heathrow and the train from London had heaters. If he could will it by the roadside at that very moment, he would have been more than satisfied with Banjhan's hovel, the bed, the quilt and mustard-oil deeva.

The metal gate to the enclosure squeaked as they entered Udho's St Leonard's Avenue home.

'Put the baggage down and knock, Kalu. I don't have the key,' said Udho.

To save himself the money and the time to get an additional key made, Udho had left his key with the new tenant. Kalu knocked but there was no answer. Udho walked to the back of the house and knocked on the back door. Jeetu, the new tenant, let him in and Udho walked through the house to the front door. The ground floor was the size of the Banjhan hovel, at the most slightly larger and not much warmer than outside.

Kalu stood in the front room where there was a fireplace with a mantle and a pole lamp beside it. A light bulb hung from the ceiling, illuminating the papered walls, a large bed and a cushioned stool. Jeetu and Kalu stacked the luggage in one corner against the wall. Banti sat down on the stool.

'Bhapa, its cold. My feet are frozen,' said Kalu.

Jeetu took the empty bucket from beside the fireplace and brought coal from the cellar. Soon, the coals were red hot. The blood streamed in Kalu's warmed-up body. Jeetu returned to his bed.

The two bedrooms upstairs were rented to three tenants. Jeetu shared a bedroom with another. Udho's bedroom was the front room. He walked Kalu and Banti to the kitchen on the ground floor.

'This is how you turn on the gas,' he said, lighting up the stove.

'There's no chullah here?' asked Banti.

'This is it. You don't have to use cow dung pathiyan any more,' said Udho and led them to the toilet outside at the end of the enclosed yard, which was small though twice the size of the enclosure at the front.

'I'm hungry,' Kalu said, coming back in.

Udho warmed up the pranthas they had packed for the trip in Banjhan. Kalu was mildly impressed by how well his father knew his way around such things. Apart from moulding and forming at the foundry, Udho had had to learn all things kitchen and sewing, among other things. They sat around the fire and ate the pranthas with chai. Udho spread the bedding from the baggage on the linoleum when he sensed Kalu was beginning to doze off.

'Bhapa, the floor will be cold.'

'No. Under the linoleum the floor is made of wood. Below that is the cellar,' Udho said.

Banti didn't say very much, happy to be away from India where she incessantly worried about Kalu getting into trouble. That he would sooner or later was pretty much a certainty to her. He was difficult; he couldn't suffer indignity silently.

She and Udho shared the bed, sleeping with their feet next to each other's head.

Udho was taken aback by the smell and wet floor of the toilet when he got up to use it the next morning. The water closet had no toilet paper. His late night instruction hadn't helped. After relieving herself, Banti had tried to clean herself with a bottle of water while seated on the toilet, but she found it impossible to do. So she had squatted as she would in Banjhan's fields and washed herself.

'Didn't I teach you last night?' he yelled at her, grabbing her by the arm from the kitchen and dragging her back to the scene. 'This thing takes days to dry,' he said, pointing to the floor.

Kalu had had the same problem. By the end of the long, halting flight to London, he had figured out how and why toilet paper was used. He wondered why Udho had no toilet paper. For some reason, he didn't feel like asking him upfront.

'It's Saturday, the market day,' Udho said to Kalu and Banti as they settled down for breakfast. 'Vendors from many different places bring their wares to sell in the Corn

Exchange Yard behind the library. We'll buy groceries for the week and overcoats for both of you.'

And some toilet paper too, Kalu thought.

They walked, father and son wearing suits, and Banti behind them in her salwar-kameez. It was his first morning in Bedford. He watched with interest the paved sidewalks, the people, the shops and the traffic. From St Leonard's Ave they had taken St John's Street which became St Mary's Street. On their right was the King's Arms pub, a hundred yards before the bridge on the Great Ouse.

'Bibi, see... Here, wives walk with their husbands. Not behind them,' said Kalu on the bridge, looking back at Banti.

'Let her be. What would people say?' said Udho.

'That you learnt something good in England.'

The street name had changed to High Street. On the left was the Corn Exchange Yard, behind it the library and public toilets, and across the street, perpendicular to and crossing the High Street, sat the Corn Exchange Hall. The yard was full of rain-proof tarpaulin-covered shops selling everything from apples to aprons and coats, most things people needed in their daily lives, and at prices cheaper than in the trendy shops on High Street. Kalu felt right at home with men and women haggling over prices. He saw a woman bargaining with a shop owner while her husband stood watching without interrupting. Bibi couldn't be that wife, he thought. She didn't know English. But neither did he, at least not enough to speak it. So it fell to Udho to argue over the price for the overcoats. They finally bought one for Banti. Not for Kalu though, for the one they found just fit him.

'For you we should get something looser, so that it can last a couple of years. You'll have eggs and milk here and gain weight and grow taller.'

'Bhapa, I'm shivering.'

'Go see if there is another vendor selling coats.'

Kalu didn't want to go home without a coat but he didn't know that Udho would not go a couple of hundred yards away to Marks & Spencer to get it. Udho's only suit, the navy blue he took to India, he had bought from the Salvation Army store. Along with the lifelong limp, life in Banjhan's Chamarli had bequeathed to Udho an obsession with saving money. Fortunately, Kalu found another shop and a looser coat.

They had bought groceries for the week and begun the walk home when Udho said, 'Oh, Kalu, I forgot the library.'

'We can go another day, Bhapa.'

'No,' said Udho and turned back.

Leaving Banti at the entrance with the purchases, Udho took Kalu to the library reception and had a library card made for him; if Mulakh could get one so could Kalu, he thought. Walking back to the entrance, Kalu saw a room on the right with its doors open. Inside it were men and women reading newspapers spread open on wooden stands. He had seen the words 'Reading Room' above the door. Udho saw him looking at it and led him in to try reading at an unoccupied stand. The *London Times* rested on it. Kalu could make out a few words printed on it. The news of the United Kingdom exploding its first atom bomb on the Monte Bello Islands in Australia and the end of tea-rationing in the country caught his attention but he understood no more than a few words. He gave up, frustrated at his inability to follow very much.

Carrying the bags of groceries as they walked home, Banti behind the men, Kalu felt small. The obstacle to his progress that a lack of English presented appeared Himalayan.

Jeetu and the tenants, Sam and Mike, were in the kitchen early Monday morning making food to go to work. Udho was packing the pranthas and daal for lunch when Banti came in to help make chai for him. She entered the kitchen, saw everyone and returned to the front room. Kalu was asleep on the floor. Udho waited for his chai in the common eating area. It didn't come. He looked in the front room and found Banti sitting on the bed. He asked her why she hadn't made tea, but got no answer. Wanting to catch the foreman before the shift began, he left without pressing her to explain.

Awoken by Udho's voice, Kalu got up and went to the kitchen. He wanted tea. The tenants were now at the eating table sipping whatever beverage they had made for themselves. It smelled different from chai. Kalu assumed it must be coffee. From the tap he poured some water into the pot, placed it on the stove and turned on the gas. But he stood in the kitchen watching the water heat up, not joining the others at the table.

'Banti chachi left without making tea,' Jeetu remarked when Sam and Mike left for work.

'You like these dirty habshis?' asked Kalu.

Jeetu knew the derision the word conveyed for black people.

'You mean Sam and Mike? I work with them. Is that why you didn't come and sit down with us?'

'Habshis are animals,' said Kalu.

Jeetu decided to not argue. He left for work too. Kalu made tea which Banti and he had in the front room.

Exiting the library on Saturday, Kalu had noticed a cinema hall. After lunch, he crossed the Ouse Bridge and checked out the show times at the theatre. Returning to the river, he walked the embankment by the Great Ouse. It looked more like a canal compared to the Satlej. What made it grand was the way the embankment, the buildings and the landscaping hugged it. Lost in the otherworldliness of the surroundings, he roamed the city centre, looking through the glass windows of shops selling clothes, radios and televisions. He glanced at Boots Chemists and marvelled at the orderliness and cleanliness of the place. There was so much to see and buy if one had the money.

With the money he did have, he went to the cinema when it was time for the 3 pm showing of *Escape Route*, a thriller in which the FBI agent George Raft teamed up with MI5's Sally Gray. Sprawled out in the seat, which was unlike any he had ever sat on other than in the plane and on the train to Bedford, his eyes remained glued to the screen. He examined Raft's car more than his actions. He found the American accent easier to make out than the English and yet he paid more attention to Sally, telling himself as he walked home that it was because he now lived in England, and certainly not because she was beautiful and a woman.

'Where were you?' Udho, out looking for Kalu, asked him when he found him on St Mary's Street near Mander College.

'I...went to see a movie.'

'I've been in England for ten years and I never even went to a restaurant! And you went to a movie? We still have a mortgage to pay.'

Kalu could do little but follow his angry father back home. They went in through the back door. The kitchen and the eating area were empty. Banti was still in the front room.

'And Kalu's mother, why haven't you made any food?' asked Udho, now even more annoyed that there was nothing on the stove or the counter.

'The habshis...how can you cook and eat in the same place?' said Kalu.

'So that's the problem! You're talking as if the goras and upper caste Indians are lining up to be lodgers in my home,' he said, adding, 'I have to pay a mortgage,' as he barged out of the room.

That evening Udho made the meal himself before he called them to the eating table. They ate. Banti did the dishes.

The front room was quiet. Little noise from the rest of the house escaped into it. Kalu couldn't sleep. He felt awkward sleeping in the same room as his parents.

'Bhapa, I want a separate room.'

'I told you I have to pay the mortgage loan. And I don't want you to work. You will go to school.'

'And you brought me here to live with habshis?' asked Banti.

'Go to sleep. I have to go to work,' said Udho, covering his face with the quilt.

10

Udho had told his foreman, Henry Ashworth, about Kalu, Banti and his dream of sending Kalu to school. Henry's brother taught math at the Elstow Abbey Secondary School, walking distance from Udho's home. The next morning, Udho, Kalu's passport and matriculation certificate in hand, walked his son to the school. Alerted by Henry's brother Edward, the school secretary was waiting for Kalu. Leaving Kalu in her hands, Udho left for the factory.

Kalu returned home before Udho. Banti was in the kitchen cooking while Jeetu did the dishes. Sam and Mike sat at the eating table, sipping tea.

'*Arre*, Kalu, how was the school?' asked Jeetu.

'Fine. But English is hard,' replied Kalu, happy to see Banti at the stove.

Banti didn't accept Sam and Mike but she had decided to make peace with them. Jeetu being Chuhra didn't matter because she did not know.

'Ah laddy, how is the new country?' asked Sam.

Kalu couldn't understand the question in Sam's Jamaican accent. Jeetu translated for him.

'Like the old country but richer,' Kalu said.

Sam didn't ask how it was like the old country. Not that Kalu could have explained it. He didn't have the language for it. The question of white, black and brown that hovered in the air was new. At least that's what he had thought at first. But it wasn't. He was wrestling with who his friends and enemies were. He knew caste. He had lived it. And here he was, grudgingly putting up with Sam and Mike just so his father could pay the mortgage. Jeetu's caste didn't bother him much. After all, he had accepted Kirti the taxi driver in Hoshiarpur in solidarity against the upper castes that victimized them both.

Udho bought Kalu a used bike from his neighbour, Harban. A handyman, he often helped Udho with home repairs and maintenance. Udho knew enough pidgin English to engage in basic conversations with him. Udho and he were 'tired of Africans and West Indians flooding Bedford'. Among the coloureds, the word he used for all non-whites, Harban preferred Indians. Having read Max Muller on Vedanta and Sir William Jones's works, he believed like the latter 'that Pythagoras and Plato derived their sublime theories from the same fountain with the sages of India'. In an ironical twist, Harban was going to Australia which, because of its white-only immigration policy, wouldn't have accepted Udho.

Sam and Mike sensed tension in the household and moved out. Jeetu moved into their room promising to find another tenant to share it. Kalu got his separate room. He took on a paper route earning a small amount, enough to pay for a movie or two and some chocolate. Udho needed help with the mortgage. Henry gave Kalu a weekend job stacking light steel items and cleaning up in the foundry. Kalu was doing reasonably well at school. He was a B student. But his English could use some help, particularly deficiencies in his speech, which were obvious to Henry whenever they spoke. So he brought an old radio to the foundry and gifted it to Kalu to listen to BBC1, the commercial free radio, all talk all the time.

Kalu placed the radio in his room. But he could still only manage a C-minus in English. He was interested in movies, the women in them, the cars and motorcycles. Once a week he was at the cinema, which was one more time than at the library. His library card sat unused, gathering dust, on Henry's unplugged radio near his bed. He told himself he didn't want to study. He needed to earn money to buy a car which would make it easier to date women.

The Elstow Abbey School was all white except him and Rodney Porier, a tall black Haitian teacher with prominent lips and a nose one could rest an apple on. He was born to immigrant parents in Britain and taught Kalu English. No one could find fault with his teaching but behind his back, many students called him 'monkey'. For over a year and a half Kalu, too, called him monkey, until he overheard others calling him 'rag-head' behind his back for wearing a turban. From that moment, solidarity with Porier took root in his heart. He felt ashamed for thinking him less than himself, less than human.

One day, he stayed behind in the classroom. The other students had left. Rodney was sorting the books and papers at his table when, standing near his desk, holding it for support, Kalu said, 'Mr Porier, sir, I'm sorry.'

'You, Kahla, why are you sorry?'

'Sorry, sir. I can't say the word I used...but I'm sorry.'

'No, Kahla, pray tell.'

'Sir, I used to believe and say that you were less than me...not a human, I mean, sir.'

'Oh that. Come on, now. Off you go. I know what some say. I'm sure glad you spoke to me. Go on home now.'

Kalu walked home. He searched the house and touched all the objects and places Sam and Mike might have made contact with. In his mind he kneeled before them and begged forgiveness. Porier had been magnanimous enough to forgive him. But lest he forget the lesson, he didn't pardon himself.

Jeetu had persuaded another tenant, an untouchable, to share the room with him. He had spoken with many but no one from the non-untouchable castes wanted to move into Udho Chamar's home.

'We'll manage the money,' Udho said as they sat in the front room one night after supper. Kalu was by now done with his A Levels. 'You should enrol at Mander College for BA.'

Udho knew what BA was. His hero, Master Hazara Singh, was a BA. Kalu refused. He had asked Henry and the latter had given him a full-time job in the foundry.

'What's the point of bringing you here? I sweated at the foundry furnaces for so many years so you could have a better life. And now you want to do the same job!' he said when Kalu told him. He felt powerless to do anything about it.

On Kalu's first day at the fulltime job, Udho walked with him to the foundry, grinding his teeth, his jaws locked.

'You look like you just came out of a coal mine. Is this what you want in life?' he asked him after the shift.

Kalu did not answer. He limped home, looking like

a lump of coal. Despite Udho's insistence, he continued at the foundry. A car was too expensive. He settled for the motorcycle and its accoutrements, thinking he would trade it in for a car as soon as he could afford one. Unlike Udho, he didn't want to walk to work or the city centre for shopping.

But there was another reason. Christine, a classmate from Elstow. She alone showed an interest in him. And she loved motorcycles. Her father, a foreman at the Stewartsby Brickyard, had one which he allowed her to ride. Kalu took her on rides into the countryside. The riverside pub at Northampton was their haunt for Friday evenings, a fireplace in one corner, a piano in the other and a dartboard on the wall between. Playing darts, they would down pints of Guinness. With their last Guinnesses in hand, she would play the piano and he would marvel at her, sipping the remaining drops of the dark brew.

One evening, before riding out to Northampton, Kalu brought Christine home. The tenants had gone pubbing and only Udho and Banti were home, at the table, eating. Kalu and Christine took the empty chairs. Udho welcomed Christine in his pidgin English and Kalu in Punjabi as Banti stared. Thankfully for her, the awkwardness didn't last long. But she let her feelings be known as they made to leave. With Christine out the door, she turned to Kalu and, wagging her nail-less left index finger, said, 'You'll see my dead body if you marry this white whore.'

'Bibi, you can't say that. This is just how Mulakh treats us. Are we going to do the same to Christine?'

'Even I don't like it. But she has no caste,' said Banti, pointing the tip-less finger at the door Christine had just walked out of.

On the road to Northampton, Kalu's mind went back to Banti asking him on the plane whether she could drink the orange juice from the hands of the white stewardess. He now understood what Bibi meant. She couldn't fit the non-Indian white stewardess into the caste hierarchy. She had no caste. Banti, who had known only caste and been made to live it all her life, had to place the stewardess in the matrix to know how to behave. The oblivion-inducing road and the cool breeze that hit their faces didn't dull the tumult in Kalu's head. The pub, the darts, the piano seemed strangers and he a charlatan, who couldn't truthfully translate Banti's reality to the woman he loved.

Christine had talked to her parents about Kalu. They hadn't met him, but her father, too, had objected to her marrying 'a rag-head'. He knew Udho's foreman and found out that Udho didn't approve of the union either.

'She's not a Chuhri or black. You should have no problem with her,' Kalu appealed to their prejudices he knew so well. Until recently, he had harboured them himself. His appeals only elicited silence. How could the loathed of Banjhan turn loathers of Bedford, he wondered.

'Your woman is worse than low caste. And the white women...they sleep with anybody,' Banti had said as Udho looked on.

Binda and the Mahilpur cobblers came to Kalu's mind, but his lips remained sealed. He couldn't bring himself to undermine his parents' relationship. But he had a decision to make.

'My father can't force me to choose between him and you. I'm yours, for the courage to marry me if nothing else,' said Christine when they next saw each other.

'I can't bring you into a hostile family. My mother hates you.'

'I'm marrying you, not your family.'

'You're marrying them, too, because I won't live away from them.'

In his heart, Kalu had given up. Their Friday evening rendezvous ceased, as did the charm of the motorcycle, which he sold not long after. The routine at the foundry too continued for a few months until Kalu got fired from the job.

'Hey rag-head cunt, go back to the shithole you came from,' a co-worker had shouted at Kalu.

He lunged at the man. Fists flew. His turban came off. And the foreman decided to let him go.

'It's their country. I'm taunted too. But to pay the mortgage one has to work. You could've ignored the bastard!' Udho said, deeply upset with his son's recklessness, as they sat having their evening meal.

'I cannot remain silent when someone says such hateful things.'

Between his temples, Udho felt his world crumble. Kalu was not in college, and now he had lost his job.

Kalu understood the situation they were in and applied for work at dozens of places. The openings were scarce. He landed a job in the quality control laboratory of the crayon factory, Krayon, at half the wages of the foundry and pedalled his new, second-hand bike to work. He stopped going shopping with Udho and Banti. As for the library card, it continued to gather dust atop the unplugged radio.

He regretted not having listened to Christine and not standing up to Banti's hatred of her. His cowardice shamed him. But it was too late. Christine was enrolled in college and had a new boyfriend.

At Krayon, his A Level Chemistry helped. In the year-end report to the management, the head of the laboratory, Brian Symonds, commended his work. The foundry and Christine began to recede into the past. After a long time he began looking forward to Friday evenings when he would walk over to the King's Arms pub on St Mary's Street near

Mander College to meet up with a couple of his Elstow classmates. After two pints of Guinness, he would walk to the bottom of Ampthill Road Rail Bridge to the fish and chip shop. The fare wrapped in old newspapers, he would come back home, and with a Scotch to down the food he would lick the wrapping and his fingers clean before going to bed. The weekends took him to the city centre to window shop and the Corn Exchange Hall for exhibitions being held there. Other than that, his life consisted essentially of eating, sleeping and washing up, reading only to keep up with the needs of the Krayon laboratory.

At home, he didn't interfere much with Udho and Banti's way of doing things. He had mistaken the transformation in Udho's attire and appearance to mean more than it did. It had taken him months of arguing with Udho and Banti for them to discard empty milk bottles filled with sink water for use in the toilet and begin buying toilet paper.

For several weeks he had been overseeing the laboratory as Brian had left the job to go teach college in London. To head the Krayon lab one required a BSc in chemistry. The management hired a man named Ravi Agnihotri. He was a Punjabi, born and raised in Bihar, but he had obtained his Bachelors and Masters in science in Britain. In his early thirties he had switched from teaching to industry. The manager, Robert Jennings, tasked Kalu with acquainting Ravi with the lab, its processes, procedures and goals.

At the end of four weeks, when Ravi had learnt everything Kalu could teach him, he caught him off-guard with a rather unexpected question.

'What's your last name, Kahla?'

'My father told me Singh. He said for a Sikh, it's Singh.'

'But what's your real last name, like some Singhs' last names are Sandhu and Johal.'

'I'll have to ask my father. He never taught me another name.'

A chill hung between the two. Kalu excused himself to go to the washroom to end the inquisition. The need to coexist became their relationship's only underpinning from then on, particularly for Kalu.

When collecting samples from the technicians, Kalu would see another Punjabi on the shop floor once every week.

'Oye Kahla, the new lab chap was asking about your caste. I told him everyone knows you're a Chamar,' said the man one day with a contemptuous smile.

Kalu could do little more than collect the sample and walk over to the next work station. The incurable birth defect of caste weighed on him. Unlike the birth mark, the turban couldn't conceal his caste.

'Bhapa, what's our last name...our gote?' asked Kalu when Udho had taken the first bite of the evening meal.

'It's Badhan. Why?'

'Someone wanted to know.'

'Guru Gobind gave us the gote Singh,' said Udho, not taking his eyes off the table.

Christmas brought a respite of cheer. Kalu went pub crawling with his classmate, Jim Jordan, consuming pints of Guinness and loads of fish and chips. He spent the last day of the year polishing shoes, ironing clothes and taking a hot bath. In the evening, he put on his best suit, tie, scarf and overcoat. Umbrella in hand, he walked to the annual dinner and dance for Krayon employees. He had missed the previous year's celebration. This year Jennings had reminded him of it before the Christmas break. At the door, the attendant took his scarf, overcoat and umbrella. She directed him to a table of six, the table for Ravi and five others of the lab team, including him. He took the only empty seat next to Ravi and asked if anyone would like a drink from the bar, since he was getting one for himself. Ravi was the only one to not respond. Over drinks, the conversation rambled from the economy and healthcare to race relations. Everyone except Ravi participated. He sat in silence. After the first half hour, Ravi left the table. Even at the factory, he had already made it a habit after the first month to have his lunch by himself in the lunch room. Sometimes even in the lab, but never at the same table as the lab team.

The evening wore on. The meal was to be served in half an hour. People were milling about, table hopping and chatting. Ravi had been at the manager Jennings's table for over an hour. Kalu walked over and sat in an empty seat next to him. The talk turned to politics. Prime Minister Anthony Eden's poll numbers were on a downward slide. In Northern Ireland, the Special Powers Act had been used to intern several hundred Republican suspects without trial. Kalu expressed concern about the lack of due process and infringement of their civil liberties.

'Who says we don't have castes in Britain? One only has to look at how we treat the Irish,' Jennings remarked.

With dinner about to be served, Kalu got up and asked Ravi, 'Not returning to our table?'

'No. In India, you and I wouldn't be seen walking together, let alone seated together and dining.'

In a flash, Kalu's right fist landed on Ravi's face. The latter's nose began to bleed, bloodying his white shirt and black suit.

'I'm sorry,' is all that Kalu said to Jennings before collecting his scarf, coat and umbrella. As he walked home he held the umbrella in his right hand, the one that had landed on Ravi's face. He kept feeling its knuckles with the left. He knew he couldn't return to work at Krayon. He went to sleep on an empty stomach that night, feeling embarrassed for losing his temper yet again.

11

'Are you not going to work? Just brought you chai,' said Banti entering his room.

'Leave it on the radio.'

He was in bed. The police had visited his home because Ravi had reported the assault. Jennings had got wind of it and accompanied Kalu to the police station. The police asked him to apologize to Ravi so they could dissuade him from insisting on proceeding with his complaint.

'I'd prefer conviction and jail to apologizing to the moron,' Kalu told the police.

'Officer, you or I in Kalu's shoes would have beaten the crap out of the man,' Jennings had said to the police, explaining what had transpired.

The police dropped the matter but not before cautioning Kalu about keeping his anger in check.

'I get that you don't want to return to Krayon. But what *are* you going to do?' Jennings had asked after their visit to the police.

All Kalu could come up with was an equivocal 'I don't know'.

Banti had left the cup of tea on the radio and Kalu's bedroom door ajar. Sitting up, he lifted the cup and sipped the chai brewed with milk, cardamom, cloves, ginger and fennel. It occurred to him how deeply Bibi must love him. For all her faults, he felt grateful for her. He also thought about Udho, who had begged him to go to college and not worry about the finances. How the father had cried the night he had found out his son had sought and accepted a job at the foundry.

'Had I known you wouldn't go to college, I'd have stayed in India and gone to jail fighting the British,' Udho had told him that day. 'I'd have been of some use to the country. I wouldn't have crossed the oceans to slave for them.'

Clutching the half-empty cup of tea in his hand, he regretted the hurt he must have caused for his father to say such a thing.

He had been rather brusque in his interactions with Banti and Udho ever since he broke up with Christine. He blamed them for it. He was an adult, able to think and act for himself, wasn't he? he asked himself. Why blame them?

The question brought forth a myriad others as he sat there examining his life, and every decision he had taken—or not taken—in it.

He turned his head to look towards the radio. He was about to place the cup back on it. It had one last sip in it. The library card caught his attention before he could take the sip. He picked it up. Making sure to finish the last bit of that delectable liquid, he dusted the card off and sat examining both sides of it. His name was written on it in the library receptionist's hand. He got it the first day he had woken up in England, after the long and fraught journey in the Westfalia camper from Banjhan to Hoshiarpur, in the taxi to Delhi, the plane to London and the train to Bedford.

He jumped up and plugged the radio cord into the wall. He smiled at the scratchy sounds that came from it. After so many years, Henry Ashworth's box radio with its round switches and bands marked SW and MW for short and medium wave had finally come alive. He slid open the window, placed the loose end of the antenna wire, screwed and hanging behind the radio, outside, and shut the window. Returning to the radio, he flipped through the bands, trying to tune in to a station.

'This is BBC,' said a voice out of the radio.

Within minutes, papers in the inside pocket of his

jacket, overcoat and umbrella in hand, he walked down the stairs to the eating area.

'Bibi, make me two eggs and bacon with toast.'

He had started eating meat regularly. Bacon, beef, chicken, mutton—it didn't matter to him. Some Indians would scrunch up in disgust when they heard he ate beef. These would often be those very people who, for centuries, had forced his people to skin dead cows and oxen and eat carrion. One could only marvel at the hypocrisy that numbed them to the memory of their crimes.

From the kitchen, Banti turned to look at him. He smiled. She did too. Soon, he was walking on St John's Street to cross the intersection of St Mary's. The Mander College admissions office was open. He was late by a few days.

'Your A Level marks tell me you could catch up if you applied yourself,' said the admissions clerk.

Admission in hand, he walked through the slush and came and stood at the bridge over the Ouse. The river looked different. The melting snow on its banks, the water connecting them, the flow—it seemed a world unto itself, on its own path. Over the centuries, it had carved its way to move with ease. He, too, had begun chiselling a course for his life's journey. But the effortlessness of the Ouse was absent from his path.

From the bridge he headed for the only bookstore that sold the prescribed texts for the college courses. Along with the texts, he bought the 1957 reprint of the third edition of *The Little Oxford Dictionary of Current English* and promptly wrote his name, the time, place and date of purchase in it. He had taken the first deliberate step of the rest of his life.

He strode over to the library's newspaper reading room. A spring in his step and an urge in his heart to engage with the world had brought him there; something new for him. According to the *London Times* headline, Prime Minister Anthony Eden had resigned. He wondered what Eden's caste might be. Were he a Chamar, he thought, the headline may well have read: 'The first Chamar Prime Minister Anthony Eden Resigns'.

The clerk confirmed that despite the passage of time, his library card was still valid; they were valid for life, he learnt. He roamed the aisles of the section on India and checked out the *Annihilation of Caste* by B.R. Ambedkar, published in 1936 and *Untouchable*, a 1935 novel by Mulk Raj Anand about the life of the scavenger—Chuhra—Bakha. Heading home, carrying the stash of books, he paused again at the bridge. He told himself he needed to be like the Ouse, which never rested and never appeared restless. He had to be for ever moving, alive, but not lashing out at others around him.

'Bibi, I want some spicy chicken curry tonight...and hot-off-the-tawa rotis,' said Kalu as he picked up the small table sitting unused in the eating area and took it to his bedroom. Udho was confused, watching him moving to and fro, brisker than ever.

'What's going on, son?' he asked from his chair near the eating area.

'Nothing much. Could you come and help me in the front room?'

Udho jumped up. It was the first time in weeks he had seen a smile on Kalu's face. The bamboo bookshelf Udho had bought for him years ago from the Saturday market of used goods had been pulled away from the corner it had stood in. An old, crumpled pair of Kalu's shorts rested on it. The shelf was not covered with the thick layer of dust Udho had seen just last night. Its glass doors reflected rays of the sun that snuck in through the windows. A grin on his face, the limping Udho helped Kalu take the bookshelf up the stairs. A radio, bookshelf, and a study desk with a lamp on it—the bedroom-cum-study was complete.

The steaming pot of curry sat on the table next to sliced onions. At the stove, Banti was rolling rotis, readying them to cook on the tawa. Kalu saw Udho at the table as he came down the stairs a few hours later. Udho smiled as he bent down and up came a bottle of Indian whiskey which he must have bought when Kalu had been busy upstairs.

'Wow, what a gift, Bhapa. Bibi, bring the rotis and come.'

They touched glasses, the whisky glittering under the lights. The men's glasses emptied instantly. Kalu didn't contort his face this time. Banti lingered with her drink. They nibbled on onions as the whisky streamed down their throats.

After dinner, they retired to their rooms. Kalu switched on the radio preset at BBC. He fell asleep listening to the news, interviews and commentary. When he woke up to the alarm in the morning, BBC was still on.

Carrying the leather briefcase Udho had bought him when he had graduated from Elstow Secondary, Kalu cycled to college. It took him a few minutes to find the room for his first class. The teacher, standing at the front of the room, nodded as Kalu entered. He went and sat at the back, feeling a little awkward. The only other non-white face in the room smiled at him. The teacher began reading and explaining William Butler Yeats's 'The Second Coming', written following the First World War and at the beginning of the Irish War of Independence. Kalu knew of Yeats and the poem. His Indianness felt a kinship with Yeats's Irishness and coming to college seemed to him his own Second Coming—being alive again.

'Mr Singh, come a few minutes before the next class

and I'll fill you in on what's been covered,' said the teacher, Robert Cox, after the class.

Kalu nodded and walked out.

'Mr Singh?' a voice came from behind. It was that of Simran Kaur, the other brown face in the class.

'Hey mate, what's the hurry? I'm Simran. And you are...?' she continued.

'Kahla. Bibi was in a hurry for me to grow up!'

'Bibis are like that. Kahlu will be its sweeter version though, won't it?'

'Yes, but not Kalu...blackie.'

'Okay. But unfortunately it fits. There're only two colours in this country. Non-white, brown, black...it's all the same.'

'Yes, with some that's true. Not all.'

'You're pretty impressed, Mr Singh, with white sahibs, then.'

'Not everyone is a racist.'

'Hmm,' she smiled. 'We'll continue later. If you'd like to, that is. Right now I must get to chemistry.'

'I have to go to history. See you in English tomorrow,' he said. 'But why chemistry? I suppose the old folks want a doctor!' he couldn't resist teasing her a little.

'They can't help it. See you tomorrow,' she said as she left.

Instead of rushing to class, he lingered, watching the tall brunette stride away. She was black-eyed and light-skinned—shades of the centuries-ago white Aryans who trekked to India evident in her. A tiny black mole on her chin accentuated her mystique. She walked erect, unbent, like the bamboo pole he had thrown into the Satlej, as if on a mission against some dangerous foe.

The smiling Kalu would return to a smiling Banti in the afternoons. She made a variety of Indian foods, sweets and snacks. On the weekends, the three of them would finish a bottle of whisky Udho would buy on the way home on Friday evenings. One evening a week, Udho met up with Kalu at King's Arms on St Mary's Street across from the college. Father and son would drink a couple of pints of Guinness each and walk home to Banti's cooking which they both loved.

The rest of the time, Kalu was to be found cooped up in his study-cum-bedroom reading, writing, listening to the BBC and occasionally lounging with songs from Indian films in the Binaca Geetmala from Radio Ceylon on the old radio.

The only class he had in common with Simran was English. Cox would catch him glancing at her and smile. Kalu would run to the cafeteria in the free periods. She would often be there, waving him over to her table. Occasionally, they sauntered to King's Arms. She would keep him company for a pint of Guinness although she didn't drink, at least as far as her parents knew.

It was one such evening at King's Arms, a couple of years into his BA. The street lights had been on for some time. The roads bustled with workers and students on foot, bicycles, motorbikes, cars and buses. They were nestled into the corner at the far end of the pub near the dartboard. Simran noticed Cathy Johnson, training to be a teacher, sitting by herself and asked her over. Into their third round of Guinness, Simran watched as Kalu and Cathy played darts, bantering about politics and life.

'O hell, life's good. I'm winning, man,' she said for the umpteenth time.

'So you believe in hell, eh?' Kalu said, curious about her habit of peppering each sentence with 'O hell' as if it was her secret ode to God.

'I do, Kahla. It's simple. I need the heaven. Without the thought of hell, heaven would be impossible to perceive.'

'No good without evil...'

'Hell, yes.'

Kalu noticed the four men that had just walked in, their heads just inches short of the pub ceiling. They looked around, ordered a round of beer and sat down a few feet away from their table. Kalu saw them looking his way. Having been at the dartboard for over half an hour, he returned to his corner to take a sip of his Guinness and decided to stay. Cathy too returned.

'How about another round?' Simran asked.

Cathy nodded. Kalu waited for the bartender to look their way and signalled the order for the round.

'Those roughnecks keep staring at us,' said Cathy.

'Eh, probably curious about the turban,' said Kalu, consciously avoiding paying them any attention. 'Cheers,' he said and raised the pint to his table-mates when their drinks arrived.

When he did look across at the 'roughnecks' though, he immediately recognized Gholi, a first cousin of the rapist, Karam Singh, and a son of Banjhan's Daulat Singh Sandhu and a white woman whom he had married in Cambridge. He made crayons at Krayon.

'He needn't be curious about me or my turban. He knows who I am,' thought Kalu. The troika raised their glasses and resumed their conversation.

'A game, you and I?' Cathy asked Simran.

'Kahlu darling, you play. I'll watch,' Simran replied.

A few minutes into the game, as Kalu was writing the numbers with the chalk and Cathy was readying to throw her next dart, one of the four men walked up and pushed Kalu away from the board.

'You, asshole with head bandage! You fucking a white woman?' he said before turning to Cathy and adding, 'And bitch, you couldn't find a white dick to suck?'

'What the fuck is the matter with you, asshole?' said Kalu, getting up from the floor and almost lunging at the man.

But he checked himself, remembering the police caution to not let his anger get the better of him. To be sure, Simran and Cathy held Kalu back, standing between him and the four ready to bash him up.

'And you? A Johal who couldn't find anyone but a Chamar to hang out with?' said Gholi.

'Hey, just fuck off!' yelled Simran.

The pub's owner called the police. Gholi and his gang left. The police station was a mile past the Ouse Bridge. The three of them waited for half an hour but the police didn't show up. Kalu wanted to leave, angry at himself for losing his temper.

Worried about both his anger and safety, Simran put her right arm around his back and said, 'Kahluji, learn not to lose your cool. If you marry me, Indians will give you nothing but heartache.'

'I can't help lose my cool at dumb shit. I feel like killing the bastards.' After a moment's pause, he added, 'But I guess you mean I should resist acting on impulse, right?'

'Right you are,' said Simran as she and Cathy walked Kalu home.

At college the next day, Simran waited outside Kalu's first class.

'We've got to tell the police,' she said as he came out.

'Maybe. But one charge or prosecution won't bring salvation. I can't wish away my caste and colour.'

'Look, Kahla. Bullies have to be confronted by law.'

Kalu was not convinced that was the right thing to do. But having grown up in England, Simran was less cynical about the justice system.

'Did I ever tell you about Reeti? It was horrible...what

happened to her,' she said, pulling him to the cafeteria, hoping to sit him down and persuade him.

Simran had never found it easy to talk about her friend from school. Reeti was an unlikely candidate for the private co-ed boarding school she was able to get admission into. She was an untouchable, on scholarship from India. Things had changed for the worse when an Indian boy she knew at school, the son of rich zamindars, found out she was an untouchable. He began harassing her as he would lower caste people in the village. Brought up in submission to the zamindars, she couldn't tell him off. He raped her. Not only did the upper-class friend she confided in offer no help, she had scoffed at and belittled her. Reeti eventually committed suicide, unable to live with the dishonour she had brought to her family and afraid to take recourse to the law, given the lack of concern of that institution for lower castes back home.

By now Simran had tears streaming down her cheeks. 'How I wish Reeti had told me,' she said. She had decided then never to let such a thing happen ever again.

They crossed the Ouse Bridge and within minutes they were sitting at the police station across from officer Chris O'Toole who was the one who had decided not to charge Kalu for punching Ravi Agnihotri at the Krayon Christmas party.

'But the half-Indian Gholi hanging out with racist roughnecks beats me,' he said.

'He wants to be considered white. He looks white, acts white and racist. The caste hatred he's picked up from his father. But how did he know my name?' said Simran.

'The daughter of the only Indian doctors in the city! And that too out and about. He and his gang are probably always on the prowl for good-looking young women. He would know who you are... Or maybe he could've seen you at your home. You know? At your dad's prayer meetings,' said Kalu.

In the expensive part of Bedford, Simran's parents' home was three times the size of Kalu's, not including the manicured gardens surrounding the structure. Every couple of months, many Indians, largely Sikhs, gathered at their home to pray before the Sikh Holy Granth in a large room designated for prayer. Kalu had been there only once before he met Simran. But he hadn't seen her there that time. The only child of her parents, and unlike them not too religiously inclined, she enjoyed a degree of freedom rivalling that only of the sons in Indian households in Bedford. More than Kalu, it was Simran who pressed, in fact pestered, the police about the assault on him. But no one could identify the attacker. And Gholi didn't cooperate with the police. That file, like many others, was perforce closed.

The final examinations of Kalu's BA and Simran's BSc were over a few months later. The ugly parts of that evening were forgotten, but they had also lost touch with Cathy. She had decided to marry and move to another town. At least that's what they knew. The two of them now spent long hours with only each other for company, roaming the parks and visiting monuments, or at the library reading rooms and the cosy pubs of Bedford. Udho and Banti had met Simran. The daughter of Punjabi Sikhs impressed them with her Indian etiquette.

'She seems a bit headstrong and stubborn. But tough people get respect,' Udho had said. He had gone to Simran's home only once, for the prayer meeting, and had taken Kalu along. He never did again because some attendees had expressed their disapproval about the presence of an untouchable.

'She is a Sikh Jatti. I hated Karam and others in Banjhan.

But then Chacha Hazara is a Sikh Jat too. She's all right. She's tough,' said Banti.

'But she hasn't talked to her parents yet,' Kalu told them.

12

The beginning of the new academic year was days away. Simran's parents, Amrit Singh Johal and Sureet Kaur, wanted her to enrol in medicine. A scion of rich zamindars, Amrit had completed his post-secondary education in England. That's where he had met Sureet, a medical doctor from Punjab who had come to Britain on a research scholarship. Those days Amrit presented himself as progressive, aiming to disrupt the slumbering Indians against all evils. And caste was one of those evils—Sikhism had told him. In time, he began leaning towards a more fanatic view of Sikhism. The tenet of equality in Sikhism got lost in his nonsensical insistence on Jat superiority.

The change in him had disturbed Sureet. But the fear of dishonouring her family kept her in the marriage. The bow-legged Amrit, a good student of mediocre intellect, wasn't beyond physically abusing Sureet. On what limits to place on Simran and what liberties their headstrong daughter could enjoy, they often differed. Those moments of differences often ended in Sureet bearing his blows.

For the Johals, Kahla Singh was an Indian, a Sikh, a Punjabi—a promising prospect for marriage for their only child—until they discovered he was Udho Chamar's son. Like an earthquake, it upended the Johals' world. Amrit was fine with Simran studying medicine in London but told her to stay away from Kalu.

His caste revealed itself quickly enough as it was bound to in the small Indian world of Bedford. Their relationship had become a topic of discussion among the Indians of Bedford and its suburbs at about the same time as the building of a Sikh gurdwara was being discussed. Probably the wealthiest Sikh in Bedford, Amrit was leading the drive to build it. That had set him on a collision course with Udho who had helped register the Sri Guru Ravidas Sikh Society for the purpose of building another gurdwara—for the untouchables.

Though a believer, Udho wasn't a man given to religious dogma. He had been stung by the experience of his only visit to the Johal home for prayers. He had lived Banjhan's bondage and the ostracism of the untouchables from its social life. He wasn't prepared to allow Banjhan's cruelty to be replicated in Bedford. The insult at the Johal home had led him to side with the untouchable Sikhs who wanted a separate gurdwara so they could pray in peace without the Jats and others belittling them.

'I'm there for you,' Kalu had told Simran a few weeks before the admissions were to be finalized. He had advised her to go study medicine in London as her parents wanted while he did his masters in Bedford.

'Hypocrites...that's what they are! All my life they lied to me...the Granth says this, the Granth says that...there's one caste,' Simran had fumed. 'How can you be so blithe about it, it's our life? Mine won't be without you.'

'Maybe I'm being a coward,' Kalu said, still ashamed deep inside of the fact that he had *escaped* to England. 'First I wanted to marry Christine and now you...almost as if I want to escape my past. To erase my caste and Banjhan.'

'Or perhaps you're able to love people for who they are. Maybe it's just that simple.'

At the Johals' home, the arguments ranged from 'Kalu's

upbringing is different. The values are bound to be too' to 'You'll have difficulty dealing with the illiterate parents of an only child' and many more in that vein. It was Amrit who always spoke for Sureet and himself. Not once did he utter the word Chamar. Yet in its absence it echoed louder than all the other words that came out of his mouth.

At the other end of town, on St Leonard's Avenue, closer to the brick kilns, factories and foundries, Banti was saying, 'Oh Kalu! In Banjhan by now we'd be in the cremation grounds lighting your pyre. I'm frightened... We'll find a Chamari for you.'

Udho nodded at Banti's invocation of the realities of life and death in Banjhan's Chamarli. After their initial approval of Simran, both had begun having second thoughts, especially now that they knew her parents were against it.

Simran enrolled in medicine in London, Kalu for his master's degree in Bedford. Every weekend she travelled to Bedford and he received her at the bus stop or the railway station. They went for walks, pubbing with friends, spent time planning their life, catching up and then waiting for the next weekend. She wanted to marry him. He wanted her to wait, to be sure. The world of London might induce a change of heart, he argued. But she had been part of London's world before. To deny the voice of the heart and soul was cowardice and she would not be able to live with herself as a coward. She issued him an ultimatum.

'Kalu, you could be letting life elude you for the second time.'

It was midnight. Simran was not at the Johal home. She used to spend every Saturday night at her home in Bedford. Amrit dialled her London apartment but got no answer. He called her close friend. She didn't know where Simran was either. Sureet stood by silently, holding on to the teak stairway post by the telephone stand. Amrit kept dialling the apartment and other numbers well past midnight. He tried again the next morning, but to no avail.

'Where were you, Simran? Your mum and I, we were worried,' he said when he got finally got through that evening.

'I'm fine, Papa. I couldn't make it to Bedford this weekend.'

Angry at her own weakness in not being able to confront her parents with her decision, she slammed the phone down; her teeth grinding so hard that her jaw ached as she tore the cover of the book in her hand and threw it on her bed.

'Were you ploughing your father's land in Punjab with oxen all night...? You look terrible,' said Rajbir Kaur, a recent immigrant and a fellow Punjabi student.

'No, it was worse. But I'm late for class,' Simran said, rushing away.

Simran had spent the entire weekend at Kalu's home. For two days, a trembling Banti walked around the house afraid of Bedford's zamindars and untouchables, parallel but separate—both detested Kalu Chamar's impudence. She imagined them marching with swords and lathis, 'How dare you disobey Banjhan?' etched on their foreheads. Frenzied, she rushed around the small house, ensuring all doors and windows were bolted and locked at all times, drapes and curtains drawn, the lights out.

'Bibi, don't worry,' Kalu said.

'Vey Kalu. I don't know the language or the ways of this place; her parents...do they know that you want to marry her?' She obviously knew the answer.

'No, they don't.'

'The doctor's probably on his way here with a gun. Send her home or go hide somewhere,' she pleaded.

Udho walked around the house as if searching for something.

'Bibi, Bhapa, we're going to be fine. I'm going to talk to my mum and dad soon,' Simran had said before returning to London without visiting the Johals.

Late the next Friday, Kalu received Simran at the train station. They spent the night and the next day at Kalu's home.

'You're sure we've done the right thing?' he asked as they walked to the Johals' home.

'Kahlu, you've got to be strong. I'm not a child. We'll be fine.'

In the dark, their shadows walked with them, unseen. Proximity to the street lampposts exposed them. At the entrance to the one-acre front yard the light recreated their embrace on the concrete floor. He felt the weight of Banjhan ease. He kissed her. She walked away into the house.

His head was filled with questions about how the news of their marriage was being greeted by Simran's parents. Instead of four eyes on the way to the Johals, only two guided his footsteps home, his own. The last eight days flashed before him as he strode. Nine days earlier, outside the marriage commissioner's office in London, an Indian friend brought to witness the civil marriage had balked. Simran hadn't told her it was Kalu she was to marry. Fortunately, there were other friends to stand in. Even at the last minute Kalu had said, 'Sim, are you sure you want to marry me?'

Inside the Johal home, the black mole on Simran's chin, her tiny black pearl, radiated in the lights. A paraffin heater ablaze in the sitting room, Simran told them she was now Mrs Kahla Singh.

'Sim, we'd have arranged tents and the Granth in the back yard for the marriage. We'd have had a party. Your mother and I are happy for you,' said Amrit, rubbing his pressed beard with one hand and his right knee with the other. Busy in the kitchen, Sureet was unable to concentrate on cooking. Her heart raced, making it difficult for her ears tuned to the conversation to follow it.

'Papa, I was afraid you'd be cross with me.'

'Why would Papa be cross with you? You're our only child,' said Sureet, her eyes fixed on the stove.

'But he argued against it like I was committing suicide!'

No answer. The aroma of the food being served in the dining room absorbed the silence. After dinner, Sureet asked Amrit to drop their daughter at 'her in-laws'. They drove her to Kalu's together.

13

Halfway through her medical degree, Simran spent weekdays in London and weekends with Kalu in Bedford. He was completing the last few courses of his master's. It was Simran's wish for him to prepare for a doctorate. Udho was working and they could manage their expenses until the two started earning.

Jeetu had found a better place to stay and moved out of their home. But Udho felt the home needed more room and privacy with Simran joining the family. He added a full bath and toilet to the house so one didn't have to walk to the water closet at the end of the backyard. Each room of the home had electric and paraffin heaters so that when studying at home or resting, Simran was comfortable. A telephone was installed at home for Kalu and Simran to stay in contact during the week. Banti would cook Indian delicacies for her daughter-in-law and keep her supplied with chai on demand as the latter lounged and studied. Amrit and Sureet visited them every month on St Leonard's Avenue and insisted upon Kalu and Simran visiting them too.

In London, she studied hard all week so she could be relatively free on the weekends she spent in Bedford. On occasion, she would insist Kalu take the train to London instead of her coming to Bedford, particularly if there was a social engagement. The crowds were often mixed with both Indians and non-Indians in them, but sometimes just Indians. One weekend, it was the medical school Indians. She had missed their last event.

'Sim, I've a paper to write and haven't I already met them?'

'No. Kahlu, I don't want to be alone on the weekend. Till death do us part, remember?'

Fifteen students, spouses and mates, wearing western and Indian clothes, sat or stood in a London house the size of the Johals' kitchen. Holding their drinks, Simran and Kalu sat in a corner talking to their neighbours. Someone suggested they play 'antakshari'. As if on cue, another sang the first verse of an Indian film song, expecting the next person—Simran—to sing the first verse of any other film song beginning with the last consonant of the verse just sung. Born and raised in Britain with little or no access to Indian films, Simran let her turn pass to Kalu. He had been to the talkies in Mahilpur, idolized matinee actor Dilip Kumar and regularly listened to the Binaca Geetmala on the radio—he left the crowd thoroughly impressed. Kalu was glad he had agreed to be part of this jovial evening as everyone now poured fresh drinks and ate sitting or standing in any space they could find.

The talk turned to real introductions—beyond first names—urged by Columbus, the convent-educated son of a well-known zamindar of Punjab. The whispered reluctance of the few did not stand in the way for long.

'Tirath Kumar Anand,' one said.

'Oh, nice to know another Anand. I'm Jagjit Singh Anand.'

'Iqbal Ahmed.'

And so it went until the person third from last said, 'My name is Manoj Kumar.'

'But what's your real name?'

'Manoj Kumar. The only real name given me by my parents.'

'There's more beyond Kumar in an Indian name.'

'You mean what the society gave me at birth? Oh, I'm from a family of Rajpurohits, Dwivedis, you know...the readers of two Vedas...? Who became royal priests... But that's family history.'

'So, what about you?' Columbus asked turning to Simran.

'Simran, Mrs Kahla Singh.'

'I'm a Singh too!' said Columbus.

'And what's your point?' asked Simran, explaining how Guru Gobind named all Sikhs who took his nectar Singh.

'What is your gote?'

'You mean caste? Why not just say that instead of pussyfooting around it? This is what the real introductions were about, wasn't it?'

There was silence in the room.

'Hey Columbus, discoverer of people who weren't lost and hadn't sought to be found, I'm not lost. I'm Kahla Singh, son of Udho Singh and Banti Kaur. For you, a Chamar of Banjhan. Where's the land or the dead cattle you want me to work on?'

Kalu could hear the birds chirping outside in the pin-drop silence. He helped Simran with her overcoat and held her arm as they walked to the Underground station. The noise of the wind, the air-blowers and the trains in the Underground mirrored the turmoil in Kalu's heart.

'You all right?' he asked, turning to Simran.

'I am. But what kind of culture do we have? Papa keeps

on about our proud traditions but there was nothing to be proud of tonight.'

'Except you,' he said pulling her in.

Kalu enrolled in courses to do his PhD at the University of London after his master's. Simran was about a year away from completing her medical degree. Through his PhD and her degree and residency they lived in London and managed to keep peace on the family front despite the strain of the ruckus about the separate gurdwaras in Bedford. For their part, the parents kept the peace too. Despite the fathers belonging to warring camps, Amrit and Sureet regularly visited Udho and Banti.

One Saturday, while Kalu was visiting Bedford and happened to accompany Udho to the market, another Indian came up to Udho and said, 'Udho, we need to redouble our efforts to raise money for the gurdwara. The Johal group doesn't have to because he's pledged to make up the shortfall.' Soon, people in the Johal group were referring to the other as the Udho group. Not that Udho was their leader or had money to give. In the small world of Bedford's Indians, the facts lent themselves to lazy and inevitable juxtapositions.

'Bhapa, we should avoid conflict with Simran's parents,' suggested Kalu.

Udho continued to put the vegetables he had purchased into his bag and said nothing. They walked back home.

Banti greeted them with, 'I don't want to lose my daughter-in-law over the gurdwara. Why can't these idiots just have one place?'

Udho proceeded to place the grocery bags in the kitchen and went to the front room to sit in front of the heater. He hadn't asked for the friction around the gurdwaras and didn't appreciate everyone losing their minds. Kalu could take the train to London but Udho got no respite from the temple talk. And Banti was on again about how she worried her daughter-in-law would be the meat in the sandwich in the battle between the untouchables and those who despised them.

The day before the meeting of the untouchable group, Kalu called Udho from London.

'Folks, I'm one of the poorest members here. I will do what I can to see that a temple for us is built. But please, for God's sake, stop calling it Udho's group,' Udho repeated at the meeting what Kalu had asked him to say. He heard some whispers but no objections. Kalu called back to see how things went at the meeting.

'Fine, son. And, oh, by the way, I'm going to attend the prayers at the Johal home,' said Udho.

'Nice, Bhapa. Thank you.'

Dressed in his Sunday best, Udho set off from home. He stopped to look at the water on the Ouse Bridge. Looking over its edge, he could see the side of the bridge reflected in the river. Many men and women in Banjhan, much younger than himself, couldn't see, nor afford glasses or treatment, let alone enjoy this picturesque county town in England. He was more fortunate than them. Striding swiftly, he reached the gates of the Johal home. He walked around the house to the backyard, took his shoes off, covered his head, grinned all the way to the Granth and bowed before it. On the men's side, there were at least fifty others seated on the ground on the carpet, and about the same number of women across the aisle. The prayers over, prasad made of wheat flour, sugar and lots of butter distributed to all present, it was time to sit on the mats in rows to share the meal, men on one side and women on the other.

'What the fuck is this Chamar doing here? Fuck off to your own group,' someone shouted, pushing Udho from behind as he bent down to squat cross-legged in an empty spot between two other men. Amrit and others stopped the attacker and walked him away. No one helped Udho, lying face down. He got up, dusted off his pants and jacket, and stood there for a few moments. Everyone was looking at him, but in the stupor of a Banjhan-like blindness, no one was seeing him. No one, not even Amrit nor Sureet, apologized to him. The only other time Udho had attended prayers at the Johal home he was with Kalu. He had detected hostility but there had been no violence. He had resolved never to come to Amrit's again but Amrit had invited him, and his son was now Amrit's son-in-law; he had to come. His fists clenched, he stormed out of the Johals' garden. His calves ached, the limp pronounced as if his calves had once again taken a beating, as if Banjhan had struck across the oceans. He reached the top of the Ouse River Bridge and halted at the spot he had in the morning. The river looked different. But it flowed with the same calmness.

He unlocked the door to their home and dropped onto the sofa. Hearing the door open, Banti, who was upstairs cleaning one of the bedrooms, came down.

'What have you done to your cheek?' she asked.

'What are you talking about?'

'The blood on your cheek...?' said Banti.

She cleaned it up. It was minor but quite obvious. He told her what had happened. In the evening, Kalu phoned.

'Some kutta Jat assaulted your Bhapa,' Banti told him.

'Nothing, nothing...it's not the Johals' fault,' Udho placated Kalu on the phone.

Simran was engrossed in preparing for her final exams. Kalu kept Udho's assault from her and cautioned his parents to do the same lest it disturb her focus. On the weekend, he travelled to Bedford. The Johals came over to their in-laws' home.

'Bhra Udho, I apologize for the idiot who assaulted you,' said Amrit.

'It's all right, Papa. Bhapa doesn't blame you. There are caste warriors galore amongst us.'

Udho nodded.

'Kutta! That's what he is. And not a simple kutta; a simple kutta has a heart,' said Banti.

Nobody said anything. They all resumed sipping chai.

'Bhen Banti, at the next prayer meet you should come with brother Udho,' said Sureet, patting Banti's thigh.

'Nah, bhen, I don't understand God. I have a portrait of Ravidas here. Whenever I have a problem, I pray before him,' said Banti, pointing to the portrait on the wall. The Sri Guru Ravidas Sikh Society had distributed the portrait.

Kalu watched his parents interact with the Johals and felt pride in the dignity they showed despite the deep hurt of the assault. As he walked the Johals to their car after the tea, he said, 'Papa and Mum, please don't mention the assault to Simran. I don't want any family issues impacting her exams.'

From inside the car, the Johals nodded and drove off.

14

India and Indians who had felt bruised by the Sino-Indian war of 1962 constantly read, listened and watched the coverage of the Indo-Pak war of 1965. Night after night, in London, Kalu too tuned in to BBC news on a small radio. The Indians' Indianness badly bruised and machismo severely mauled in 1962 stood somewhat restored in 1965. Kalu's thoughts now turned to the British home front. Having emerged victorious yet weakened from the war years, London was into the Swinging Sixties, with more freedom for the young, music and drugs. Kalu and Simran appreciated London's openness to diversity, but after years of classes, notes, papers, lectures and exams, they were homesick.

Bedford was home.

The Johals had paid for the London living expenses and fees for Simran. Kalu didn't want to accept their money. He was confused about the Johals' view of his marriage to Simran. Sometimes they appeared quite accepting of it. At other times they, in particular Amrit, since Sureet was always quiet, appeared distant and uncomfortable.

Udho had retired and had jumped into renovating the house. He added a bedroom on top of the bathroom built earlier. The small eating area was expanded to accommodate a formal dining room, a sitting room for the family and the daily eating area. The front room with sofas and chairs served as a place for special occasions and to welcome guests.

'Why are you spending so much on the house? It was already a million times better than the one in Banjhan,' said Banti.

'Our only child and his wife, it's their home. We put our thumb prints for signatures. They are both doctors.'

The renovations were complete with a few days remaining before Kalu and Simran were due home. Udho and Banti were sipping chai in the new sitting room off the kitchen. There was a knock on the door, which was odd because they hardly ever had any visitors.

'Oh, probably a registered letter from Chacha Hazara Soonh,' said Udho walking to the door. He rarely pronounced Singh as Singh, often using the lazy version, Soonh. Despite Udho expressing his helplessness in dealing with the trust proposed by Master Hazara, the latter had pressed ahead. The trust deed was expected any day in the mail.

He opened the door.

'Sir, I'm here to speak to Udham Singh about a complaint that's been made against him,' said a cop dressed in the official blue.

Udho understood enough English for the foundry, the Saturday market and the pub but not to converse with the police. 'Not enough talk, my son talk. Your name and telephone please,' he said.

The cop gave him his number and left.

'What was he saying, that kutta pulsia? What was he doing at our door?' asked Banti who had snuck up behind him to take a peek at who Udho was talking to.

'No, Banti, the police here are good. They're not like the corrupt officers in Banjhan.'

After finding out why the police had come she said, 'What have you done now?'

Seeing him slump into the recliner Simran had bought him, she poured him another chai. After drinking the chai he called Kalu, who in turn called the police. The forty-five-year-old Gurbachan Singh Hundal, who had pushed him at the Johal home, had filed a complaint with the police accusing Udho of assaulting him.

'Bhapa, in three days Simran and I are going to be home. I've told the cops we'll go see them then,' said Kalu.

A moment after speaking to his father he called Amrit.

'Papa, did you know your friend Gurbachan is making false allegations of assault against Bhapa?'

'No. Why would he do that?' said Amrit.

'Papa, in Punjab we do it all the time. False complaints against people to cause trouble and expense. I'm sure you know that.'

'Kahla, I'll speak to Gurbachan.'

'Papa, it's your group doing this in the name of gurdwaras and prayers. Defeats the purpose, no?' said

Simran, taking the phone from Kalu, her right index finger wagging in the air.

'I'm going with you,' said Simran in the sitting room of the Bedford home as they discussed the impending visit to the police station.

'Puttar, what are you going to do there?' asked Udho.

'Are you not my father too? Does a daughter not have as much right as the son to defend her father?'

'Women don't go to police stations,' said Banti of Banjhan.

'Bibi, the world is changing. Women are cops, lawyers, judges and doctors,' said Simran.

The following day, in a small cubicle at the police station, they sat opposite the moustached and balding officer Warrington. Udho narrated the incident. Kalu translated for him.

'Why would the complainant lie?' asked Warrington.

'That's what they do in Punjab. Police and the courts are used to settle scores with each other,' answered Kalu.

'Mr Singh, you say your father and the complainant had no ongoing feud.'

'No feud, except that for my father and the complainant, my father-in-law happens to be from the wrong caste. My father-in-law is an untouchable, you see,' said Simran.

'Caste, Mrs Singh? I've read about it...untouchability and the rest of it.'

'That's the nub of it. My parents didn't want me to marry my husband. Lower caste, et cetera. They relented. But then, my father hangs out with these macho Jats. And now there's also this tension over the planned temples they're building. They want separate temples...them and the untouchables both.'

The police meeting over, they walked out and set off

towards home, uncertain what the outcome might be.

'Bhapa, how about a Guinness at the King's?' asked Simran.

'Why not, we're in Bedford, not in Banjhan!' said Udho.

'In England, daughters are like sons too. Why not daughters-in-law?' said Simran walking close to Udho, placing her hand on his back.

Udho smiled and limped along. As they walked over the Ouse to the pub he wondered about the wisdom of a Guinness with Simran. He didn't want to set more Indian tongues wagging. But he always found it impossible to say no to Simran.

'Bhapa, are you sure it's okay?' It was unlike her to second-guess herself but she asked.

'Absolutely!' Udho said, pleased at the same time about how perceptive she was of his doubts.

Kalu thought the affection between them heavenly as they sat in their corner near the dart board. The round of Guinness arrived. Taking the first sip Udho asked, 'Puttar, did your parents ever bring up caste when you told them you wanted to marry Kahla?'

'Well, Bhapa, they did, but not directly. They argued different culture, different values, but never caste. They'd never tire of the beauty of the village culture. But when they met Kahlu they began to talk of different values and cultures. Suddenly, a village with one culture had many different cultures. They obviously meant castes.'

'I wish you'd told me how serious your parents were about this caste thing before we got married,' said Kalu.

'It was my fight, Kahlu. Had I lost it, I wanted it to be my loss. I couldn't bear to see you lose,' Simran replied.

The traffic was at its peak as they left King's Arms that afternoon. Kalu and Simran had to make a visit to the bank before going back home to work out further plans for the opening of her medical practice. Kalu didn't want her to rent. Udho had saved some for 'our Simran becoming a doctor', as down payment for an office. But the rest had to be borrowed. As with everything else in their life, it involved clearing a minor hurdle.

'We don't lend to women. It can be done if you sign as co-owner,' the bank manager said to Kalu.

'Why? The money that I'm going to be earning... probably a lot more than my husband, isn't it good enough for the bank? Or is it our colour?'

'No, madam, it's our gender,' said the manager, Janet Simpson.

'But this is stupid. You're a woman. How can you let this happen...treat women as second class?' Simran was livid.

They went to several banks in Bedford, all at short distances from each other, only to get the same answer. They had ultimately to return to Mrs Simpson and sign the documents for a joint loan, with Kalu as the main applicant.

As for the search for Kalu's job, he made it a habit to scour the local evening newspaper every evening, keeping an eye out for teaching vacancies. He spotted one, not long after their return, for a history professor at his alma mater Mander, and yelled it out to Simran.

'I'll type up your application right away. Bhapa was prescient in buying the ancient typewriter from Sally Anne's,' shouted Simran.

'Old-Remington-for-a-shilling Sally Anne's!' added Kalu.

'That's where I had bought my first three-piece suit from; from the Salvation Army's used goods store. The navy blue one that you were so proud of,' said Udho.

With paper and carbon already purchased for the purpose, Simran sat at the Remington pounding the keys.

The banging of keys, the carriage return and the space bar, the myriad movements of the typewriter made music in the house.

Always the first to arrive in the morning, the receptionist Darlene McIntosh opened the college office. She was surveying the room to make sure she had everything in place for the day when, envelope in hand, Kalu entered.

'Oh Kahla, how've you been? Long time, no see. Someone said you have done your PhD.'

'I'm well. PhD...yes, I'm glad you asked. That's why I'm here,' Kalu said, a tad hesitant as he handed her the application. 'I saw the advertisement in the paper for the History professor's position.'

'If I could will it, you'd be it,' she said.

A fifty-year-old, separated single mother, Darlene had been in the job long before Kalu had enrolled at the college. She remembered the only student with a turban in the college at the time, his smile and the reverence he had for her and the office staff, even more than some elementary students had for their teachers.

Happenstance or synchronicity, the telephone rang twice at their home the next day. Simran's loan had finally been sanctioned—Simran's, for she was the sole and primary applicant, not secondary to Kalu. Janet Simpson had gone to bat for her. She had been a manager for several years now. Their confrontation had awakened her to the inequity of their policy. And at Mander, Darlene the receptionist had walked into the office of the administrator tasked with hiring professors and repeated what she had said to Kalu about 'if she could will it'.

Kalu was interviewed by three men the next morning and offered the position to teach history. As an alumnus, he was welcomed with open arms by the faculty and students, in particular by Dean Robert Symes, a graduate of Durham

University, further distinguished by his longish, curly locks of blond hair.

'Nice to have another Indian teach at the college, and also in the department, where this other Indian, yours truly, is Dean.'

'How's that?' Kalu asked.

'Born pre-Independence, my friend! My father served in the British Indian Army. Have fond memories of Mother India.'

For her clinic, Simran had bought a small home in Queen's Park. Bedford Council allowed her to turn much of the ground floor into a doctor's office, allowing the rest to be rented out as a residence.

Kalu would drop by her office once a week after she began her practice to see how it was going. 'Sim, my magician wife, not a seat vacant in the waiting room today,' he remarked one day, about two months into it. A packed crowd of patients—white, brown, black and everything in between—kept streaming in. The untouchables in particular, young and old, made a beeline to the clinic of Doctor Simran Kahla Singh.

He taught five days a week while she practised another half-day on Saturdays. Her parents lost all the untouchable patients to her, as well as some other Indians. Simran tried, but failed, to dissuade them from abandoning her parents. Some of the Johals' friends would try luring the patients to return by saying to them about Simran, 'She's a Chamari hiding behind the name Singh, married to a Chamar.' One such patient reported back to Simran. To make it less ambiguous, in a further act of defiance, the new nameplate outside her office now read: Dr Simran Kahla Singh Badhan. That removed any doubt about Kalu's caste and her embrace of it and him.

'A stubborn child,' said Amrit when told of the new nameplate by a member of his group.

'If she was my daughter, she would've been long dead,' the man told him.

Amrit looked at the man and then down at his own feet.

15

The Johals' prayer group, now the Guru Nanak Society, bought a house for a gurdwara on Goldington Road. The untouchables, called the Udho Group by everyone except Udho, legally incorporated Guru Ravidas Society, and bought a house on the opposite side of Bedford town centre on Bromham Road near Queen's Park. Despite both groups being Punjabi Sikhs and in Bedford, they were worlds apart. Not just that, in naming the societies they had separated Nanak from Ravidas, conveniently forgetting that their Holy Granth contained the teachings of both. The two groups applied to the town to authorize alterations to the houses to turn them into gurdwaras. The Goldington Gurdwara was bigger, both the built and un-built areas twice the size of the Bromham Gurdwara.

'One would think having your own gurdwara would calm things down,' Kalu remarked once to Simran.

'That's if they believed in anything cogent. Their faith is what anyone makes of it. One is being charitable calling them fanatics,' said Simran, troubled by the fissures in the community. 'They're lunatics.'

Come Baisakhi, the first day of the Nanakshahi Calendar, both societies requested permission to hold a Baisakhi parade, a first for Bedford. It was the day the tenth guru is said to have administered nectar to his first five Sikhs, all five from different castes—though none a Jat, the Johals' caste—thus founding the Khalsa. The Bedford

Council suggested they take out a joint parade. Failing to convince them, it allowed two parades on two different weekends, their priority decided by a coin toss.

'Bhapa, you don't need to go to the temple or the parade. You lived without a temple when there was none, not even a prayer group. I'm concerned the tension may get out of hand again,' said Kalu to Udho at supper.

'I'll think about it.'

Udho wasn't on the board of directors of the Ravidas Society that ran the Bromham temple. But because he was the father/father-in-law of the professor/doctor duo, the Society roped him in to volunteer on different committees and sub-committees as renovations to turn the house into a temple got underway. Bringing him in was a way of involving Kalu and Simran in the work around the temple for which they had shown scant interest. Not that he had any interest in formal religion otherwise, but there was the added concern Kalu had about mindless controversies and rumours a la Banjhan in Bedford. As a clever diversion to keep Udho from immersing himself in these affairs, he encouraged his father to accompany him to the meetings and activities of the Labour Party in which he had become active lately. The manoeuvring by Kalu failed, however. Udho was the unanimous choice to head the building committee and he accepted, though he did so reluctantly. The Goldington Group responded by making Amrit the head of its building committee.

The committees' main task, Kalu discovered, was to raise funds. Kalu hated the perceived rivalry between Amrit and Udho. He feared a competition would ensue as to the amount raised and a bidding war on how much money one or the other would raise and/or donate.

The tension between the Johals and the Badhans was on the boil. The trial for the criminal charge of assault against Udho was to be held in a few months. The police had tried to make the charge go away. Hundal, a younger man full of hate for the untouchables, wouldn't recant the allegations though.

'Asking is begging. I'm not begging him. Can't he see it himself? It hurts me that he hasn't put an end to this already,' said Simran of her father at the dinner table.

Kalu hadn't asked her to approach her father. Nor would he do it himself. He couldn't bear the insult of asking, particularly if the man didn't even have that much fealty to truth or his own daughter.

As the renovations progressed, the Ravidas Society began to hold prayers in the finished portion of the Bromham temple. Banti began attending the Sunday sessions.

'Dheeay, come with me to the gurdwara,' she said to Simran one Sunday morning. 'The idiot women keep asking about you. They're beginning to blabber that maybe you and I don't get along.' She added, changing tack, 'It's all right to go sometimes to the house of God.'

'I'll go with you, Bibi. But whether it's the house of God, I don't know.'

Kalu stood outside the door, watching them get into the car. Banti ran to it, a smile on her face like Kalu had never seen. Simran drove Udho and Banti to the temple. A limping Udho being driven by a doctor daughter-in-law in England to a gurdwara where he was respected was a far cry from his calves being broken for asking to be treated with respect in Banjhan.

'Dheeay, I'm so blessed. Here you drive me to the temple. They want me there. I'm in heaven,' he said.

'In Banjhan, they would have killed your Bhapa. The idiots treated us worse than dogs,' added Banti.

Banti walked around, introducing Simran to every woman she met at the temple. 'Banti bhen, she's my doctor,' said most of them.

They were walking to the car after the prayers when someone said, 'Your father donated five hundred pounds for the Goldington temple. You're a doctor too.'

'I don't believe in bribing the gods,' said Simran and drove away with Banti.

Udho had stayed behind to discuss the progress of renovations with members of the building committee. It was obvious what they wanted from him.

'Our numbers aren't as good as the numbers of the Goldington temple,' said a middle-aged man who worked at the brickyard, as they sat discussing funds.

'The Johal doctors have given lots of money. We need to work harder,' said another.

The meeting went on for a while, with little coming forth by way of solutions, and Udho unable to offer much beyond lending a concerned ear. As he exited their small office and walked out into the common area, he overheard someone say, 'The Chamars have only one rich doctor, Jatti Simran. And she's a Chamar only by marriage.'

But Kalu was there to rescue him. 'Bhapa, time to go home,' he said, finding Udho standing by himself in the main hall. He had been dispatched by Simran to fetch him. She was alive to the contest being set up by the temple committees between Udho and Amrit, and worried constantly for her father-in-law.

In the car home Udho told Kalu what had transpired. How the members of the committee expected the family to pitch in, though they only hinted at it in his presence.

'I have no money. My savings went into the house. My small pension won't help the gurdwara!'

Kalu understood from Simran the sentiments of the untouchable group, many of them her patients. They would spill their guts in her clinic: She made money off them and she should give some to the temple.

'Bhapa, there's already too much religion in the world. I've been urging you to stay away from all this stuff. Some people have nothing better to do than being at the temple or seeing you fight the Johals. A Chamar fighting a Jat, his own daughter-in-law's father...they just want to see some drama.'

Udho was quiet on the sofa in the sitting room. Kalu asked Simran for some chai.

'I think Bhapa will have a cup too. Right, Bhapa?' said Simran.

'No, Dheeay, had enough at the gurdwara.'

'Lots of other stuff at the gurdwara, too,' added Kalu.

'What?' Simran asked as she lifted the tea cosy to check if the pot was still hot.

'Like money...they're suggesting Bhapa should contribute to the untouchable Bromham temple because your father is contributing to the Jat Goldington.'

'We can, but Papa has been practising a long time... can't compete with him. It would be foolish to get sucked into a bidding war one couldn't win and that too for this ungodly feuding over God,' said Simran, placing four cups of chai on the table.

Banti had walked in from the front room by now. 'Don't say that, puttar. God's everything,' she said, dismayed by the suggestion that the gurdwara was somehow ungodly.

'Yes, Bibi. How's the chai?' said Simran, ignoring Banti's comment.

'Chai is good but there is too much God in the family. Bhapa and Bibi, we should want to be known for doing something for Man rather than God. We could give money here to a good charity or to Chacha Hazara's trust in Banjhan. There are many others here who will make up the shortfall for the gurdwara. Why not transform jhuggis into habitable homes for people in Banjhan?' said Kalu.

'Bedford is my world now. I have to live here,' said Udho.

'This is my world, too. But I don't have to belong to its parts I don't agree with. Even you don't agree with the separate temples but you're still helping them...?'

'The Jats hate us. The whites look down upon us. And you're telling me to stay away from the only people who don't hate me?' said Udho.

'Yes, I'm suggesting we find good people and keep our doors open for them, be they white, black, brown, untouchables, Jats or whatever else.'

'You mean like the Labour Party people you've begun hanging out with? They are good but I'm sure some of them too are racists,' said Simran.

'Sure, Sim. Like many of us Indians think dark-skinned people are inferior, like darker Indians...and blacks,' said Kalu, glancing at Udho and Banti.

16

Kalu stood outside the bathroom waiting for Udho to come out. Udho had been in there a bit too long. Kalu didn't want to go downstairs to the other bath Udho had had put in when Simran came into the family. He was just feeling lazy. He knocked on the door.

'Come in.'

The door opened. His pyjamas on, face turned, Udho was looking at his left cheek in the mirror, examining the scar from his fall at the Johal house.

'Bhapa, the scar shall be there long after the trial is over. You can meditate on it then. Let's get ready. We've got to see the lawyer in his chamber.'

'I want to go with you. I've shut down my office for the morning,' said Simran, who had overheard them.

'Sim, I told you, you don't need to go.'

'Kahlu, I know the difference between need and want. You don't need me there. I want and need to be there.' Simran was determined not to lose the argument begun the previous night about going with them to see the lawyer.

'I want to be there for Bhapa. And dealing with lawyers is not a men-only domain. Aren't I right, Bhapa?' asked Simran as she drove them to Arthur Taylor Q.C.'s office.

'My dhee, you're always right.'

Simran wanted to physically stand with Kalu's family. With Amrit denying seeing Udho being pushed, the tension between the two families had only worsened. 'I won't add anything of value to the testimony,' Simran's father had maintained in refusing to stand witness for the defence. The bow-legged doctor had stood amongst his Goldington temple group and declared he wouldn't testify. By talking to other people present that day, Simran had learnt that her father was a mere ten feet away and had certainly seen Gurbachan Hundal assault Udho. She knew her mother had seen the whole thing too. But she didn't want to place Sureet in the awkward and difficult position of having to contradict Amrit. Though she had in the months leading up to the trial insisted she was above begging, Simran did appeal to Amrit to testify. But he firmly denied he saw anything.

'He could be compelled to come by an official summons, but often witnesses brought in to testify against their will choose to lie,' said the barrister Taylor.

The prosecution planned to call two witnesses corroborating Gurbachan's lie. Taylor suggested they canvass others present to find at least one, possibly two witnesses to what had happened. Kalu and Simran, she more than him, had in fact been canvassing the people present without any success. Following leads to find witnesses occupied much of their time outside work now that the trial was a mere month away.

On the way home, the honks and the whirring of the cars whizzing by could be heard uninterrupted in the silence inside the car.

On Monday mornings, Simran opened her office at 8:30 am so she could begin seeing patients at 9:00. Today, she had to write two brief reports before the deluge of patients started. It would inevitably be a deluge because most people didn't have phones to make appointments. While some did, it was hard for the recently immigrated, country-bred Indians to get used to the idea of booking appointments. They just showed up. Often, when she got to the office, the patients were already lined up, hoping to be seen before nine to be able to get back to work.

Pandit Karam Chand greeted her at the office door as she got out of her car.

'Uncleji, you're early. Everything all right?'

'Yes, beta. I've had a back problem for many days. There is pain in the lower back which shoots down to my toes. People tell me there is no cure for it. I thought I'd see my doctor dhee. She would surely do something.'

Once inside, Simran wrote a request to an orthopaedic specialist for a check-up and handed it to Karam. He got up to leave, but then sat back down.

'Dheeay, I understand Udho's case is coming up. Bloody liars. He's the victim. He did not even provoke Hundal; he did nothing. He was bending down to sit. That idiot just pushed him. And now, just like in the feuds in India, they're lying to prosecute him in court.'

'How do *you* know, uncleji?'

'I was three spots away. I was eating when it happened. But Udho is a nice man. He just walked away. Your father... I don't understand this nonsense about my group and your group, the divisions... They build and run gurdwaras...for what?' said Karam. He was among the many Hindus who would regularly attend the prayer meetings at the Johal home. To them, the tenth Guru had ordained the Khalsa as an army to protect Hindus.

A trade unionist active in Bedford's Labour circles, Karam knew of Kalu's involvement in local Labour politics.

'One day Kahla Singh should run for the parliamentary seat for Bedford. You and he make a great team, Dheeay,' he said before leaving.

Kalu showed up at Karam's home in the evening. A copy of the Indian Constitution rested on one end table and on the other a photo of Karam with Prime Minister Attlee peered at him. A poster of Nehru with a rose and pen tucked in his pocket, too, hung on the wall. Karam had come to England well before India's independence. He had followed the ups and downs of the freedom movement from afar.

'Uncleji, we need a witness to the assault on Bhapa... No one wants to testify, not even my father-in-law.'

'Feudal and caste loyalty, Kahla... Without his group, Amrit believes he'd have no friends. But Udho is part of his family now. What's the matter with him?'

'We've tried. He won't agree. It'd help if you could testify. You'll be a better witness. You're not related to us like Amrit. That's in fact better.'

'If I testify, I'll become an enemy of Amrit and his friends.'

'I understand that. But please, uncleji!' said Kalu and left to pursue other potential witnesses they had yet to visit.

The evening before the trial, there was silence in the sitting room as if it were empty. The visibly pregnant Simran drinking water, Udho sipping a beer, Banti drinking chai and Kalu watching them—his small family, they were all there. They had talked to all possible witnesses. Some had agreed to consider. None had promised to show.

'I want to talk to papa once more, my last attempt at extracting the truth from him,' said Simran.

'No, Sim, you've begged enough. I can't see you crawl.'

'Dheeay, it's all right,' said Udho, taking the last sip of his beer before turning to the food Banti had placed on the table. 'We'll let God be the witness. You've talked to brother Amrit so many times. If he was going to he would have melted by now.'

Kalu saw Simran pick up the car keys and walk to the car. He followed.

'Kahlu, I don't want you there. This is between me and him.'

'Sim, I don't want you to stress about it. Our child is more important than anything else right now. Please don't go.'

She started the car.

He got in and said, 'I want to go with you. I'll wait in the car.'

Simran promised to be out in half an hour. She had been gone an hour. Kalu got out of the car and began walking the hundred-foot pathway to the house. He was halfway when the front door of the house flung open, shattering the serenity of the lawns. Simran ran out wiping her eyes and blowing her nose. Sureet followed saying, 'Sim puttar, you shouldn't leave like this. Come back. He's your father.'

'No, Ma, I want to have nothing to do with him any more. He doesn't deserve my respect. How can you go on living with such a coward? You taught me to be brave. Show some courage for once,' said Simran as she threw herself into Kalu's embrace.

'Sorry, Mum. I've got to take her home now,' he said before turning around with Simran and walking to the car.

'People *lie* for loved ones. My father won't even tell the truth.'

'Sim, we've done our best. It's going to be all right.'

Kalu kept turning his head to look at her as the car breezed along the empty road. Moving through dark spots between the street lights, her face would periodically emerge into their glow before being obscured again. That was the only movement he felt. They had spun their wheels endlessly in search of a single witness with the fortitude to bury caste and walk into the courthouse to speak the truth. She continued shedding tears, oceans of them still inside her.

Banti was waiting for them in the sitting room.

'Your Bhapa went to sleep. Dheeay, don't lose heart. You're all that matters to us,' she said, seeing Simran's moistened, red eyes before placing her hand with the nail-less index finger on Simran's head to bless her.

'You carry our next generation inside you...that's all that matters,' continued the woman from Banjhan about the only thing she understood women to be—vessels for carrying the seeds of the future in their wombs.

The exhaustion drowned Simran into sleep. Kalu lay awake staring at the framed portraits of Nehru, Ravidas and Ambedkar he had requested Kirti to forward to him from India. Along with the portraits, Kirti had written a note that said, 'Hazara Chacha is well. The trust is functioning. I live with Chacha and help him. Sadhu is good, Sondh dead, the gun returned to Chacha.' As Kalu looked at the portraits, fragments from events long past swirled in his head—the scar on Kirti's wrist, Sadhu's tears and the last words he spoke to Kalu: 'I'm a Chamar too.'

A deep contentment coursed through him too. A smile crossed his lips before he turned to touch Simran as if to reassure himself she was still there, next to him.

But that took him to the scene outside the Johals' home. Apprehension replaced the smile as the thought of the looming trial consumed him. No one present at the scene of the assault on Udho had put a determined foot forward on their behalf. The world of Bedford's India seemed no better than Banjhan's. He put his arm over Simran's pregnant belly and curled up against her. He wanted to trade places with the foetal being inside her, eager, in ignorance, to unleash itself upon the world.

Hearing the noise of the up and about, Kalu got out of bed. The 5:30 am train rolled into St John's station. The morning shift brickyard workers boarded it. He went downstairs. Banti was making tea and Udho was in the bathroom. Simran was up when he returned to his bedroom.

'I'm going with you,' she said.

The train was still there. It seemed to be in no hurry to leave. He went back downstairs and brought two mugs of chai from the kitchen. He tried to persuade her as they had their chai to go attend to her patients rather than witness the trial.

'Bhapa is a good man. When I met him before deciding to marry you, I knew he would stand with me even against you if you were wrong. I must stand with him. It's not *his* need, it's mine.'

Banti served them pranthas with yogurt.

'Dheeay, half a prantha isn't enough for you and the child. You should eat two like every day,' said Banti.

Kalu had another chai and no pranthas.

17

Kalu took a sharp turn from St Leonard's Ave onto St John's Street, prompting a car on St John's to honk and come to a screeching halt. Kalu braked to a stop himself. Simran screamed.

'Son, we have a lot of time. Don't rush,' Udho said.

'Sorry, Sim. You okay? Yes, Bhapa, we'll take our time. And by the way, there're bound to be lots of provocations. Let's keep our focus. Concentrate on the goal, winning an acquittal,' he said, more to himself than the others.

Kalu found a parking spot not too far from the courthouse. The tall, moustached Arthur Taylor Q.C. was waiting.

'Udho, I hope you had a good sleep. It could be a long day ahead...and you too, Doctors Badhan,' said Taylor.

Simran's defiant adoption of the last name 'Badhan' had persuaded the family to begin using it. Kalu had reasoned it out thus: the Sikhs' Singh was meant to hide caste for all the Sikhs and the world. But it never did. Despite the vehemence of claims to the contrary, caste mattered to most Indians, including the Sikhs. Confronting caste couldn't be done without proclaiming it, Simran had told him. Adopting what one was battling did not at first make sense, but he had agreed to begin using last name.

The portrait of Queen Elizabeth above the judge's chair greeted them in the courtroom. Simran and Kalu found front seats in the gallery behind the defence counsel's table. Regina v Udho Singh Badhan also known as Udham Singh was the only case listed for the docket. Taylor took Udho out for a private discussion. Kalu went with them to translate. They had been speaking to each other when the complainant walked by with three others. Udho didn't look their way. Kalu did and said, turning to Taylor and Udho, 'There goes hate.'

'Dr Badhan, let's not be distracted,' said Taylor.

The discussion resumed and continued until Kalu spotted Amrit walking up. He walked over to him, unable to heed Taylor's advice.

'Papa, I've shied away from talking to you about this

but a victim is being tried as the perpetrator of a crime because you won't speak the truth. He was an invited guest at your home for a prayer meet. You had an obligation to ensure his safety. You failed. The least you could do now is speak the truth and urge others to do the same. There's still time.'

'I'm helpless...and I didn't really see it happen.'

'Papa, that's a lie,' Kalu said, watching Amrit walk into the courtroom without looking back.

The judge had come out of his chamber now and was moving towards the bench. The three of them quickly took their places before the clerk called the case. Several other men from the Johal group entered the room soon after they did.

Kalu glanced disdainfully about the room as he turned to look at the newcomers. There were none who, he felt, might stand up for the truth. He did find one though, a student of his who had shown up and was seated behind him. Unfortunately, he was not a witness.

'Hey Gurbat, you've classes, don't you?'

'Yes, Dr Badhan. But what's happening here is more important. I needed to come, for myself.'

Kalu smiled and turned his face back towards the bench.

A recent immigrant, Gurbat Gill observed everyone and every move in the court. He had entered England on the pretext of continuing his education. In India, he had begun skipping classes to go watch movies and journey by train to various places, things only the affluent could afford. His father saw Gurbat's future doomed, got him a passport and took out a loan for the plane ticket to England.

He had met Kalu at a pub and took an instant liking to the professor.

'My father gave it to me,' he had said once when their conversation veered to the oddity of their names, Kahla's and his own, Gurbat—poverty. 'He thought I could be the Gur, the Guru, for the poor and lead them out of poverty into prosperity. He had dreams for me. But my destiny was to slave in Krayon.'

Kalu encouraged him to enrol in the evening classes at the college. A freedom fighter in his extended family had impressed deeply upon him the idea of equality and a passionate abhorrence for the caste system. And so, here he was, to stand by a friend in his fight against caste.

The Punjabi-to-English court interpreter for Udho was sworn in. The prosecution called the complainant Gurbachan Hundal as its first witness.

'Udho shinned me while I stood talking to Ranbir Singh,' he repeated his allegation to the court.

'Did anybody see the accused shin you?' asked the prosecutor.

'Yes. Ranbir saw him do it and Dr Amrit Johal was close by, too.'

Simran turned and stared at Amrit who was looking down at the floor.

'Mr Hundal, what did you do after you were shinned?'

'I pushed Udho away and he fell.'

'Did you see any bleeding or other signs of injury on your shin?'

'No bleeding but the bone was tender for a few weeks.'

'No residual effects of the shinning now?'

'None, but the insult still hurts.'

The examination-in-chief over, Taylor began the cross-examination by asking Gurbachan if he had ever been convicted of a crime.

'Yes,' answered Gurbachan, followed by the prosecutor advising the court of the three-year-old common assault conviction.

'Who did you assault, Mr Hundal?'

'A bloody Chamar...untouchable...' said Gurbachan. 'He came and sat at the table next to us in the pub. I told him to move away. He said he'd sit where he pleased.'

'You hated his kind, his caste, as dirty and untouchable?'

'Yes.'

'So you punched him, Mr Hundal?'

'Yes...the Chamar, he'd never dare sit next to me in India.'

Taylor put it to Gurbachan that he assaulted Udho Chamar for the same reason, 'for daring to sit in the spot near you to partake of the food after the prayers'.

'No, I wouldn't assault Udho. Unfortunately, Doctor Johal's daughter is married to his son, otherwise...'

'Otherwise what?' asked Taylor.

'Otherwise I wouldn't want to sit near him, either.'

'And why is it unfortunate for Dr Johal's daughter to be married to Kahla Singh Badhan?'

''Cause he's a Chamar, simple as that.'

'Mr Hundal, I suggest you did hit Udho the Chamar at the Johal house and further suggest you did so *because* he is a Chamar.'

'No, I didn't hit him.'

'But you did hit him and then used the police and the prosecution to lay false charges to fend off any complaints by him.'

'No, I didn't.'

'Yes, you did, because you'd have done the same in India. Am I correct?'

'Lots of them do it in India. I'd have done it too, sure... so the other chap doesn't do it first. But only in India, not here.'

'But in the case at the pub you did try to file a case against the "bloody Chamar" but he beat you to it, didn't he,' said Taylor, brandishing a bunch of papers.

'Yes, the bloody Chamar beat me to it.'

The prosecutor didn't ask any further questions of Gurbachan. Prosecution's next witness, Ranbir Gosal, corroborated Gurbachan's account of the assault. Under cross-examination by Taylor, he too admitted his compatriots frequently used criminal courts to initiate and prosecute false accusations against individuals. The court took a recess for lunch.

Kalu looked back and a smile broke out on his face. Karam Chand sat next to Gurbat. Unknown to Kalu, Gurbat had been talking to Karam about the case against Udho. Karam was a Brahmin. With his top-caste lineage he had felt awkward about meddling in a case between a Chamar and a Jat. He didn't want anyone to believe he had an axe to grind against the Jats.

'It's not about you, me, the Brahmins, Jats or anyone else. It's about justice. Without truth, justice will lose out and you do know the truth,' the idealistic young Gurbat had told Karam, whose house he was a regular visitor to. Twice during the testimony of prosecution witnesses, Gurbat had slipped out of the court to phone Karam.

Kalu hugged Karam and Gurbat before they sat down to lunch with Taylor in a nearby cafeteria. Six of them, plus the six customers that had already been served, filled the place. Savouring the cream of cauliflower soup, Simran said, 'Arthur, thank you for exposing the fraud Gurbachan is. I wish you'd call my father...the coward, huh.'

'We can't call him. We don't know what he'd say... might damage our case,' said Taylor.

'Sim, let's not focus on the negative. I believe we're winning so far,' said Kalu.

As they ate, Taylor quickly went over what Karam's testimony might be before they rushed back to court.

It was time for Udho to take the stand. Taylor let him

tell the story of the assault and the fact that he was an untouchable, a Chamar, and how he had been treated in Banjhan. The prosecutor asked him pointed questions, some of which implied he might be lying. After the prosecutor's cross-examination of Udho, the judge asked Udho if the practice of laying false charges was common in India. Udho affirmed Gurbachan's testimony on the point.

Taylor asked the judge for a brief recess as he hadn't been able to fully prepare Karam for his testimony.

'Truth demands no preparation. Proceed,' said the judge.

Karam explained why, being a Brahmin, he was hesitant to testify. He corroborated Udho's testimony. The prosecutor decided cross-examining Karam would weaken his case.

'Caste in India...in Punjab...is there no inter-dining, intermarrying or even touching between untouchables and others?' the judge asked.

Karam affirmed his assumptions as fact and said, 'Not just that, we used to kill the untouchables as sacrifices to our gods. I distinctly remember the complainant saying, "In India I'd have gladly slaughtered you for coming near me," when he attacked Udho.'

'Any redirect arising out of my questions?' asked the judge.

'None, your honour,' said Taylor and the prosecutor, in unison.

The prosecutor then rose to make the summation.

'Judge, my father, Amrit Singh Johal, saw my father-in-law, Udham Singh Badhan, being assaulted. He's in the court. Ask him to stand up and speak the truth. He won't, because he's a snivelling coward,' shrieked Simran, wiping her tears.

'Madam, any more outbursts and I will ask you to leave the courtroom,' said the judge.

The prosecutor summed up the crown's case as Simran sat back down. Taylor concluded arguments for the defence. The prosecutor didn't avail the chance for the last word.

The judge adjourned and left the court, saying, 'I'll pronounce judgement tomorrow morning.'

'First, your daughter insulted us all by marrying the Chamar, setting a bad example for our children...and you did nothing. Now she's insulted you in the court. If she was my daughter, I'd have beheaded her long ago,' Kalu overheard a turbaned man of the Johal group say to his father-in-law as everyone cleared out of the court.

'Arthur, you did a great job,' said Simran.

'I'm optimistic about what tomorrow may bring,' he replied.

Udho ahead, Kalu with his arm around Simran, the trio walked to the car.

'Bhapa, you were brilliant on the stand. Had you gone to school...' said Kalu, his voice trailing. Drowned in thoughts of Udho persuading him to be educated and labouring in the foundry to make it happen, he let the sentence hang.

The aroma of the sarson saag with mukkay ki rotis greeted them as they entered the home. Banti was in the sitting room, watching TV. She watched anything moving on the screen, her only connection to the fast-changing world outside. For her, it was the TV and cooking for the family, in particular for her daughter-in-law whose womb carried the Badhans' next generation. Simran was particularly delighted by the aroma and warmth of the food and the kitchen. She hugged Banti, turned to Udho and hugged him too.

'Bhapa, I love you even more. You were so dignified in court, so without malice,' she said.

Kalu saw Udho's eyes moisten. Simran's words were a welcome thing after the stressful trial, he thought. Udho requested Banti for a cup of chai before the meal as he sat down on the sofa. There was indeed no rancour in him. In India, he was a Chamar, which was as good as a death sentence following life imprisonment. Here, he may have been a *coloured* man for the whites, but at least not a Chamar. As for Simran, he knew there was no trace of pity or altruism in her decision to marry Kalu. She was a pure soul. He only wished at times he had more words to express his gratitude for who she was.

'You've brought us so much happiness,' was all he could manage today as he tried to suppress the lump in his throat.

The next morning, Banti voiced her desire to go with them to the court to hear the verdict.

'Bibi, it's going to be over in a few minutes and we'll be back soon,' said Kalu.

'Bibi, it's going to be fine. The lawyer did a good job,' chimed in Simran.

'Because I don't speak English doesn't mean I don't have fears,' replied Banti, putting away her chunni and sitting down on the sofa, turning on the TV, clutching her chai.

The car drove off. Unlike the day before, there was only one seat unoccupied in the gallery. Simran took it. Kalu, Udho and Taylor stood against the rear wall near the door. In addition to the parties and witnesses of the other cases listed for the courtroom, there were several more members of the Johal group present, the tall, heavy Gurbachan sitting next to the shorter, bow-legged Amrit. Amrit looked smaller than usual, the squint of his left eye hidden from those standing or sitting behind. Kalu had never thought twice about Amrit's squint before. But as he stood at the back of the full gallery he thought back to Amrit's image in his mind. There was always something shifty about him, Kalu now concluded.

The judge entered. Udho's case was called. Taylor and Udho went forward. Taylor sat at the counsel table, Udho beside him. The judge ordered Udho to stand up. Taylor stood with him and the judge began reading the judgement.

'I find the complainant's story to be incredible. The assault is alleged to have taken place at Dr Amrit Singh Johal's home. Throughout the trial he was present in court. The complainant testified that Amrit witnessed the assault. The Crown chose not to call him. This leads me to believe his testimony would have weakened or killed its case. The aggressive animus the complainant expressed towards the untouchables leads me to conclude he would have been prone to assault the accused. I believe the accused's version of events. I find the accused not guilty. I do find that an offence was committed, but by the complainant and he may have committed perjury before this court. I urge the police to conduct a thorough investigation.'

After celebrating the verdict, Kalu thanked Taylor for representing Udho again as he handed him a cheque. 'Here's a little more money. Please send me the final bill,' he said.

The Johal group quickly marched out of the court to gather outside and engage in a heated discussion, which could be overheard by Kalu, Udho and Simran.

'You and your daughter demeaned us. You did nothing when she married him. Her example will lead our children astray. A man like you can't be our leader...!' said someone.

'If I were you I'd have killed her and the Chamar that fucks her,' said another.

Kalu tried to stop her but Simran broke away, walked over to where the voices had come from and said, 'All of you, including my father, are cowards. Lying is cowardice and you all lied, even those who remained silent. I married of my own free will. I don't need your permission.'

No one said anything till she walked away. Then the shouting resumed. Everyone seemed to be saying something.

'This is what you get when you don't kill the bitch,' Kalu heard someone say in the pandemonium, before the three of them left the building.

18

The tension of the trial over, the Badhan household resumed its rhythm. Simran's patients had her full attention. And Kalu got busy with the college and his students once again. Udho singlehandedly painted the entire house to welcome his grandchild. He had learnt to paint the walls when he came to England—to save money to bring Banti and Kalu here, and then to educate Kalu.

The Johals still visited them, about once every month. When they did, the Badhans received them with affection. No one talked about the assault or the trial. Their visits became more frequent when Simran gave birth to a baby boy. Simran and Kalu had considered a number of names and settled on Angad, meaning 'my own limb'. Guru Nanak had given the name to his follower and the second Sikh Guru.

Simran returned to work after a few months off. Banti and Udho gladly took over the job of looking after the ever smiling baby.

It was time for the Bedford municipal elections. There was a range of candidates backed by the local Labour Party. In addition to these candidates themselves canvassing door to door, attending public meetings and gatherings at private residences, members, activists and volunteers went about the neighbourhoods taking the message of the campaign to the constituents individually. At an organizing meeting, Kalu suggested pairing up a white person, possibly a woman, with an Indian who spoke Hindi or Punjabi to canvass the area of Bedford home to a large Punjabi population. He believed his idea to be practical and linguistically appropriate.

'I'm told lots of Chamars live in the Queen's Park area. It'd be good if you went to all the Indian homes there. That way you'll hit all the Chamar and Chuhra homes, too. We'll give you the lists to identify Indian names,' said organizer Richard Levitt.

'So I guess even in the Labour Party I'm a mere Chamar. An Indian, to be sure, but a Chamar first.'

'The treasurer, Ashok Dwivedi, suggested that. He's Indian too.'

'Well, it doesn't come as a shock that he made the suggestion. I'm sure he volunteered to canvass the area around the Goldington temple,' Kalu replied, the sarcasm lost on his interlocutor. Goldington was where lots of Indians from upper castes lived.

'I'll canvass Goldington, in the company of Pam Wright,' Kalu said firmly.

At college, Dean Symes, the blond, curly-haired 'Indian' was livid when he heard about the incident at the organizing meeting.

'How can they do that to my Indian brother?' he had yelled, a Labour supporter himself. He was of course glad Kalu didn't take it lying down. Labour had done well in both Queen's Park and Goldington, but in the latter it exceeded all expectations. He now began to canvass his friends and contacts in the Party for Kalu as a potential parliamentary candidate. The results at the municipal polls spoke for themselves, he felt.

The Labour Party and its affiliates soon began inviting Kalu to meetings to speak. An untouchable with experience of Banjhan and Bedford, caste and race, of Krayon and the foundry, of college and university, he was passionate about workers' rights, better wages and working conditions and addressing inequalities faced by women and people of colour. Simran began to hear through the grape-vine that the Labour Party rank and file wished to see Kalu as its next parliamentary standard bearer. She encouraged him to run. But Kalu shunned the limelight.

'I don't need it to feel fulfilled,' he said to Simran.

'It's not limelight, but power, for public good. This is not about self-cultivation... If anything, not thirsting for power distinguishes you for public service,' she argued.

Dean Symes convened a group of friends and supporters to persuade Kalu. He agreed to throw his hat in the ring.

Not long after, some Indians from Bedford with connections to the Indian Labour leaders in Southall, the town with the highest percentage of Indians in Britain, began a whisper campaign: If any constituency deserves a candidate of Indian origin, it must be one that includes Southall.

'It's racism to say an Indian should be given consideration only in an area with an Indian population, large or small. For all I care, Labour can have an Indian in Southall. Why should that prevent Kahla being considered for Bedford? Why should there be a limit on how many people of colour can run for parliament? Why not a limit on how many white men could run? I'm not batting for Kahla because there're Indians in Bedford. Black, brown, white or some other colour, Kahla is a formidable candidate,' said Symes to a meeting of power-brokers in the Labour Party.

'But there are Indians who are objecting,' said John Darling, an influential Labourite on the selection committee.

'Have there been any whites that have ever opposed a white nominee? Yes. But that's never stopped the committee from choosing the white candidates it saw fit to do. Whites don't agree on anyone or anything. Why must all Indians approve of Kahla's candidacy?'

Banjhan had pigeonholed Kalu as an untouchable in perpetuity. Now, England, and which was more troubling, the progressive, left-leaning Labour, was permitting caste to tarnish British society by adding it to the toxic mix of ethnicity, race and class. Bedford was plummeting towards Banjhan.

'Bhapa, when you came to England, did you flee poverty or caste?' Kalu asked Udho at home that evening as they sat talking local politics.

'One could confront poverty and win. But for caste, if I fought, I was sure to lose. The only other option was flight. Perhaps I was a coward to run away. I didn't know our caste would stick to us like a leech even across the seas.'

Kalu, Symes, Darlene the secretary at the college and many others worked hard preparing the application and canvassing support on the ground for Kalu to be the Labour candidate in Bedford for the parliamentary elections. Word came down from on high that his candidacy wouldn't be approved. What considerations were taken into account neither he nor Symes was told.

A few days passed before Kalu met his friend Raghbir Singh Jawanda for their regular monthly beer at the King's Arms. After each had a sip of Guinness, Raghbir said, 'Sorry, Kahla, the Jats of the Goldington temple lobbied the Southall Indians to tell Labour that if you're nominated they'd go all over the United Kingdom to tell Indians to vote against Labour.'

'You mean they'll tell *non-untouchable* Indians to vote against Labour.'

Both looked at each other and sat sipping beer and fiddling with the pints in front of them. An immigrant like Kalu, Raghbir, a science graduate from Punjab, was brown like Kalu but clean shaven. He had married Sheila, also a science graduate from Punjab. Childless, they worked in the

Texas Instruments factory in Bedford. Raghbir, who often attended the Goldington temple, broke the silence.

'Oh, I forgot to tell you there was a brawl at the Goldington. Fists rained and turbans flew off people's heads. Several men had to be taken away in ambulances and panda cars. The police have charged a few of them. Amrit lost his turban...but otherwise he escaped unhurt.'

'Ah! Amrit hasn't visited us for a long time. I've been asking Simran to go see him and her mum but she won't listen.'

'I'm sorry, but how is Angad. I haven't seen him for some time. Sheila and I'll drop in one day soon.'

'Do come soon. It might also help change Simran's mind about her father... Angad is well, by the way. Growing up fast.'

Raghbir gave Kalu a ride home and left. Once inside, Kalu fell onto the sofa.

'Everything all right, son?' asked Udho from the rocker, a Scotch in hand.

'Raghbir just told me Sim's dad lost his turban in a fight at Goldington.'

'They've taken his money. The temple is complete. He is of no use any more. And on top of it they wanted him to kill you and Simran, which he didn't do,' said Udho, but after scratching his head in a moment of silence, continued, 'But why has he stopped coming to our home?'

'Simran told me his idiot friends keep pressing him to beat her,' said Banti. 'She told me what they said at the courthouse. He never fights back. But our Simran should still go and see her parents.'

Working late, seeing more patients than ever, Simran had just walked in and overheard Banti.

'Papa doesn't have the courage shun these idiots. What kind of a father is he?' she said and slumped onto the sofa next to Kalu who was holding Angad.

Banti would have preferred Kalu marrying a Chamari but Jatti Simran was preferable to Christine or a lowly Chuhri. She had made Simran feel completely welcome. That was one reason Simran didn't miss her parents. But Banti could be stubborn about what Simran wore or ate.

'Your dress doesn't suit you, Simran. Everyone can see your legs.'

Simran looked at Kalu and smiled. Unlike the one-day plane ride that got them from Banjhan to Bedford, he thought, a lifetime was too short for Bibi to bridge the cultural gap between the two.

The phone rang. Sheila Jawanda was calling for Simran.

'Sim, the boys at their beer session were complaining that we hadn't seen each other for far too long. If it's okay, we'd come later this evening.'

'That would be lovely,' said Simran.

Kalu was reminded of how he met Raghbir, a couple of years ago. Seeing Kalu, Raghbir had walked over to the corner table at the King's Arms and said, 'Do you mind if I sit here?'

'Sure, if you don't mind sitting with a Chamar.'

'As long as you don't hate my village Punjabi or my face, I'd sit with you even if you were a goddamned Brahmin,' Raghbir had said with a huge grin.

Angad scratched Kalu's nose, bringing his thoughts back to the room. Banti and Simran got busy with preparing the food, and Kalu with preparing notes for his classes for the upcoming week. He handed Angad to Udho to keep him entertained and out of the kitchen. A couple of hours later, there was a knock on the door.

'Come in, puttar,' said Udho, carrying Angad.

'Oh uncleji, Angad's grown so much. He'd soon be a big man,' said Raghbir.

Sheila took Angad from Udho into the kitchen. Hanging

their coats on the racks, pointing to the bar room he had added after Simran came into the family, Udho said, 'It's all self-serve.'

The women took one light Scotch each for the evening. The men polished off quite a few. The norm for their get-togethers was discussion on politics and parenting, and everything in between. Angad went to sleep in Udho's lap and Simran put him to bed.

As she returned, Kalu said, 'Sim, do you know? Raghbir told me Papa was involved...or at least his turban fell off during a fracas at the Goldington. I thought he should tell you what he knows. He was there when it happened.'

'A patient said something about it in passing but nothing about Papa. He wasn't hurt or anything?'

'No. From what I saw he's fine. But it's dangerous in the temples.'

'Temples...!' Simran said, exasperated. 'How can you learn anything from Gurbani when your minds are so numb?' said Simran.

'No one goes to learn... It's funny how they gather and complain about racism and exclusion by the whites and then do the same thing themselves,' Raghbir said, before adding, 'But you must go see your parents, Sim. Angad should know them.'

'I don't want to think about temples and castes and colours any more. My small world is big enough for me. But you're right. I'll go see Papa and Mum. They are Angad's grandparents. He's entitled to know them.'

'Excellent! Now let's turn to politics, Kalu bhaji,' said Sheila, sensing Simran's unease. 'Don't give up on Labour. It doesn't realize what it rejected when it said no to your candidacy.'

'Yeah! This import of caste into British politics...it's

quite depressing. But I agree. The Conservatives aren't an option,' said Kalu.

They talked late into the night before the Jawandas left.

The noise of the train braking at the St John's station for passengers to board and disembark awakened Kalu. Simran didn't like that sound and he turned around to look at her on the other side of the bed and Angad lying between them. The night hung in his brain like a fog. He went down to the kitchen.

Udho was already up, savouring the chai Banti had made. She was kneading dough for potato and cauliflower pranthas. He salivated at the thought of the pranthas, sipped his chai, reviewed his notes for the classes and contemplated Simran's visit to the Johals.

'Is Angad up, puttar?' asked Udho.

Angad had become Udho's project in retirement. He woke up early each day to play with him, and took him out for strolls up to the train station. Angad would jump with joy seeing the train come and go as if he had made it happen.

'Still sleeping next to his mother...he's such a lovely kid. I can't imagine how you must have felt leaving Bibi and me behind in Banjhan.'

'It wasn't a choice. Poverty and oppression don't allow much room for free will,' Udho said.

Visits to the Reading Room at the library, Punjabi books and a habit of glancing at *The London Times* the household subscribed to had enabled Udho to articulate the ravages of Banjhan in the language of books. But Kalu felt depressed for what lay inside the man that was his father which never got an opportunity to blossom—a waste of the man he could have been.

Kalu went upstairs. Simran was up.

'Oh, now I've got to go see Papa and Mum. Why did you make me promise?' asked Simran.

'Sim, it's good for us and Angad to remain connected with them. They're your blood, the nearest thing you and Angad have.'

He took Angad down with him. She too got ready. Joining the others for breakfast, she devoured her prantha and was off.

'Bibi, that was heaven. And now I'm going to hell.'

'Puttar, people don't say such things about parents,' admonished Udho.

The car sped away to get to the Johals' home before they left for their Sunday gurdwara visit. But past the Ouse Bridge, Simran stopped the car.

'Kahlu, I want to go by myself. If I say something stupid, I don't want them to think ill of you. Even though they don't like your Chamarhood, they like you. I can't explain that so don't ask me how...but they like you, and it makes me happy.'

She drove away. He walked towards the library. The image of Udho getting him the library card and the morning's conversation about free will not being so free haunted him. The urge to walk in his father's footsteps entered his mind. He had walked all the places Udho had been known to frequent except Bedford's red light row. He walked on, scuffing his steps. The clouds hovered above, not a hint of the sun behind them. Tied in a knot of emotions and thoughts, he kept going.

'Hey!' a voice shouted to him from a doorway. 'It's too early for anyone to be up.' The man lay in front of the door under a mound of torn, soiled blankets. Kalu read the street name on the corner building. He was walking the road Udho had once walked, desperate for the touch of female flesh. He stopped and looked at the cement slabs beneath him, as if searching for his father's footprints, the past pulsating under his soles.

'Hey, I told you it's too early,' the voice from the mound spoke again. Kalu had not moved much beyond the doorway. He began walking towards the end of the street; the houses were squished together like sardines and lumps of flesh covered in blankets lying in the doorways stared at him. He turned around and headed to the bridge over the Great Ouse. The calm river had become a symbol of the divide between the Badhans and the Johals. For them to meet it had to be crossed. At the moment, Kalu perceived the Ouse and its bridge as icons of impotence in the face of the caste gap. Neither the bridge builders nor the Great Ouse could have ever imagined becoming vessels of division for denizens of an erstwhile colony thousands of miles away. He walked the High Street. Across the bridge was St Mary's Street, a different name and a different world, his world. As he walked by the King's Arms, the Johals' world was behind him, his own ahead.

He turned onto St Leonard's Avenue. In front of his home, the car stared at him, inquisitively, he thought, about his secret pilgrimage to the place of hard labour for women who earned a living pleasing flesh-eaters. He fumbled around in his pockets. Lodged in their recesses, the key eluded him. He persisted and found it. His hand trembled as he inserted it into the hole, his feet unsteady, his ears eager to hear from Simran.

She was at the eating table, lost in the leftover prantha.

'Hungry again so soon, Sim!'

'Yes.' She looked at the prantha, then away at the wall and said, 'Bibi and Bhapa are out walking Angad.'

'I guess it didn't work. Papa is still angry with you?'

'I can't tell who he's angry at, me, the temple idiots, the world or himself.'

'Sim, he needs you. You're the only counterweight to the feudal nonsense around him.'

'Papa's head is filled with this Jat thing. He couldn't shut up about the beauty of his village when I was growing up. Now it's Jat culture versus all others. It shows in how he speaks...the Jats are braver than anyone else nonsense. And he says he won't come and see us. No reason, he says, but I suspect his temple gang is giving him a hard time, questioning his manliness... Can't keep his daughter in check and whatnot.'

Her eyes brimmed, her obsession with seeing crying as weakness preventing the tears from flowing. Kalu felt responsible for the dammed flood inside her. He pondered again whether it was his desire to escape caste that made him wed her. Was he ultimately responsible for her tears, which refused to flow? He wrestled with doubt.

19

Kalu attended to all the burning fires inside him and doused them. The ones he couldn't put out, he ignored. His life moved on. Students, even from the pure sciences if they had the time, flocked to his lectures that infused life into the past, shed light on the present and pondered the future. The student body had voted him the most popular teacher in the social sciences as well as the college. Invitations streamed in from universities and colleges for him to speak on history, to help people understand the issues facing the country, particularly with respect to class, race and the colonial experience.

He had become part of the fabric of Bedford. Yet the ghosts of Banjhan were never too far away, as Udho's trial had reminded him. An integrated Briton and yet disjointed, he was no stranger to being pigeonholed and excluded by race and caste.

One place he had felt totally accepted was the faculty lounge where the professors and lecturers gathered during breaks for tea, coffee and lunch. Among the faculty and students he had many friends. One such was the fifty-five-year-old Michael Carrington. His short gray beard and frizzy hair gave him a softer academic look. Though a professor of Chemistry, he knew quite a lot about India and its history.

Michael was his partner for articulating thoughts on—and often venting his annoyance about—Indian politics. The wars of the past few years, like the one with Pakistan which had concluded not too long ago, had occasioned long and rambling conversations on sabre-rattling among the neighbouring nations and the West's unprincipled approach to geopolitics, as evidenced by its support of the un-democratic belligerent.

Most days, however, others joined the table and the discussion would often turn to domestic politics. Michael unwaveringly encouraged Kalu to not give up on parliamentary politics or his activism. He recognized how important his friend's voice was on the various issues they would talk about and promised to help him mount a campaign for nomination for the Bedford seat next time.

But Kalu wasn't sure about it any more. 'Life moves on,' he would say. Not that he was giving up his activism around racial equality but, for him, the parliamentary ship had sailed long ago.

Michael and Kalu were joined one day at lunchtime by Madan Lal Verma, a recent addition to Mander's Chemistry Department. Michael had been reading a book on sati, the practice of widows jumping, or being forced to jump, alive into the pyres of their dead husbands to burn with them.

'I find many faults with the British colonial era in India but banning sati was definitely not one of them,' he said.

'It was an illegitimate intrusion upon the cultural sovereignty of Indians. No one forced women into sati. It was purely voluntary,' countered Madan.

'Sati and voluntary? My foot! Cultural sovereignty... that's sheer fantasy. India's been independent for over twenty years now and I haven't noticed a rush to reinstate sati. Nor should it be,' said Kalu.

'You see, the Muslims got Pakistan. The Hindus didn't get a country. If India was a Hindu country governed for them, you'd see sati back,' said Madan.

'Well, in that case you may also see a return of the untouchables being slaughtered as sacrifices to the gods. If that happens, I'd return to India to fight that menace, with violence if need be,' stated Kalu.

'Well, nobody condones untouchability. You see, Manu's idea of castes...he only gave us a good way of organizing roles in society. He didn't mandate their religious sanction or perpetuation. We can reject untouchability. We could reject him and substitute something else, like class in this country,' said Madan.

'Madan, it's mad to compare classes in a secular society to caste blessed by religion in an endemically religious and feudal society. And by the way, nobody proposed a roadmap for class,' said Michael.

'The bloody castes, a good way of organizing, you say!' said Kalu. 'The abuse, the oppression, the slaughter in sacrifice and the untouchability, all a good bloody way of managing society in perpetuity! I've had enough of this discussion.'

Kalu wasn't unaware of Madan's sentiments on the subject, though that hadn't made their conduct towards each other less cordial. But he hadn't quite expected a colleague to dig in his heels on as indefensible a position as had been aired today. Unlike Michael, he was in no mood to indulge caste as a rational argument. He had lived it long enough to know better. He got up and left.

'Sim darling, I feel like a Guinness. Come and join me please. Janice Charlesworth may be there, the chemistry teacher. You know, your old friend from elementary...?' Kalu said, calling Simran after his classes one evening.

'I've late appointments at the clinic. I want to go home and spend some time with Angad. Bhapa and Bibi need a break from him too, you know? And we need to begin teaching him more than just the alphabet and counting. He'll be in school soon.'

'Sim, you're making me feel guilty.'

'No, darling, you go to the King's. Say hello to Janice. I'll see her another day and you at home.'

He hung up the phone. But as he prepared notes for tomorrow's classes he found himself being pulled in opposite directions by home and King's Arms. The thirst for Guinness won. Street lamps lit his path as he walked the pavement to the pub. Its door creaked as he opened it. With his white handkerchief he wiped the top of his turban and his beard. Taking his raincoat off, he shook it on the mat and hung it. The fireplace was aglow. Instead of going to his corner near the dart board, he sat in front of the fire to dry out. Seeing him, the bartender poured his pint of Guinness Stout, using the two-part pour method. Kalu saw the colour of the pint slowly change. The creamy light brown became dark ruby red, bits of its longer than half-inch head slithering down the sides of the pint. He rested his head back against the chair took after the first sip, extending his feet forward to take in the heat. Until Simran had explained it to him recently, he didn't know why his extremities felt hot in the summer and cold in winter: low blood pressure and bad circulation.

Gurbat walked in.

'Dr Badhan...you seem lost in another world.'

'No, my young friend, I was thinking of the here and now. How Simran came into my life and changed it. I'm probably the freest person on earth. I have the love of a wonderful woman yet no constraints on what I can or can't do in life. I feel lucky!'

'Simran madam is good...but she's lucky too.'

'Oh, I don't know how lucky I make her. The marriage has been torture at the hands of her people. She's guilty of the crime of miscegenation! You know, breaking caste bonds...so-called interbreeding. I guess for these idiots it's not enough that we are shunned by the racists in this country.'

'One would think the white racists would make us unite with all good people. But no.'

Gurbat's pint of beer arrived and he excused himself to play a round of darts with his friends from the college who had just walked in. Kalu turned his chair a bit to watch them play. About five minutes into the darts, Janice came. The entry of the long-haired, five-eleven, spectacled blonde turned many heads.

'Hey Kahla, where've you left Sim? Or did she abandon you?'

'My friend, it's the latter!'

'I guess she's pretty sure you're safe with me,' said Janice, signalling the bartender.

The coals in the fireplace were dimming. She stoked them and poured more on top before dropping into a chair saying, 'The college is getting bigger and busier. I can't keep up with marking and preparing. Is history any easier?'

'Not if you want to do it well.'

'I hope you're still thinking about running for the Labour nomination though, with all your teaching and speaking engagements. They lost the seat last time because they didn't allow you to run.'

'With me the loss might've been worse.'

'Sim's right, you're always selling yourself short.'

'One's worldly worth is the net of others' view of it. If for most others one is worthless, in public life one can never much matter.'

'For elections, yes. But then the voters have been known to be idiots. Take Churchill, for example. The colonials have a lot to hate him for but he led Britain brilliantly in the war and soon afterwards we turfed him out on his rear. How's that for gratitude?'

'Granted. But forget about me for now.'

He ordered another beer for himself, having emptied the first in that short interval before Janice joined him. Gurbat and his friends were still playing, sipping beer between their turns. But the pub fell silent for a moment as the entrance door creaked and burst open. Four scruffy Skinheads entered. They placed their order with the bartender before heading to the empty table against the wall a few feet from the fireplace.

A few minutes later—almost as if on cue, Kalu thought—one of them walked over to Kalu's table and yelled, 'Who the fuck allowed you in 'ere with that bed sheet on your head? You belong on a camel in the Arabian desert!'

'Please mind your own business. Go join your friends,' Kalu said, holding his pint which he had lifted just before the onslaught.

'And you, f...in cunt, you need a white man to sleep with?' the tall Skin in dirty leather pants said to Janice.

That drew Gurbat and his friends' attention to the table. They rushed over as the man pushed Kalu's chair. It fell to the side, Kalu with it. He tried saving the pint in his hand but the beer splashed and wet the Skinhead's pants.

Infuriated, he raised his arm to hit Kalu, now standing before him. Gurbat and his friends tackled him to the ground. Overhearing the owner dial the police, the trio of Skins bolted. The police managed later to arrest the attacker though he too had followed his friends and made a run for it.

'I remember calling the cops for you once before,' the pub owner said. 'I was much younger then and the police took hours to come. Sorry you've to put up with these scum, you know. Please do keep coming to King's.'

Not that Kalu had any intention to ever stop coming there. After the dust had settled, they were treated to another round of drinks on the house.

'This bloody Skinhead business...' Kalu said. 'I don't understand why they hate us. Fine, you're angry. So take it out on the ruling class. You know, the real culprits? Instead they hate us. Idiots! How convenient for the rulers! They can just go around pleasing everyone mouthing platitudes about human brotherhood and whatnot.'

'Sisterhood too, Kahla, don't forget us.'

Kalu smiled at being nudged to be more inclusive in his choice of words. Janice and Gurbat, who both lived a walking distance from Kalu's, had insisted on walking him home. He invited them in when they got there.

'Oh Janice, Gurbat, so nice to see you. You've come at the right time. I just put Angad to bed and Bibi's got everything ready for dinner.'

'Lovely to see you, too,' said Janice.

'Janice, what would you like to drink? And Gurbat, you?' asked Udho.

'Bhapa, we had lots of beer.'

'After beer you can have a shot of whisky, no?'

'Yes, uncle, why not?' said Gurbat.

He had become a frequent visitor to the household since

the trial and felt little hesitation. Udho poured six shots and gave one to each with a grin on his face.

'How have you been, uncle?' asked Gurbat.

'Quite well and happy when the house is full like now.'

The talk turned to how Janice and Gurbat ended up accompanying Kalu home.

'It's either the racists or the caste warriors. Wasn't the first time and won't be the last. No reprieve from the idiots on the cards for us,' said Simran.

'Talking of caste warriors, how's your dad?' asked Janice, bending to look at Simran over her glasses.

'Oh, he'll be fine if he ever stops stewing about Kahlu. Why people become so consumed by hate, I'll never know.'

'Yup, me neither. From Skins to Singhs...how does one even begin to make sense of it?' chimed in Kalu.

'Have another shot. Any takers?' asked Udho.

Janice and Simran's hands went up. Udho who should've been in bed by now poured and served the shots within seconds and settled in his seat on the rocker.

After Janice and Gurbat left, the household felt much quieter than it did on other nights.

'You look puffed out,' Kalu said to Simran when they were alone in their bedroom. 'Thankfully tomorrow is a holiday. No patients. Just Angad and us,' he added, putting his arms around her.

Ever the conciliator, Kalu tried again to persuade Simran to reconnect with her parents, gently this time.

'Why should the onus always be on the child to reach out to the parent?' asked Simran.

'The onus is always thrust upon those who understand and are prepared to accept the challenge. Fighting caste is a challenge you took on when you married me.'

'Okay, Baba, will do,' said Simran, addressing Kalu with the honorific for paternal grandfather as she always did whenever she conceded an argument to him.

Over the next few days, Kalu talked often about the need for Simran and Angad to visit the Johals; they were family, Angad's grandparents. 'So what if they're stubborn or stupid. It's not as if one gets to choose grandparents,' he argued.

Simran saw the wisdom of the argument but was exhausted just thinking about having to face Amrit. She wanted to see her mother. But seeing her meant seeing Amrit. Simran was prepared to ignore him and his presence. But Sureet was afraid of crossing Amrit. And he didn't want her to see Simran because it undercut his authority in the Johal house and influence at the Goldington temple. So mother and daughter only ever spoke on the phone secretly. Kalu finally accepted defeat and stopped pressing her to see Amrit and speak to him. He knew she wouldn't budge, and nor could her father.

20

The Race Relations Bill was under discussion in the country. Kalu was at the forefront of the forces arguing for its passage by the Labour government. In the Conservative ranks, there was opposition to the legislation. Kalu happened to be in Birmingham when a Conservative friend told him Enoch Powell, a onetime Tory Minister of Health, was about to make a speech to a meeting at his Wolverhampton constituency. The speech promised to be quite unlike his famous speech Kalu knew of, the one Powell had made in 1959 about eleven Mau Mau rebels killed at the Hola Camp in Kenya for refusing to work. Kalu thought of it as 'the greatest speech he ever heard'. Powell had criticized government actions, arguing British standards of fairness must apply to all British actions. Kalu wanted to hear the scholar of classics in person. With the help of a Conservative friend, he stole himself into Powell's constituency meeting which was open only to the members and the invited press.

The speech turned out to be about coloured immigrants and immigration. Alluding to the Roman poet Virgil's 'Aeneid', Powell spoke of seeing 'Like the Roman...the River Tiber foaming with blood' if immigration to Britain continued unchecked. The audience cheered the speech. It repulsed Kalu. It made Powell a pariah in the official Conservative circles and popular with the vast majority of Britons. Known as Powell's 'Rivers of Blood' speech, it gave oxygen to racism and the Skinheads, who had now begun to lean decisively towards a brand of white supremacy and didn't simply hate Asians. In the bars and streets, attacks against the coloureds escalated.

As a witness to the speech, commenting and speaking on it, Kalu became a star in the country and among the Labourites. Teaching history while attempting to shape it meant a busier calendar for Kalu, who was now often away from home. Simran, assisted by Udho and Banti, ran the household in his recurring absences.

One evening, a patient told Simran about a dispute at the Goldington Gurdwara where turbans and fists again flew. The patient knew of Amrit being present but couldn't offer details of his involvement. Simran asked the receptionist to lock up the office and jumped into her car. The driver's seat froze her skin through her thin trousers as it took several attempts to start the vehicle. She got out and cleared the snow from the windshield. As she drove on the Ouse Bridge, she noticed that beyond it the snow was knee deep and still falling. She was less than a mile away from her clinic but it felt a different world. She thought of turning back but didn't.

The car made it to the door of the Johal home. Inside, she encountered Sureet's smile and Amrit's silence. Sureet made her tea and asked whether she needed something to eat. Amrit remained mute about the incident at the temple. Simran phoned Kalu to come over.

'It's snowing. Probably won't be able to get a taxi. It will take me half an hour to walk over. Come home, we'll talk to them another day,' he said.

'No! You're the one eager for me to talk to the man. He seems to have lost his voice. I want to know what happened at the temple. Don't I even have a right to know and ensure my father's safe?'

'No, you don't. You're married. You're independent and on your own as are we. We don't owe you any answers,' Kalu overheard Amrit bark.

'I'll be there soon, Sim,' he said and hung up.

'Son, it's dangerous to be out in this weather. The cars slipping and sliding...not safe,' said Udho as Kalu began to get ready to go.

'But Bhapa, I've got to go support Sim.'

Wrapped in a hooded waterproof raincoat covering him from turban to snow boots, Kalu walked into the storm. The cars wove and swerved, the cyclists slipped and slid, the pedestrians glided and stumbled over the surging mounds of snow as his boots navigated its treachery and the road beneath. But he was focused on Simran, the Johal house and what might be happening there. He stood gasping for air at the Johals' door before knocking on it.

A quiet, restrained fear in her wider than usual eyes, Sureet opened the door, welcoming him in.

'How are you, Mum?'

'All right, puttar. They're in the sitting room.'

Freeing himself of the boots and the coat, he walked over.

'Papa, Sim, sorry it took me some time. It's freezing and there are no taxis around.'

'You think it's cold outside? Worse in here! Even our tongues are frozen—especially Papa's.'

'Sim, give the man time.'

Kalu discerned a suppressed smile on Sureet's face. He had suspected all along what her faint expressions of joy conveyed—she was an ally of her only child but one who wasn't courageous enough to defy Amrit's abuse, caste pride and the dumbness it entailed.

'Papa, except by marriage, I'm a stranger to you, but Sim and Angad are your blood. For their sake you should come and see us as often as you can. You're always welcome in our home. It's Sim's and Angad's home. I know the caste business is something your friends poke you about, but you're an independent and educated man, above the narrowness. I'd love to see you and so would Bibi and Bhapa. They don't have any other family here, just you and Mum.'

Amrit looked at Sureet and Simran, both of whom had quietly listened.

'Okay, if you ask we'll come and visit you,' said Amrit.

'O Papa, I love you so much,' said Simran running up and squeezing him in her embrace.

Sureet prepared soup and quick sandwiches for a late snack which they all had as they chatted. She insisted they call home and stay the night but Simran hadn't seen Angad all day. As she looked through the window of the sitting room she heard the sound of rain drops falling on it. In the slush, Kalu drove as Simran rested her head on his shoulder and dozed off.

Everyone was home Sunday morning. Tired of travelling, staying at hotels and friends' homes and the last evening's exertion, Kalu slept in. Angad was kicking up a storm, insisting he wanted sweet pranthas, Bibi's specialty, which she got busy making. Simran was having chai, chatting with Udho and watching Angad.

Udho hadn't gone to the gurdwara. Lately, he'd been staying away from it. The building was complete. Without the hard work of collecting money to build, there were many new aspirants to power within the organization. The feuding over control, discord and arguments regularly turned into bloody brawls. He had lost interest in the temple and turned away.

'Everyone calls us adharmi, without religion, then why do we need temples?' he'd begun saying.

Kalu thought he had a point although adharmi could have been Adi Dharmi, of the original religion, coined by the Aryans for the original inhabitants of India, shortened over time to adharmi. Whatever the meaning or the history of the word, Kalu was thankful for the change in Udho's life. While it did serve a social and cultural purpose, the temple also ghettoized people in ancient fanaticisms, which Kalu detested.

'You should take Angad over to his nana-nani's home every week. It might give them a new focus, something to do. Like Bhapa, Papa might walk away from religion. It'll be good for him. And he won't have to put up with his chauvinist gang of Jats,' said Kalu to Simran, watching his own household at peace with itself. 'Part of the reason he doesn't want to see you is because they taunt him for his Chamar son-in-law.'

'I don't know what's happening to him. The once rational man I grew up admiring has gone nuts. I can't bear the thought of him sitting there like a Buddha statue... devoid of Buddha's wisdom obviously.'

'That's why you must try to peel him away from his obsession with the temple. Perhaps it's control he's afraid of losing. He's lost it with you, already.'

'Okay, stop psychoanalysing him. They should be here any moment. Remember, he said they'll come?'

'Oh, he's coming to see us? Wonderful!' said Udho, clutching his chai.

'I should make kheer for them,' chimed in Banti, before quickly walking away to take out rice and milk to make it.

It was 11:30 am. Banti had washed the rice and placed the pot on the stove. The telephone rang.

'Hello,' Angad picked up and spoke into it before anyone else could.

'Who, Angad? Angad, Nani,' the caller said.

'Nani,' Angad said, holding the phone away and looking at it.

Udho took the phone.

'Sorry, Bhaji Udham Singhji, we won't make it today. There was a fight at the temple and the police have taken Amrit away,' said Sureet and hung up before Udho could ask or say anything.

The pot of kheer had boiled over. Banti was busy cleaning the stove. Simran was sitting on the sofa next to the phone. She called the Johals' home and office. No one picked up her call.

'Kahlu, do something. I don't know who else to call,' she said.

'Come with me, we'll drive over to see your mum,' said Kalu, getting up and lifting her by the arm.

The Johal house stood in the middle of the acreage, like a morgue enveloped in dead quiet.

'Let's go,' said Kalu to Simran, who sat in the car with the door open. He walked over and pulled her out by the arm. Holding her as they approached the door, he said, 'Papa's going to be fine.'

He didn't know that but he compelled himself to say something, anything to lighten Simran's anguish.

The door opened. Sureet stood before them wiping her eyes and blowing her nose into a handkerchief. She put her arms around Simran and continued wiping her nose and eyes. In between the tears and the sniffles, Sureet described to them what had happened.

Still in the lobby, Kalu said, 'I'll go to the police station and find out. Sim, you stay with Mum.' Shutting the door behind him, he jumped back into the car.

His turbanless hair hanging down his back, beard tousled and dried maroon gashes on his forehead and nose, Amrit was sitting in a cubicle with a police officer. He noticed Kalu at the front desk and looked away. The cop at the reception told Kalu he couldn't see Amrit until the questioning was over.

'He needs a lawyer. You can't talk to him without a lawyer,' said Kalu, and then shouted towards the cubicle, 'Papa, don't talk to them without your lawyer present.'

'I don't know the man. He doesn't speak for me,' Amrit shouted back.

'Of course you know the man. I'm your son-in-law.'

'I don't have a daughter therefore you couldn't be my son-in-law.'

The officer interviewing Amrit recognized the professor from Mander College. He knew enough about Kalu to know he must be telling the truth. He ploughed with the interview. Kalu waited on the bench in the reception. After the interview was over, Amrit was handed his turban which he quickly tied over his head. His hair hidden and the cut on the forehead covered by the turban, he walked out to the reception.

'Why the f...k are you here?' he said, squinting at Kalu. 'You're the reason the whole town is laughing at me. I'm a nobody at the temple now. The whore Simran has brought me nothing but shame by marrying a Chamar. Any two-bit idiot feels free to make fun of me.'

'Papa, please, don't create a scene. I'll drive you home. We can talk there.'

'I'm not riding with a Chamar,' said Amrit and walked out.

Kalu drove up to Amrit and drove alongside him as he walked, pleading for him to get into the car.

'F...k off. Leave me be,' said Amrit and walked on.

Kalu sped away to the Johal home.

'Mum, please send Simran out, we've got to go home,' said Kalu to Sureet when she opened the door.

'Your Papa, where's he?'

'Papa doesn't want any help,' he said.

Hearing them, Simran walked up and said, 'Papa didn't come with you?'

'No, he didn't want to come in a Chamar's car.'

'You're not serious, Kahlu?'

'Yes, Sim, Papa's serious.'

'Kahla, please don't go, wait,' said Sureet.

Sureet stood at the door clutching her wet handkerchief, watching them leave. In the car, Kalu described the scene at the police station to Simran.

'Why does he have to humiliate you or me? He's lost any spine he ever had. That Jat spine of his... That's all he ever was, a stupid Jat.'

'Sim, he was angry. I didn't think he meant any of it.'

'He can't stand up to his Jat chauvinist friends and defend you and me. Were he not ashamed of us, things would be different.'

Simran's shoulders slumped into the back of the seat. She exhaled loudly. She didn't want her disquiet to show at home, which was a mere hundred yards away now.

'This isn't the time to be angry at him. He needs help,' Kalu said and turned the car to head back.

In the headlights, Kalu spotted Amrit, a silhouette on

foot on the pathway to his morgue of a home, heading to the door. He slowed the car down, parked it. Simran and he got out. Amrit unlocked the door, swung it open and walked in. He didn't shut the door.

Kalu and Simran walked in and over to the sitting room to be greeted by a sniffling Sureet, clasping a large white handkerchief, and Amrit shouting at her, 'Why are you bawling your eyes out like a newly minted widow. I'm not dead yet.' Sureet hid her face in the handkerchief and sat rubbing her eyes.

Simran hugged her and said, 'Mum, everything will be all right.'

'No, Simi, it won't be. You don't know,' said Sureet, still holding the handkerchief to her face. Amrit, who had been walking around the home as if searching for something, came and sat in the recliner.

'Papa, it's okay to be mad at Sim and me but you shouldn't have spoken to the police without a lawyer. I hope they haven't charged you.'

'They have but I didn't attack anyone. Niranjan Singh lied to the police about me assaulting him. *He* slashed me with his kirpan,' said Amrit.

'Papa, false charges, your friends did it to Bhapa. Now they'll do it to you,' said Kalu.

'These are my friends. You know nothing about them. I'll talk to them. They'll withdraw the charges.'

Sureet was cooking in the kitchen. Nobody had eaten anything for hours.

'You come here, Seet...I want to say something,' Amrit yelled.

She walked up to him.

'Now you listen to me, Seet. Either you're with me or with them. I want to have nothing to do with them. I've lost all my friends. I'm being boycotted by all the Jats. Simran's marriage did this. And you two...I left the doors open for you because one never turns away even a stranger from the door. I don't want to see you or have anything to do with you. As far as you are concerned we're dead for each other. Do you hear? Now get lost... You can go with them too since you always side with this slut who couldn't find anyone but a Chamar to marry.'

The large handkerchief was drenched. Sureet was sniffling and wiping her already red eyes and nose with it.

Kalu got up and said, 'Sim, let's go. No need for us to stay any longer.'

'Kahla, wait. Your papa has been rude but please don't go like this. Please...' pleaded Sureet.

Kalu held Simran's hand and pulled her to her feet. They walked out the door as Sureet screamed, 'Beta Kahla, don't go, please don't.' Kalu revved the engine and drove away, the rear tires kicking up gravel from the pathway.

21

With a cup of coffee in front of him, Kalu sat staring through the windows at the afternoon traffic one day during lunch. The once cheerful and chatty Simran talked less and less. Kalu noticed her isolating from friends. Though civil with Udho, Banti and Angad, she floated through her days detached. He began to hear from her patients about her missing smile. He reached out to Janice who took her to lunches and pubbing. But he couldn't stop worrying.

'Oh Kahla, my friend, long time no see. Of course a star has no business down on earth and that too in the Mander cafeteria,' said Michael Carrington, joining him at his table.

'Just busy with the earthly dumb shit, my friend,' said Kalu taking a sip of coffee.

'The inferno of Enoch's utterances has pulled you into its orbit. I've been following it, quite unfortunate for Britain.'

'Yeah. Been wondering. His repatriation of immigrants' scheme... Let's say I left. What do you do with Simran and Angad, both born and bred here, who don't know anything about India?'

'You're not going anywhere, my friend. I see Heath's kicked him out of the shadow cabinet. The country will change. It has to. It needs your labour. It can't go on treating immigrants as flown-in slaves.'

They were joined by their colleague Madan. Over the years, they had learnt to extend a guarded civility to each other and, happily for both, there was no pretence of warmth. Kalu found his excuse to leave. He was not in the mood to talk, and certainly not for another argument about the glory of India's ancient past. There were more pressing things on his mind.

He didn't know the specific charge but he heard Amrit was about to be tried for inciting, aiding and abetting violence at the temple. Simran had taken the whole affair very badly. She was physically deteriorating, yet she wanted to attend the trial.

'No need to punish yourself, Sim. Your presence is bound to anger him and he's going to need to focus on the proceedings,' Kalu said at home that evening.

'Kahlu, I haven't seen Mum. I'm sure she'll be there... This way at least I'll have a chance to see her!'

'Sim, he hates you. He could hurt you just to impress his caste buddies.'

'For God's sake, he's my father. If he wants to hurt me, so be it.'

From the kitchen, Banti overheard the argument occurring on the second floor. It being in English she understood little and alerted Udho. He went upstairs and tried to mediate.

'Son, Simran dhee wants to see her father and mother. So what if it's at the court house? Let it be.' He came back down soon after, having made his opinion known.

The Goldington crowd had never approved of Simran's marriage to Kalu. They didn't like Amrit ignoring their indignation and resigning himself to the fait accompli. They asked him for a public condemnation and disowning of her in the Punjabi weekly *Des Pardes* which came out of Southall, and was known for its vulgarity and biting feudal commentary on any 'erring' Punjabi woman.

'Caste infidelity is the worst crime a woman could commit. If it were my daughter I'd have cut her to pieces long ago,' a member of the executive had yelled at Amrit in a recent meeting. The latest violence was itself a result of the vitriol long spewed by many against Amrit for not punishing Simran. They wanted to impose and reinforce the rules of their villages in Bedford, on their own children and those of others.

The trial drew nearer. Kalu heard about the dilemma Goldington now faced and their efforts to resolve it. The group wanted to make an example of Amrit because of Simran. It didn't mind insulting Simran's father but hated losing its chief benefactor. The new granthi, the priest, an educated man unlike most granthis, offered to mediate. Everyone knew Amrit held him in high regard. He sat the two down, the complainant and Amrit, the accused, in an attempt to resolve the matter. The granthi and Amrit came to an understanding, and the executive attempted to persuade the complainant to drop the charges.

The complainant was none other than Gurbachan Singh Hundal, a onetime friend of Amrit and the complainant in Udho's case. He refused to budge unless Amrit denounced

Simran at the temple's large Sunday congregation followed by the publication of his disowning of her in *Des Pardes*.

The trial would proceed on schedule.

Simran rushed with Kalu to the courthouse. Quite a few turbaned and clean-shaven brown men milled about outside it. An object of curiosity for having married Kalu, Simran turned heads, even more so now because physically she was a mere shadow of her former self, a skeleton walking on two legs. Absent was the sparkle on her face. Instead, her eyes had dark bags under them. She walked right through the crowd looking everyone in the eye. Her gait screamed, 'I don't give a damn about what you think or say.'

Inside the courtroom, the prosecutor sat at his table thumbing through the file in front of him. Kalu took a seat at the back of the gallery. Simran walked over and put her hand on Sureet's shoulder. Sureet looked up and pressed her daughter's hand, not saying a word. Amrit sat at the counsel table with his back to the gallery, speaking with his bald lawyer.

The judge entered the room. Amrit was asked to stand and the clerk read the charges. Amrit entered a plea of not guilty. Gurbachan was the first to be called. The prosecutor elicited the evidence-in-chief from him. Gurbachan was a much better witness against Amrit than he had been against Udho. Amrit's lawyer began the cross-examination. Simran prayed for Gurbachan to stumble, but he didn't. He reaffirmed his testimony-in-chief. The temple committee was in the gallery watching. A few of them walked out. Kalu followed. He watched as they huddled together, speaking to each other for a few minutes before returning to the courtroom.

When the court recessed, some committee members and the defence lawyer approached the prosecutor while others gathered round Gurbachan. The group around Gurbachan haggled for several minutes before joining those around the prosecutor. Kalu and Simran watched it all from the gallery. Holding a handkerchief that alternated between wiping her eyes and nose, Sureet glanced at Simran, then immediately turned her face away, taking the handkerchief to it. Simran walked out of the court clutching her own handkerchief and wiping her eyes. Though he wanted to follow and comfort Simran, Kalu desisted as the court was being called to order.

The judge took his seat. The prosecutor arose and said, 'Your honour, the crown wishes to enter a stay of proceedings in the matter before you.'

'So ordered,' said the judge.

As Amrit talked to his lawyer, Sureet walked out. On the way out, she patted Kalu's back. She spotted Simran outside and ran and hugged her. In each other's embrace, their eyes undammed. They just stood there for a while uncaring of what anyone might say.

Sureet separated herself from Simran and stood to the side as Amrit came out. All the Goldington brown men gathered around him, whispering to themselves. Kalu and Simran watched them leave before going to their car.

The telephone rang in Kalu's office at the college within a few days of Amrit's day in court.

'Puttar Kahla, Sureet. Calling you from my office, can't do this from home. Your Papa's gone quiet. He doesn't go anywhere, misses days from practice. A couple of men come from the temple and they go for long walks,' she informed him. 'I'll call Sim, too, but tell her not to worry. Time may bend him and heal everyone,' said and disconnected before Kalu could say something.

Days passed. Sureet would frequently unburden herself with these short and ambiguous phone calls to Kalu at college and Simran at her clinic. Until one day when she sounded surprisingly upbeat.

'He's returned to his previous self,' Sureet reported to Kalu. 'He's seeing patients. Stays home the rest of the time. And hear this: he wants to see you and Angad.'

A few hours later, it was Amrit himself on the phone.

'Kahla, I'd like to see you. May I, perhaps at college?'

The very next morning, before classes, Amrit sat opposite Kalu in the college cafeteria.

'Kahla, I'm sorry for being an ass. I shouldn't have acted so foolish. This caste business, you know...so hard to get out of my head. The temple, sorry, temples, I mean the separate temples...it all just makes it difficult to ignore people's caste.'

'I know. One would expect a medical doctor, a scientist, to be more rational. Lucky for me your daughter is.' Kalu was glad, though guarded in his approach, suspicious of this sudden change of heart.

'Can we forget and forgive and begin de novo?' asked Amrit.

'Wonderful to hear you ask. Why not? But tell me, where did you pick up Latin?'

'Oh, the lawyer used it once, explaining a possible new trial even after a stay of proceedings. I'd asked what it meant. By the way, since brother Udham doesn't go to the temple and neither do I, can we meet Sundays at the Badhan home?'

'It's a deal,' said Kalu extending his hand.

Amrit shook it. With no more coffee in their cups to sip, they parted.

The Johals began visiting the Badhans every Sunday for brunch and stayed till late afternoon.

'Papa, I've never seen you so relaxed,' observed Simran one Sunday afternoon in the sitting room of the Badhan home.

The Johals had been there since the morning. Angad, the centre of the conversation, enjoyed the attention and the banter over who he loved most.

'I love you all, Mummy the most,' said a grinning Angad, the young soul learning to mediate the elders' attention.

'Hey little man, what about me?' asked Kalu.

'Papa, you love your mum, Dadi. Mum's special, no?'

The only child in the family was growing up speaking adult-like. Simran did try baby talk with him. She was obviously not succeeding, nor was his school. He had begun his first year at the neighbourhood's Ampthill Elementary School. It fell to Banti to get him up and ready and to Udho to walk him to and from school. Simran was dealing with an ever increasing number of patients and Kalu was hopping about the British Isles arguing for political and social change, in particular for the inclusion of immigrants. On the occasional Saturday morning, Sureet would pick up Angad and bring him back on Sunday when they came for their weekly visit.

Kalu found Simran more at peace with the world and family. Gone were the blemishes and bags under her eyes and the restrained smiles. It had taken a few years, but the Simran of yore had freed herself from the aura of sadness that had hung over her. At least once a week after work, she drove over to the Johal home for a cup of tea. The Badhans had been to several dinners at the Johal home. The Johals drove Kalu, Simran and Angad in their car to weddings and other events where they were invited. Life had returned to Simran the happiness Amrit had previously snatched from her. Having long failed to conceive, despite trying, she found herself pregnant again. The Badhan household buzzed with excitement. Udho made plans for another extension to the house to make room for the new arrival. Janice and her lunches with Simran were back.

It was the first time since the 1930s in Britain that the number of unemployed claiming state support crossed a million in January 1972. On Bloody Sunday, the thirtieth of that same month, the police shot and killed thirteen people and injured many more at a demonstration against internment without trial of people suspected of having ties to the Irish Republican Army who were fighting an armed struggle for a united Ireland. Violence, unemployment and poverty were tearing at the fabric of communities throughout Britain. Having learnt to take the likes of Madan Verma and their 'caste is a good way to organize society!' in his stride, Kalu returned to the circuit, speaking on poverty, violence, class, caste and race.

Amrit frequently travelled to nearby places such as Luton to hear Kalu speak.

'Kahla, some of my friends are interested in attending your events and hearing you. Give me your schedule for the next six months,' said Amrit one Sunday at the Badhan home.

Kalu was happy to oblige, looking through his diary and copying all the entries for speaking engagements. Amrit would show up every now at then at these events with friends.

Several weeks later, in Northampton, after Kalu's remarks and the Q and A session following, Amrit and a friend approached him.

'Hello, Kahla,' he greeted him, 'I see you're busy next Saturday night. There's a wedding at a friend's in Southall. He's always asking to meet you and Simran. In case your event cancels let me know. Simran and you should come with us.'

'Papa, Saturday night won't cancel; it was fixed a long time ago. You take Sim with you. I better attend to these people. You and I can always talk at home,' said Kalu, turning to speak with members of the audience wanting to chat with him.

Most always offered ideas. Ideas nourished his will to continue. Many like Carrington and Symes persevered in their push for him to consider the run for parliament. Would he ever run, again placing himself at the mercy of the Labour bosses anointing the nominees? He wasn't sure. But the fight for fairness propelled him and kept him on the hustings of ideas, if not of elections.

Kalu had planned to take Simran to Leicester for the Saturday speech. But he didn't want to disappoint Amrit who had been making up for hurting his daughter with his intransigence on caste. Even though the years of hell he put his daughter through could not be forgotten, Kalu wanted her to savour the present. He drove her to the train station on Friday evening. The Johals were waiting for her. Together, they took the train to London for Southall. Kalu took Gurbat along on Saturday morning for company on the train to Leicester to address the long scheduled public meeting.

Angad was home watching the Sunday cartoons on TV. Banti had prepared everything for dinner. She and Udho were lounging, waiting for Simran and Kalu to return from their trips. Kalu and Gurbat walked from the station, parting at the intersection of Prebend and Cauldwell Street near the college to go to their homes. Even from under the umbrella, Kalu could see the light of the lamp posts, dancing on puddles of water, creating a thousand images. By the time he reached home, his shoes and socks were soaking wet. He took off the raincoat, shook it and the umbrella, wiped the top of his turban off with his hands and entered through the back door.

'Puttar, while you dry off I'll warm up dinner for all of us. Or do you want to wait?'

'Wait, Bibi. Sim should be here any minute. She has to see her patients in the morning. It's Monday tomorrow.'

Kalu went upstairs. Briefly distracted by Kalu's arrival, Angad returned to the cartoons, Udho and Banti to watching him.

22

It was past midnight. Sunrise was several hours away but Monday had already dawned on Bedford. On the sofa in the sitting room, Kalu was awake. Exhausted, waiting for Simran, Angad had gone to sleep next to him. Kalu had carried him up and tucked him in bed before coming back down.

'Puttar, if they weren't returning tonight they should've called,' said Banti.

Udho nodded. Kalu picked up the receiver and dialled the phone. This was the tenth call he had made to the Johal house. There was no answer.

'Bibi, maybe they decided to stay one more night and have no easy access to a phone,' said Kalu, reassuring himself more than Banti. It was quiet again in the sitting room.

'You should go to sleep. I'll stay up and make some calls,' said Kalu, his eyes focused on the phone.

They didn't listen to him and remained on the sofa and covered themselves up with blankets. Kalu dialled again, still without success. He went to the kitchen after a while, poured some water in the pot, and lit the stove and placed the pot on it. The lid fell on the floor as he opened the small canister of tea. Banti got up to see who had invaded her domain.

'Bibi, I'm making chai. I'll make extra. You and Bhapa can have some if you can't sleep.'

Kalu saw Banti put her head on the sofa and close her eyes. Udho hadn't opened his. He was lying face up on the sofa. His body was taut. Silence was his tool to resolve tension, Banti's were words, words she expressed out loud, or those she wanted to but didn't. Tonight, it was the latter. Kalu noticed that she didn't say much. Sipping the chai, he dialled the phone. Silence again.

The cup in hand, he dozed off. As his hand went limp in sleep, the cup tilted, wetting his pants and the carpet below. Udho opened his eyes as he got up to clean it.

'Anything I can do, son?' he said.

'No, Bhapa. Sleep will do some good. But I can't... Where could Simran be?'

He had had several cups of chai. He could hear the birds outside now.

'Bhapa, I'll be back soon. I'm going over to Sim's parents,' said Kalu, taking the car keys and walking out. He started the car, wiped the condensation off the inside of the windshield, revved the engine and drove away. The gate to the Johals' yard was closed. He got out of the car to open it. It turned out to be locked. They never locked the gate! He jumped over it, walked to the door, knocked and waited. He knocked again. Rubbing his eyes, wearing a night gown, Amrit opened it.

'Oh sorry, Kahla. So early. Is everything all right?' he said, squinting at Kalu.

'Simran...she didn't come home. I called over a dozen times, you didn't answer the phone?'

Sureet had come to the entry. She stood there, without a word.

'Oh, Sim wanted to stay over and see a friend, she said. I thought she was coming by the late train. I thought she'd have called you,' said the turbanless Amrit, running his hand through his beard, further dishevelling it.

Kalu didn't know what to say. The nonchalance of the father about the daughter's whereabouts shocked him. Sureet looked away, then down towards the floor but said nothing.

'I'm sure she'd have returned or at least phoned you,' said Amrit.

'But, Papa, why didn't you answer my calls?'

'Oh. I couldn't hear them in the bedroom.'

'If you were in the bedroom now how did you hear the door knock? The telephone ring is as loud if not louder.'

'Oh, I had lowered the volume on the ring. Sometimes it's hard to sleep. The patients keep disturbing us, hers and mine,' said Amrit pointing at Sureet.

'All right. I think I'll go to the police on the way home.'

'No, Kalu. You know a report of a missing person becomes public record. Won't be good...for your political prospects. I suggest you wait a day at least. She's an adult and police won't do anything in a hurry anyway. They'd ask you about spats you might lately have had and put it down to marital discord, at least initially. Sureet and I can tell you from experience with our patients,' said Amrit, turning to Sureet to back him up.

'Papa, did she tell you which friend she had gone to see?'

'No, Kahla, privacy for adult kids, you know.'

'All right...by the way, I've never seen the lock on the gate before?'

'Oh, Sureet's been quite afraid of thieves lately.'

Kalu noticed Sureet's blank face before turning and jumping over the gate.

Banti was bathing Angad. He was crying and insisting

on being bathed and readied by Simran as was the routine before she headed to the clinic. Kalu took over from Banti and bathed and dressed Angad as he sobbed. The thought of Angad deprived of Simran sent shivers through Kalu. He hugged his son and said, 'Puttar, Mum will be here soon. Papa will go get her.'

Soon, Udho was walking Angad to school. Banti had returned to the kitchen. Kalu left for college, a stone's throw away. Less than a hundred yards from home, he turned back, took the car and drove to the college. He spoke to the office about his class for the morning and drove off.

'Good morning. I need to speak with someone about a possible missing person,' said Kalu to the police officer at the reception of the police station.

'How long has the person been missing?'

'She was supposed to return last night from Southall with her parents. They're home but she's not returned.'

'And what's she to you?'

'She's my wife.'

The officer went into an office and a burly six-foot-four chap came out and asked Kalu to follow him. Inside the office, Kalu sat across from Sergeant Dave Abbott.

'You say your wife's missing,' he said, wasting little time. 'I'm told she was supposed to return last night. It's only been a day. We don't start searching for an adult unless we know she's gone for an unreasonable time and it's quite unlike her to disappear.'

'Yes, I understand. She's a medical doctor. She's never gone without telling me.'

'Are you sure you didn't beat her up. You people...I've seen some of you beat your wives and daughters to pulp, and kill them, and report them missing.'

'I beg your pardon, sergeant. Are you going to take down my report or are you going sit there and imply that I beat or murdered my wife? Are you in the habit of beating yours?'

'Sir, I was just saying it's too early for me to take down a missing person's report. Give her a couple of days and come back if she hasn't returned.'

He drove to the college. In his office he took out his diary and began searching for Simran's contacts in London and Southall. He found two and dialled them. One hadn't heard from her in months. The other didn't pick up the phone. He walked over to see Janice. She was teaching a class but it was about to end in a few minutes. So he waited outside the classroom.

'Kahla, didn't expect to see you waiting for me early in the morning. Things all right?' asked Janice, spotting him.

'I hope they are. I'm not sure though.'

They talked as they walked over to the cafeteria. Sitting down with coffees, they continued the conversation.

'Other than the two names you have, there's another mutual friend of mine and Simran's. I'll call her.'

'Let's do it from my office...it's closer,' said Kalu.

'Yes, let's. I hope she's home. I don't have her office number.'

Kalu stood as Janice sat down and dialled the number. The friend was home, but no, she hadn't heard from or seen Simran.

'Kalu, take the day off. I will too and let's go see your in-laws.'

Janice went to her department head and Kalu to Dean Symes to inform them of their absence, promising to meet back in the cafeteria.

'I'm sure she would've phoned if she was held up. I'm worried, Kalu,' Symes said when told about Simran.

Janice was already back in the cafeteria and free for the day.

'We should get to the Johals' office around lunch time,' said Kalu as they got into the car.

'Where're we going now?' asked Janice.

'To the police, to make the missing person's report. Sim won't have stayed away without telling me.'

'I know. But it's almost lunchtime. Let's head to your in-laws' office first,' said Janice, glancing at her watch.

The Johals were seeing patients even though it was lunchtime. Kalu and Janice found the waiting room had no space to sit as they walked in through the office door.

'Overbooking, walk-ins perhaps,' whispered Janice.

'Dr Badhan, I'll tell the doctors you're here,' said the receptionist.

Amrit came out with the patient leaving his room. 'Oh, Kahla and Janice, what brings you here?'

Sureet heard Amrit's voice and came to the door of her own office when her patient left.

'Got to talk about Sim, I just need five minutes. Then you're free to see your patients.'

Kalu took Amrit by his arm into Sureet's office. Janice followed. Behind closed doors, looking directly at Amrit, Kalu asked, 'When and where was the last time you saw Sim?'

'From Southall she travelled with us to King's Cross station. There she said she'd come in a later train because she needed to see a friend.'

'No, the car at—' blurted Sureet before Amrit cut her short.

'You don't even remember what you ate this morning!' he yelled. 'Just ignore her, she's confused.'

Sureet turned her eyes away and then towards the floor.

'Papa, how does she look after her patients if her memory is failing? Anyhow, you say Sim left you at King's Cross and the car, you say, is Sureet's imagination or some hazy memory?'

'Yes, yes, Kahla, that's right.'

'All right then, Papa, if you hear anything let me know.'

Kalu rushed out and jumped into the car. Janice got in and the tyres screeched, leaving a trail of tyre marks on the road and smoke in the air.

At the police station, the woman behind the reception desk asked Kalu, 'Sir, you were here this morning. Do you want to see Sergeant Abbott?'

'Yes, if that's who I have to see,' said Kalu.

Abbott wasn't in. Constable Paul Sweeny took Kalu and Janice in. Kalu explained the circumstances to him, the last alleged sighting at King's Cross and Sureet's reference to a car. Sweeny asked how Janice came to be involved. He had to rule out the tall blonde being the reason for the missing wife.

'If you come across any new information, please call me. Here's my card. If we find anything, we'll immediately inform you,' was all Sweeny said to Kalu once he had made his report.

23

Kalu drove home after dropping Janice at the college. He got out of the car and saw Udho walking from school with Angad.

'Any news, son? Angad keeps asking.'

Kalu shook his head and kissed Angad. Angad looked up at Kalu and asked, 'Papa, when is Mum coming home?'

'Soon, son,' Kalu said, looking away into the distance.

At home, Banti had the same question as Udho and got the same answer. Sitting near the phone, Kalu sipped chai, his eyes alternating between the phone and Angad eating a snack. Abruptly rising from the sofa, he placed the cup by the telephone and walked out without answering as Udho shouted, 'Kalu, where are you going?' He drove to the college and found Janice was still in her office.

'Can I trade my car with yours for a few days? Everyone that knows me knows my car. Pretty difficult to hide,' he said.

'Hide from whom?'

'I need to talk to Sim's mother alone. Some nights Amrit goes pubbing or I could wait for Saturdays when she's alone grocery shopping, but I can't wait.'

'Why trade the car, Kahla? I'll drive you.'

Kalu and Janice decided to wait for some time at the college before heading to the Johal home. Stopping the car on the street a few yards away from the gate, they waited. Janice sat up in the driver's seat and Kalu slouched in the passenger seat. Shortly after 6:00 pm the Johal car drove in through the gate. About half an hour later, Kalu saw in the light of the streetlamps the complainant in both Udho's and Amrit's criminal cases, Gurbachan Hundal, walk in with another man. Another fifteen minutes had passed when Amrit walked out with them. Kalu walked the pathway to the door and knocked. Sureet opened the door.

'Kahla, you shouldn't be here!'

'Mum, please tell me about the car you mentioned.'

'I can't...Amrit...he'll be angry. You should leave. I'd be in trouble.'

'Mum, please. For Sim and Angad's sake. I haven't heard from Sim and Angad keeps crying.'

'Two cars picked us up at Southall station. Amrit said he needed to see a friend. So we went to his house. Sim went to the home of the family whose wedding it was.'

Sureet was silent.

'Mum, please, then what happened.'

'You should leave.'

'No, please, Mum, tell me.'

'I don't know. I don't know but...'

'But, but what?'

'No, I don't know.'

'What don't you know, Mum?'

'I don't know why she never made it to the wedding. She never showed up... You should leave. I'll be in trouble!' said Sureet, pushing him out and shutting the door.

Kalu came back to the car in tears. Janice drove him home.

He showed up at the police station the next day after taking his only class for the morning. Sergeant Abbott received him in his office. The police had no information to share but they had questions of their own.

'Is there anything abnormal about your marriage I should know?' Abbott asked.

'What do you mean? Is your marriage normal? What's a normal marriage? I assumed a marriage between a man and a woman without anything more was normal!'

Told about a missing married Indian woman, Abbott's father-in-law, who had served in the Indian Civil Service, had alerted him to religious and caste differences.

'Any caste or religious differences, I meant?' said Abbott.

'This bloody caste shit...I can't even shake it off at a police station in Britain, can I?'

'Didn't mean to offend you, sir. I didn't know. Just asking because it's my job to look at all this.'

Kalu calmed down. It was a reasonable request. He explained the difference in their caste and the fact that Amrit wasn't very happy about the marriage. He also told Abbott that, having gone with her parents for the wedding, she had never made it to the house she was supposed to go to.

Next morning, Abbott phoned Kalu and met him in his office at the college. Kalu was comforted that Abbott looked like any other professor, dressed as he was in plain clothes.

'I assume yours was a happy marriage, sir?' Abbott asked.

'Yes.'

'The caste thing initially upset your father-in-law. Didn't that disillusion you?'

'No.'

'Why didn't you go to the wedding?'

'Amrit told me only a week before it and I was scheduled to address a meeting at Leicester the day they had to be in London. Why are you asking me all this? Am I a suspect in a crime and if so, what crime?'

'No, sir. No crime I know of at this time, but if there was one, everyone would be a suspect. And Dr Janice Charlesworth, sir, what's your relationship with her?'

'None. She's a colleague and a friend and the best friend of my wife.'

'Oh, all right. Thank you for your help. I'm in touch with London and Southall...nothing from them so far.'

Abbott walked away, resurfacing a few minutes later at Janice's office.

'Hello, Professor Charlesworth. I'm Sergeant Abbott of Bedford Police. You were with Professor Badhan when he made the missing person report about his wife.'

'Yes, she is my best friend. I hope you find her.'

'We're trying. May I ask about you and Professor Badhan?'

'What about him? What are you insinuating?' she asked, her large light blue eyes peering over the frame of her glasses at his arched nose.

'Nothing, Professor, it's my job to ask.'

'No relationship other than as colleague and best friend's spouse.'

'Thank you, ma'am,' said Abbott and left.

Kalu heard that things had picked up at the Goldington temple. Once ostracized, Amrit had been elected president of the temple society without a contest. His erstwhile enemy Gurbachan, now his new pub buddy, had placed his name in the nomination for it. Amrit had his weekly pub outings with Gurbachan and the other man Kalu had seen the day he spoke to Sureet. He had forgotten to ask Sureet if she knew the other man. Prior to Simran's disappearance, Amrit used to go for long walks with him. But Kalu didn't know that.

Kalu wanted to speak to Sureet again. The last time he talked to her she was pale. Her eyes were dilated. She spoke fast. She wanted him to leave. Amrit's pub night was after the weekend. He couldn't wait that long for Sureet to be alone at home. Not knowing what had happened to Simran was killing him.

Kalu sat near the phone, fiddling with the empty mug from which he had just finished his chai. He picked up the phone and dialled.

'Hello, this is Kahla.'

No answer.

'Hello.'

'Ye...s,' Sureet mumbled after a few seconds.

'Mum, I want to see you.'

'Come to the office at eleven tomorrow. Wait north of it, round the corner,' she whispered.

The next day, Kalu drove from the college and waited in his car at the agreed spot. Dressed in a trouser suit, blemishes and bags under her eyes Kalu had not seen before, Sureet walked up and got into the front passenger seat.

'Can we drive away from this place?'

Kalu drove for several blocks, into a dead end and stopped.

'The other man is Harjit Singh Athwal, one of the two who went on long walks with Amrit. Simran never made it to the wedding. Amrit had prearranged the cars. No one answered the door at the house we visited...the house we went to before going to the wedding home. I don't know any more. Please, Kahla, please, find my daughter, my only child.'

'Thank you, Mum. Call me if you find out anything more.'

Kalu dropped her back at the corner and drove straight to the police station. He conveyed the new information to Abbott.

'Please, Sergeant. Pass the information on to Southall and ask them to go to the house which didn't answer the door.'

'All right, Professor Detective, I'll do it right away. I truly appreciate your sleuthing.'

'It's my wife. I'm not doing it for you. Please find her.'

In fright and anger, itching to lash out at the slightest provocation, Kalu found himself regressing to his Elstow Abbey School days. Cursing himself for crumbling under anxiety, he drove to the college to teach his only other class of the day. After parking the car, he stopped off at the cafeteria. Though not a heavy coffee drinker, he ordered one. He had had three cups of the instant, two at home and a quick one with Abbott at the police station and nothing to eat all day. The caffeine sustained him but was destroying his insides. Simran had told him to ease up on it because he was in danger of developing stomach ulcers. In his head, Simran was admonishing him. He gulped it down before entering the classroom to teach the history of democracy, in particular the suffragettes' struggle. The phenomenon of caste and his place in it imbued in him an appreciation for the plight of the serfs, peasants, the working class and women in history. Caste had reduced the Indian immigrants in Britain to artefacts of history, their minds frozen in the stillness of time, constantly acting out the past.

24

'I don't know what kind of trouble Simran is in. I can only imagine. She had no enemies except those who hate me for my caste. There are many of those, of course,' Kalu said to Janice and Carrington in the cafeteria the next day, tears flowing down his cheeks. 'I loved her but... I tried explaining to her but she didn't listen.'

They had come to see him and discuss what, if anything, had happened in the investigation. They followed every lead and phoned every person Simran could have gone to see in London and Southall.

'She was born and raised in Britain...untouched by caste until she met me, the untouchable. I tried telling her there'd be troubles in our path. She didn't care,' Kalu continued.

Swept along by the hip and modern Britain of the fifties and sixties, Amrit and Sureet had been blind to the hold caste had on them. Kalu's entry into their lives awakened the evil within which they pretended they had overcome.

'And Amrit focused his contempt on her. How dare she dishonour him in the eyes of the community? You see, we never kill our sons for dishonouring us, always our women. We may kill the other's son but never our own. Killing me would've been too obvious. Killing her, even though many years have passed since the marriage, will expunge the dishonour without raising much suspicion,' Kalu explained, as much to himself as them.

Early Saturday morning, unable to sleep, Kalu went down to the kitchen. It was quiet. He sat down with the chai he had made. The phone rang. Having taken one sip, he put the chai down and picked up the receiver.

'Hello, may I speak with Kahla Singh?' said the voice.

'Speaking,' said Kalu, listening for a few moments before saying, 'Yes, I'll be there in a few minutes.'

The tea sat near the phone. The car engine revved. Leaving the household asleep, Kalu was out and off.

The lights inside the police station had lit up its glass front entrance. The place was barely awake. Abbott received Kalu. His eyes immediately focused on the cop's arched nose peering at him. Janice had brought it up once; it had been burned into her memory. Abbott and another officer sat him in Abbott's office; its size meant he was only an arm's length away from them. Still angry at the way they had targeted him and Janice as suspects, he laboured hard to control his temper.

'Dr Badhan, Birmingham Police have recovered a body in a suitcase from a train. They've had it since Monday, three days after you say your wife left with your father-in-law. We believe it to be your wife's body. She wore a trouser suit; nothing distinct about it. But the police discovered a tattoo that reads "Kahlu" on her pubic area. Dr Charlesworth told us that's what your wife called you as opposed to Kalu or Kahla.'

The coffee Abbott had poured Kalu sat untouched. His hands fiddled with the cup without lifting it or his eyes. Then he looked up. Abbott saw the tears that had welled up but were refusing to flow. He offered Kalu tissue paper. Kalu wiped his eyes with it.

'When can I see the body?'

'It's quite disfigured. Sure you want to see it?'

'Yes. She's my wife, the mother of my child. She deserves at least that much respect.'

'All right. We'll arrange it and let you know. Obviously, you've to go there and see it. In the meantime, we've some questions. Do you mind if we ask them?'

'Go ahead.'

'Can you give us the exact time and the trains you took to and from Leicester and where you stayed the night?'

'You just told me my wife's been murdered and now you're accusing me of killing her?'

'Not accusing, sir. Until we find the murderer or murderers, everyone that had anything to do with her is a suspect. Simple policing, sir.'

Kalu gave them the information they wanted and answered some more questions about Janice.

'Strange policing, Sergeant. You haven't spoken to the man who took her to Southall.'

'Sir, we did before the body was found and we will do so again. As I said, everyone is a suspect.'

Kalu took leave from college for the day and drove to Birmingham. Abbott's questions regarding his whereabouts reverberated in his ears. His temples throbbed hard. Was he capable of murder? He could concede to being an angry man, given to outbursts. From there to murder wasn't a threshold too high, he thought. Or was it? He tried to fathom the rage that must have thrust Amrit into the dark alley of murder.

Birmingham seemed to gaze at him like a colossal question mark. He introduced himself at the police station. The short, rotund man in police uniform, a bunch of keys hanging from his belt, asked him to wait at the reception. The doors of the mortuary room creaked open and the attendant ushered him in. The head had been hacked off. The chest and abdomen without arms and the legs amputated at the knees to fit the body in the suitcase lay before him. The rest, including the pelvic girdle, was intact. The tattooed 'Kahlu' stared at him. The attendant stood close by. He perhaps didn't feel the need to give Kalu privacy, believing no one would embrace so disfigured a body. But Kalu asked him to leave. The door creaked shut. He put his lips to the 'Kahlu'. Five minutes on, the attendant opened the door a crack to see. Kalu was still there, on his knees, his lips on Simran's body.

Before their marriage, she had gone with Janice to a tattoo artist 'to have Kahlu engraved on her vagina'. Kalu had argued against it. At the time, it reminded him of the branding of black slaves in America, like farm cattle. She meant it to be a rebuke to her father's paternalism and a flag of rebellion planted against the male culture that dispossessed her of her sexuality and dictated who she could marry or sleep with. For her, her vagina most symbolized the sexual repression of women; it was as well a potent weapon for a woman's freedom. That is where she had wanted 'Kahlu' engraved.

At the morgue, the police showed Kalu the strips of the trouser suit she was wearing when he dropped her at the Bedford train station. Her purse, shoes and jewellery were missing.

'This is the suitcase I had bought for her parents. They said they wanted to go to India for a visit. Simran thought a suitcase would be a nice gift for them, since they had never left Britain after immigrating and apparently didn't have any good suitcases,' Kalu told the police as he examined the suitcase.

The police showed him the lock they had taken off the suitcase soiled in blood.

'No, I didn't buy them a lock,' said Kalu.

When the police were done getting the information they wanted from him, he asked when he could transport the body for the funeral in Bedford.

'Not finished yet with the body, sir. Sergeant Abbott will let you know,' the police officer said.

Outside the police station, Birmingham city was awash in light as Kalu got into his car. Mingling with wet roads and the constant drizzle, the lights produced a zillion reflections, making driving difficult. Focused on finding Simran while continuing to show up for work, he had not been sleeping well. He kept dozing off. Afraid that he might get into an accident, he pulled off to the shoulder, turned the ignition off and went to sleep. He was woken up by a police officer at four in the morning when he noticed the car parked by the motorway.

Banti had got up and put the water for chai on the stove when Kalu scuffed into the house.

'Son, we were worried when you didn't come home.'

'I'd asked Janice to call and tell you I was in Birmingham.'

Udho came hurtling down the stairs when he heard them talking. 'Son, don't go away anywhere without telling us.'

'No, Bhapa, I didn't mean to. But...'

'But what, Kalu?'

'Bhapa, Simran...Simran's no more...killed. Somebody murdered her.'

'Oh my God, Kalu,' said Udho, secretly hoping this was a bad dream.

'The idiot Johal killed her,' cried Banti, beating her thighs with her hands, wailing as she would in Banjhan when someone died, joining other women in mourning the deceased.

Angad heard the wailing and walked down to Banti, 'Dadi, don't cry. Mum! Where's Mum?'

Kalu had tried to protect him. He knew Angad had seen fear in his Baba and Dadi's eyes ever since Simran had gone missing. But he couldn't find the strength to comfort his son right now, or his parents. He was shell-shocked, too jolted to admit his tragedy even to himself. He didn't share his grief with his family that day. He couldn't. Dazed beyond comprehension, beyond tears, he could only fall back on his daily routine.

He had a cup of tea, washed up and was ready to head to college when the phone rang. It was Abbott.

'Doctor Badhan, we've spoken to your father-in-law. Could you come in at 11:00 am?'

After teaching his first class he reached the police station. He entered the building as Amrit was walking out.

'Hello, Papa, I'm sorry for our loss, yours and ours.'

Lips sealed and eyebrows curled, Amrit squinted at him and walked by. With his squint, one couldn't tell where his eyes were focused. But Kalu was sure he didn't even try to look him in the eye. From behind, his bow legs seemed to have sharper angles, as if his knees were ready to fly away sideways, no longer willing to carry the burden. Abbott poured two cups of coffee and took Kalu into the office. A plainclothes detective joined them.

'Amrit Johal says neither you nor Simran ever gave them a suitcase,' said Abbott, handing Kalu the cup of coffee.

'We did. Simran thought such a suitcase could hold a lot of gifts for the trip. People carry lots of British-made goods for relatives in India. We bought it from one of the High Street shops and Simran delivered it to them less than six months ago. And then they never went anyway...'

'Dr Badhan, Amrit says it never happened.'

'Sergeant, did you speak to Simran's mum?'

'No, because whatever she says, we can't use it in court. She can't be compelled to testify against her husband.'

'Well, Sergeant, you may or may not be able to use her testimony but at least you'll know the truth about the suitcase...and many other things. And come to think of it, Janice went with Simran to deliver the suitcase to the Johals.'

Kalu got up to leave, walked a few steps, turned and said, 'By the way, when could you release the body, or whatever is left of it after this butcher was done with it?'

'After one more week you could set the funeral for any day,' said Abbott.

At the college cafeteria, Janice was sipping coffee when Kalu came in, hungering for the fix. He could see in her eyes that she knew about Simran's body having been found. He went and stood by her table. Neither said anything for a while. It was Janice who broke the silence.

'Bring your coffee and join me,' she said. 'Abbott phoned, asking about the suitcase just as I was leaving the office to come down for coffee.'

'Checking out who delivered the suitcase, wasn't he? The bastard...still doesn't trust me.'

'It doesn't shock me at all, being from the wrong side of the tracks myself.'

Though she didn't have to put up with racism and casteism, Janice knew well the disadvantage the wrong class or gender could put you at. In her youth, at parties in the posh part of town, when someone deemed it appropriate to include her, she'd had 'Are you somebody?' thrown at her all the time. She understood that one didn't have a right to just be. You had to prove yourself worthy of whatever you were being judged for. As for criminal justice, on her side of the tracks, you were presumed guilty until you proved you weren't.

'They'll never let you forget you're brown, turbaned, immigrant and guilty as hell until proven otherwise, Kalu.'

'Amrit planned it. There can be no other way she'd be dead. He knew my schedule. He found a perfect moment when Simran could be lured away without me,' said Kalu, retracing Amrit's conduct from the time he found out Simran was seeing him.

'Kalu, you must tell Abbott everything about Simran's father... Poor Sureet. How she must be feeling! Unless of course she's in on it. She can't be though. Simran was very close to her.'

'She's afraid of him. Simran never told me outright but hinted at it. He is an abuser. He gives her a hard time. Sometimes he'll get violent also. She rarely looks up or smiles when he's around. I've told Abbott everything but the bastard is obsessed with me. I don't know why.'

'Well, in England husbands kill wives, boyfriends kill girlfriends...jilted lovers kill anyone that rejects them. But, you know, here no one's ever heard of fathers killing married daughters. Did you explain the caste thing to him?'

'I did, Janice. I've been doing it from day one.'

'Have you confronted Amrit about how he chose to ask Simran out to Southall by herself?'

'I didn't, Janice. And he lies. He lied about where he last saw Simran. You know how Simran wanted to be close to him. He played the long game...couldn't handle the heat from his Jat friends.'

Feeling helpless and exhausted, he got up and dragged himself to the last class of the day. After the class, he went to his office and sat staring at his desk, books, telephone and Simran's diary with all her contacts written in it. He thumbed through the diary. There was nothing more to do. He had contacted everyone. No one had seen or heard from her after she left for London. He returned to the cafeteria. It was full of students and faculty. He sat down at the only empty table, the one Janice and he had occupied that afternoon, and ordered an egg sandwich and coffee. As he dug into the sandwich, he noticed Raghbir enter the cafeteria. Their eyes met. Raghbir got a cup of coffee and joined him at his table.

'I've been looking for you all over Bedford. No one is answering the phone at your house,' he said hesitantly, not sure how Kalu was dealing with the trauma.

'Oh, Bibi and Bhapa, I told them to not pick up the phone. Already enough on their hands with Angad. And their English isn't great. Everyone that needs to reach me has my office phone. Forget that. How are you?'

'Me, I'm okay. I just learnt about Simran bhabhi. I'm so sorry.'

'Been racking my brains over it. I need to talk to Amrit. Will you come with me?'

Soon the car was crossing the divide to the other side of the Great Ouse. Kalu saw the Johal car drive through the gates. He followed, stopping his car behind theirs. Stepping out of the car, Amrit looked back. Kalu and Raghbir had already come out of theirs, Kalu standing holding the open door.

'Were you following us?' asked Amrit.

'No, Papa. Just drove up to speak to you,' said Kalu.

'Come in, Kalu and Raghbir,' said Sureet as she unlocked the door.

'Sureet, they don't need to come in as I've nothing to say to them. I've already talked to the police,' said Amrit, walking into the house, pushing Sureet in with him before the door was shut in Kalu's face.

Kalu banged the door with his fist, yelled and screamed. But that morgue, now more so than ever, remained closed.

He dropped Raghbir and drove home. Angad was asleep. Udho sat watching TV. Waiting for Kalu, Banti had cleaned up the kitchen. She was about to put the food away.

'Kalu, are you hungry? Food is ready.'

'No, Bibi. I ate at the college. We'll have it tomorrow.'

He sat near Udho, watching him and Banti.

'It should've been their time to enjoy themselves. Now they're raising my child,' he thought and shut his eyes. He sat with them, all silent, for a few minutes before heading upstairs to bed.

On a Sunday afternoon, a week later, was Simran's funeral. There was a large crowd at the crematorium, including many Indians, members of the college community and Labour activists. Abbott, accompanied by two others in civilian clothes whom Kalu didn't recognize, was in attendance. As the time to commit the body to the incinerator neared, Kalu kept turning his head towards the entrance. At last he saw Sureet walk in; still no sign of Amrit. Kalu nodded to acknowledge her. He hated the idea of Simran going into the incinerator spurned by both her parents. He patted Angad sitting between Udho and him. He needed to touch something of Simran; Angad was of her.

The closed casket rested in front of them. At Udho's insistence, Kalu relented and gave consent to the Sikh prayer. The granthi from the Bromham temple recited it. It was time to wheel the casket to the incinerator. Kalu and Raghbir stood up. Kalu glanced at Sureet. She slowly got up. He waited for her to walk over. She put her hand on the casket. They slid it into place. The attendants closed the doors of the incinerator and pressed the button. People dispersed after the granthi offered the final prayer.

Outside the crematorium, Kalu spotted Sureet briskly walking away. He ran, caught up with her and said, 'Thank you for being here, Mum. Simran would have liked it...'

Sureet remained silent.

'But we need your help, Mum. You have to tell the

police about the suitcase Simran gave you. Otherwise, it's my word against Papa's.'

She stared at him for a few moments. Her eyes showed hurt and anger, but she said nothing before walking away.

Janice noticed Kalu walking back, his eyes fixed on the ground below his feet. 'What happened?' she asked.

Kalu had been absent from college for a week now. Janice had hoped to catch up with Kalu at the funeral since he'd been avoiding calls from colleagues as well. He told her about his visit to the Johal home as well as what he had just said to Sureet. Janice promised him she'd help but also told him he should get back to work soon. Simran would have wanted him to move on with his life.

Janice spent all her spare time the next day at college in her office, dialling and redialling the Johals' office and home phones. After being repeatedly told by the office receptionist that Sureet was busy, Janice succeeded. Sureet was on the phone with her.

'Aunty, Janice, Simran's friend. Don't say anything. Just listen. Aunty, you remember Simran and me bringing the new leather suitcase over, don't you? I've already told the police about it. Uncle is lying. You're a mother...Sim's mother. If Amrit is the killer, he doesn't deserve a verdict of innocence from you.'

Sureet said nothing but didn't hang up.

'Aunty, please tell me. You must say yes or no. Will you talk to the police?'

There was a long pause. Each could hear the other breathing.

'Yes, if they come talk to me. But not at home,' said Sureet.

Soon afterwards a plainclothes detective showed up at the Johals' medical office. Gesturing to the receptionist to say nothing, he showed her his card with a note: 'I want to see Dr Sureet Johal. Please tell her, no one else.' Sureet confirmed the truth of what Kalu had told them about the suitcase and the cars arranged by Amrit at Southall and how Simran never made it to the home where the wedding was taking place.

'But you can't force one spouse to testify against the other if the crime is in relation to a third person. My husband's told me that,' she said and opened the door for the detective to leave.

25

Early one morning, Abbott and Sweeny appeared at the Johals' home. Amrit did not offer any resistance. Sweeny handcuffed him. Sureet helped gather and pack whatever Abbott suggested Amrit might need in jail because 'The judge may not look too kindly on the brutality, the grisly beheading and chopping of the legs. So he might not get bail.'

For Amrit's first appearance before the judge, Sureet was present in court. The matter was adjourned for a week for Amrit to retain a lawyer. With the help of the Goldington crowd led by Gurbachan, Amrit decided on Robert Jenkins, the most expensive defence lawyer in town. No one paid any attention to Sureet who had argued, 'Pleading before a judge isn't the same as shouting slogans at the temple. In court the loudest isn't necessarily the best. Jenkins is more bombast than brilliance.'

Kalu walked into the courthouse on the day of the bail hearing. Janice, Symes and Gurbat were already there. Several members of the Goldington temple milled about.

'Bloody Chamar. He has the audacity to marry a Jatti

and then tries to send her father to jail,' Kalu overheard Gurbachan say to the men around him. Within earshot, Sureet stood by herself. She didn't look in his or Gurbachan's direction or say anything at all. The hearing was over within minutes.

In denying Amrit bail the judge said, 'Given the cruelty and the gruesomeness of the crime, I hold Amrit Singh Johal to be a flight risk which can't be completely alleviated by the surrender of his passport.'

The trial date fixed some weeks hence, the court adjourned.

Kalu resumed his political activity. Its scope and intensity grew to fill the void the murder had etched into his life. He drowned himself in reading and writing for politics and teaching. Symes, Carrington and Janice Charlesworth teamed up to create the opportunity for him to contest the next national elections. Simran's death and the consequent public awareness of caste cruelty and the cultural depredations borne by the untouchables in Britain lent Kalu and his life story a certain intrigue and charisma.

Kalu would take Angad with him to political and other outings on the weekends. The aging Banti and Udho, though doting grandparents, weren't equipped to offer Angad the intellectual stimulation Simran or Kalu could. Her absence made his presence in the child's life indispensable. Travelling with Angad to public and political meetings humanized Kalu for people who might have previously felt awkward seeing the turbaned political activist.

Engrossed in teaching, political activism and childrearing, for Kalu time went by in a flash.

It was the Monday morning of Amrit's trial. Kalu, Raghbir and Gurbat reached the courthouse well in time. Charlesworth, Carrington and Symes were already seated in the courtroom. The court was called to order as the judge entered. Dressed in a grey suit, blue tie and turban, beard coiffed and pressed, Amrit stood up when asked and entered a not guilty plea. The prosecutor, a balding Ian James, looked around as if searching for something. In a white sari with a flowered border, Sureet entered. She looked at Amrit, his mouth agape. She had told him not to expect her in court. Kalu detected a smile when she glanced at the prosecutor.

Abbott and a police officer from Birmingham testified about how, where and in what state Simran's body was found. Their evidence, including on the specific suitcase containing the body, went uncontested.

'May it please the court, the crown now calls Dr Sureet Kaur Johal,' said James.

'She can't be compelled to testify against her husband,' said Jenkins, jumping up.

'May it please the court, she's neither been compelled nor coerced,' said the prosecutor.

The oath to tell the truth taken and preliminary questions about name, age, relationship to the accused and the victim answered, Sureet began her story:

'My husband had another lawyer advise me that I can't be forced to testify to the truth about the matter before the court. I'm here of my own volition. The only person entitled to call me mother has been taken away from me. I've been deprived of my right to enjoy the fruits of motherhood. In fact, motherhood hangs like a curse over my life. Doctor Kahla Singh Badhan is a murderer. He knew the consequences of this inter-caste union, of marrying my only child, my beautiful daughter. A Chamar marrying a Jat woman, one or both could be harmed or killed. He knew that. Yet recklessly he married her. She was in love with him. Her murder was the consequence of him marrying her, despite what may have ensued and in fact did.'

'Direct your witness to the issues at hand. The last I checked the indictment says nothing about Dr Badhan,' interjected the judge.

'Dr Johal, please tell us about the relationship between your daughter and her father and what happened before she went missing.'

Sureet related how Amrit's love for their only child turned into loathing once she told him about Kalu. His attitude was not consistent though. It swung from hate to accepting the marriage. But he began hating his daughter once again under the influence of his Jat friends, many of them now associated with the Goldington temple. She described the long walks he used to go on with Harjit Athwal and Gurbachan.

'They met regularly. Instead of going pubbing, which Amrit liked very much, they would go for long walks, return and whisper to each other at home. It continued up until a few weeks before the murder.'

She recounted how he began going to Simran's home and attending public meetings where Kalu spoke.

'After the murder, he was elevated to the presidency of the Goldington temple. He stopped seeing Angad and Kahla. It bothered me. Angad reaffirms my motherhood. But Amrit wanted to have nothing to do with them. The Jats and the temple were all he cared for. Many taunted him as weak for not killing Simran immediately upon learning of her intention to marry Kahla.'

She went on to describe the arranged car rides from the Southall station and how they travelled separately, Simran never making it to the wedding to which she had reluctantly agreed to go—reluctantly, because it meant going without Kahla due to the latter's speaking engagement in Leicester.

'The suitcase with the body, I saw it. It's the one that Simran had asked Kahla to buy. Simran and her friend Janice delivered it to us. Amrit wanted a new suitcase to go to India. My child didn't know she was arranging a casket for herself.'

She took an ironed handkerchief out of her purse to dry her eyes. The judge adjourned the trial for a few minutes for her to compose herself and the shocked courtroom to calm itself.

Sureet's evidence-in-chief was over with two hours of court time left in the day.

'Is the defence ready for cross-examining the witness?' the judge interrupted Jenkins and Amrit whispering to each other. The room was cool and aerated but perspiration had saturated the lower folds of Amrit's turban. The sweat was descending into his beard, washing away the hair fixer holding it in place.

'Your honour, the defence requests a half-hour recess,' said Jenkins.

Seeing the perspiration wreaking havoc on the accused's face, the judge said, 'So ordered.'

Everyone except the sheriffs, Amrit and Jenkins left the courtroom.

'I'll be outside the courtroom in case you need me,' said prosecutor James before leaving. In about five minutes, he was asked back inside. There was a proposal from the defence for Amrit to turn Crown's witness and give up the persons who carried out the murder at his behest. The court reconvened. The case was adjourned for a month, pending discussions between prosecution and the defence.

Amrit was taken away to jail to await the outcome of those discussions.

Kalu smiled at Sureet when they saw each other outside. Though not pleased with what she had said about him on the stand, he appreciated her honesty and in particular her bravery in defying Amrit and Jat arrogance.

26

The loss of Simran was not only the loss of a mother, wife and daughter-in-law. She had been the financial mainstay for the family to flourish and Kalu to be free to engage in public activism. Her death had created a deep void that frightened Kalu but he kept his personal burdens to himself. Though he had leaned on Janice in pursuing leads on Simran's murder, at home, he had placed a cone of silence over her death and its effect on their lives.

Inside 2 St Leonard's Ave silence reigned day and night, punctured only by Angad's smiles, utterances and actions. Udho and Banti were his full-time attendants. Though there was no lack of care, love and attention for Angad, he did throw the occasional temper tantrum. He missed his mother but didn't know what to make of the situation, perhaps because he didn't hear anyone in the family talk about her except in connection with the death, the adjourned trial and what could happen next.

Early one morning, Kalu came down and placed a pot of water on the stove to make tea. Udho was on the sofa staring at the television on mute, showing an American Western starring John Wayne.

'Bhapa, here's some money to pay the gas and electricity bills. You could do that when you walk Angad to or from school.'

'Yes, son, I'll do that... I've been meaning to say something,' he spoke quickly lest Kalu get busy with other things. 'We have a big house now. And my pension...it doesn't help much. I was thinking I should do some business like, er, money exchange...transfers.'

'What money exchange, Bhapa?'

'Oh, people send money to India. We take pounds

here and deliver more rupees per pound in India, more than the official exchange rate. In India, the rich pay a lot more rupees for pounds sterling to make their black money white.'

'How long have you been thinking about it? No, Bhapa, it's illegal to do that.'

'Son, it's legal here. Maybe illegal in India, but lots of people are doing it. A bit of extra money won't hurt. I've been trying to understand this system for some time. I wanted to be of some use in my old age...long before dhee Simran was... And now we need the money also.'

'But, Bhapa even you say it's illegal in India. Let me think about it.'

'No, I don't want to be a burden. It'll give me something to do. Soon, Angad will not need anyone to walk him to school.'

Kalu poured Udho and himself a cup of tea.

'I see father and son having tea without me. I am just an old village woman, agootha chhaap, who never learnt to read and write,' taunted Banti, walking down the stairs and pointing her left thumb at them, exposing the index finger with the nail missing.

'Your thumb print was spared the trouble because Bhapa put his for the loan to come to England,' said Kalu and poured her a cup as he stole a glimpse at the silent TV screen. John Wayne had successfully killed the cattle thieves and wrested control of his herd. Kalu could only wish and pray for such prowess to control his world.

Banti turned her attention to breakfast for the family as Udho reached halfway up the stairs to hug Angad walking down, rubbing sleep from his eyes. Kalu was on the toilet when the telephone rang.

'Phone,' Banti screamed.

It rang several times before Udho answered it.

'Hello.'

'Could I speak to Dr Badhan?'

'Just a mint,' said Udho and shouted, 'Kahla, phone.'

Kalu ran out and hastened to take it from him saying, 'Bhapa, the word is minute, not mint.' Banti and Udho stood rapt as he spoke to the caller. After putting the phone down, he took a deep breath and exhaled.

'It was Sergeant Abbott. On Monday, Amrit is pleading guilty to the charge of conspiracy to commit murder. He's also agreed to testify against his former friend, Harjit Athwal, and another. They've been charged with murder. Bibi, give me a big mug of spicy chai with a lot more sugar and milk than usual,' he said, slumping onto the sofa next to the phone.

Udho took Angad to school. Banti was making pranthas and Kalu sat cupping the mug with his hands sipping hot chai when he returned. Kalu had only an afternoon class to teach. He ate several pranthas followed by another mug of chai and lay himself down on the sofa. Soon, he was snoring. Udho woke him up at noon and he got ready and took off to the college for his afternoon class.

In his office after the class, he sat looking at Simran's diary and the pinned note in Simran's hand on his message board reminding him to come home for Angad's birthday celebration. Ever since Abbott's telephone call, he had been feeling a certain load off his back and a spring in his step. But Simran was no more. Someone pleading guilty or being charged for the murder wouldn't return her to life or to him. How could that ever be cause for any relief or happiness? he thought. Yet he was no doubt less sad than the day he first learnt of her death—an improvement of sorts.

Kalu walked over to the cafeteria to ponder death over coffee, hoping that exploring the wound might help him.

He joined Carrington and Janice who were already seated at a corner table. They sipped their beverages as Kalu told them about Abbott's call.

'I think that calls for a celebration, don't you, Janice?' said Carrington.

'Sure. It's sure to help bring closure.'

'Will it, really? Does one ever get full closure? I don't know,' Kalu said.

'You're analysing things too much. A beer or two might help. Come on. It's Friday. I'll make you a deal. We'll be at the court with you on Monday if you come to the pub with us this evening,' said Janice. 'Ah...we'll be there anyway, Kahla. Come, let's go.'

The King's Arms' low-ceiling cosiness was alive with human presence. Janice spotted an unoccupied table in a corner away from the bar. Kalu plonked himself in the corner on the bench seat and Carrington shouted an order for Guinnesses. From the bar the owner smiled and waved at Kalu.

'I think he's saying it's good to see you, Kalu,' said Janice.

'First time in a pub since Sim's death, eh.'

The owner walked over and said, 'Hey mate, sorry to hear of your missus' passing,' placing their glasses on the table.

'Thanks, mate. She loved this place, the banter, the Guinness, the ambience.'

The owner nodded and returned to the bar. He was a man of few words. Kalu looked into his Guinness. The darkness appealed to him but its head more so. The head was like light rising out of the dark below it. He was soon distracted by the talk of politics. That was the topic foremost on Michael Carrington and Janice Charlesworth's minds.

'Heath's Tories have made a mess of this country.

Unemployment, Northern Ireland... I can go on and on. Quite depressing, frankly,' said Janice.

'Well, Labour didn't do so swimmingly on jobs, either,' said Carrington.

'I know. But Kahla isn't launching a new party yet,' she said, bringing some cheer to the table before they got serious again. 'So, Kahla. The Bedford seat. Skeet would be easier to beat than Christopher Soames. The Churchill connection is still a source of charisma. So we're lucky Soames is no longer the MP.'

'More doable, Janice,' said a tepid Kalu. 'But given the state of my family, I'm wondering whether I could do it. Or whether I even should.'

'You must,' said Carrington.

'You're more than your caste, colour and turban, Kahla. Your candidacy isn't just about racial diversity in representation,' pressed Janice.

'Precisely,' Carrington backed her up.

Kalu looked into the second full glass of Guinness that had just arrived, the head still rising to the top.

'I don't know. I'll keep mulling it over. More of us around now,' he said, looking towards three other Indians in the pub, a rare sight at the King's Arms in the fifties and sixties. There were more Indian faces at the college too. For all he knew, they could have been Pakistani. But for Kalu, they too were sub-continental Indians.

A few moments later, one of the three Indians walked over.

'Professor Badhan, my name is Pardeep Kumar. I've seen you around at college. I too came at the same age as you to this country. I'm doing my BSc. Very sorry about Dr Badhan.'

'Thank you, Pardeep. Great to meet you. Keep in touch.'

Pardeep returned to his friends. Kalu and his friends left the pub not long after.

Out on the street he looked up. He could see no stars. Perhaps the dark Guinness had cast its shadow on his eyes. Despite the darkness within it, a canopy of a million bright stars would shine over Banjhan on most nights. When he did see them, the stars of Bedford were dull, although, unlike Banjhan, they had much less darkness to hide. But it did exist in Bedford. It had devoured Simran. Without the darkness' pursuit of him and his marriage, he wouldn't be heading to the courthouse on Monday. He didn't believe in fate. Perhaps he should, he thought. Despite not wanting to live by caste, fate had forced him to confront it.

He was at the rear door of his home. He found the keys in the inside pocket of the overcoat after fumbling around for a bit. With his fingers, he felt the keyhole. Resting his left index finger by it he pushed in the key.

'Son, you're late, everything okay?' Udho said, watching TV.

'Yes, Bhapa,' said Kalu, walking to the kitchen where Banti always had his dinner waiting for him. Udho helped heat it.

'Bhapa, you were saying about the money exchange business. You should think about it a little more. More money will help. The problem is its being illegal in India,' said Kalu taking the first bite of roti with chicken curry.

'But son, we won't hurt anybody. The hardworking immigrant will get more rupees per pound for his family in India and we'll make a little bit for every transaction. It won't be much but it'll be enough.'

Kalu nodded and fell silent as he ate. He wasn't comfortable talking about this business.

'By the way, we received a letter this morning,' he told

Udho after dinner. 'Hazara chacha's not well, I forgot to tell you. He wants to see you once before he passes. He's very old.'

'I want to see him too, Kahla. If I go I can also set up the delivery system for the exchange if we decide to do it.'

'Okay, Bhapa, I'm going to bed. I guess you want to watch TV.'

'Yes. It's my connection with the outside world,' said Udho, as Kalu went up the stairs.

27

On Saturday, Angad insisted Kalu take him for his weekly walk. After Simran's passing, Angad demanded more of his time. Weekend walks had become the rule.

'Papa, Dadi says India killed Mum?' Angad asked, as they stepped out of the house.

'Son, countries don't kill, people do.'

'So who killed Mum?'

'I don't know, son. I'll tell you when I find out.'

Kalu didn't want to tell him his Nana was one of the murderers. Nor did he want to burden the child with the weight of caste.

'Papa, older people know everything. How come you don't know who killed Mummy?'

'I don't know. Perhaps your Papa isn't old enough.'

The walks didn't always help resolve difficult questions, he thought as they arrived back at home. The phone rang. It was Raghbir. Gurbat and he had been talking to each other. They would be at the court house on Monday.

For the rest of the weekend, Kalu tried losing himself in preparation for his classes. He failed, and turned to the

Sunday Times. But nothing gripped him enough to distract him from thoughts of Simran. He gave up escaping. For hours he sat sipping chai and meditating on caste, death, the past and Faulkner's words, 'the past is never dead'. That 'past' rhymed with 'caste' had occurred to him before. For him, caste hadn't died. He had the urge to rent a large hoarding in Bedford near the Great Ouse Bridge and write on it: 'Caste is never dead.' Like past and death, it was a constant in his world, the world of the untouchables.

Kalu awoke Monday morning, calm, without rancour, ready to drive to the court house. On the way they could drop Angad at school, said Udho.

'Bhapa, Angad is going with us to the court. He keeps asking me who killed his mother. Hopefully, this will begin to answer his questions. For too long we've shielded him from the truth and it's not helping.'

'Up to you son, but I wouldn't do it just yet,' said Udho.

Fewer Indians than last time stood outside the courthouse. They were bunched in three groups: Amrit's supporters, opponents and a breakaway group of the carpenter caste, Tarkhans.

Amrit had a group of diehard supporters. The other group of Jats believed he had brought disrepute to the community. The third, of the Tarkhans, was tired of the Jats lording it over them and wanted to have nothing to do with the infamy wrought by Amrit. They were building a separate temple just like the Chuhras who split from the Chamars of Bromham Gurdwara to build their own. Raghbir and Gurbat understood the local caste dynamics, and wanted to associate with neither; they stood to the side, away from the three groups.

A few minutes before the court was to be in session, Sureet, dressed in a white sari with light green flowers on its border, walked into the open space in front of the courthouse. For the first time ever, her eyes were not darting around. She seemed serene.

'Hey son, your Nani,' Kalu said to Angad, pointing her out.

Angad didn't react. He hadn't seen her for a long time. She stopped when she spotted Angad. Kalu walked him over.

'Mum, Angad. Hey, give Nani a hug.'

Angad moved forward and clung to Sureet's sari. She crouched and embraced the child, kissed his head and held him close for quite a while, her long, slim fingers feeling his cheeks. Kalu smiled at her when she stood up, letting go of Angad. But she wiped her eyes with a tissue and walked away.

'Why did you do that, Kahla?' asked Udho.

'Bhapa, she didn't kill Simran. And even if she did, he has a right to know who his other grandparents are,' Kalu replied emphatically.

Everyone walked into the courtroom. By the time Kalu and others got in, only the back row seats were available. The judge took his seat behind the bench. The bailiffs then brought in Harjit Singh Athwal and Rajinder Singh Sajjan.

Over six feet tall, clean shaven with oily hair on their heads and a muscular build, they looked as if they were siblings, the terror twins—all brawn. If they had any brains, they were twisted and enmeshed in the centuries-long sinews of caste in which they were imprisoned. The clerk read the charges of murdering Simran against them. Both pled not guilty. The bailiffs took them away in handcuffs. Amrit's name was then read out. The bailiffs now brought him in handcuffs. The charges were read and the judge asked him how he pled.

'Guilty,' he said, looking at the wooden bar of the dock.

James, the prosecutor, read the statement of facts agreed between him and Jenkins. James and Jenkins both made submissions regarding the appropriate sentence for the accused. Noting the abhorrent nature of the crime, the involvement of caste and the sheer brutality of what was done to Simran, the judge sentenced Amrit to ten years in jail.

Outside the courthouse, Kalu waited with Angad. Sureet walked over to them this time. Bending to kiss Angad's head and patting his back, she said, 'Thank you, Kahla beta. Thank you for forgiving me for not being there for Simran. Angad is all I've left,' and went away, once again wiping her tears.

Kalu wished he could wave a wand, wipe away the past and the pain with it.

28

Though not much time had passed since Simran's murder, Kalu had concluded there could be absolutely no closure for a life taken by human depravity. If closure was acceptance of the fact of death, he didn't need sermons on it. He had confronted the suitcase full of flesh, blood and bones. Nothing could surpass that as evidence of death, Simran's end and the closure of his life's chapter with her. All else was sequel.

Banti, who missed the headstrong Simran, pined for a daughter-in-law.

'Son, I'm alone now. Your father has his money exchange. The home feels empty,' she repeated daily, like a mantra for her life after Simran.

Udho was anxious to be of use in the household, to

help raise Angad. Through postal correspondence, it took him a few months to arrive at the basic arrangements in India. Kirti owned his taxi. He would become the person to receive and deliver money upon instructions from Udho. For security, Kirti would carry Master Hazara's gun. To formalize the arrangements in India, Kalu drove Udho to London to put him on the plane at Heathrow Airport. It brought back old memories, some good, like the smell of coffee and chocolate at Paris and the train to Bedford, but also others more dreadful.

Angad was old and big enough to walk to school with the neighbours' children. The school, playing on the street and St John's station with his friends, books and TV kept him occupied. Kalu had reconnected with Sureet. She was a doting grandmother. Every couple of weeks, Angad spent the Saturday or Sunday with her. He asked questions about his mother, about Nana, and demanded answers. Sureet was frank about her powerlessness and cowardice in failing to protect her daughter.

After Simran's funeral, Kalu rarely used the car for local errands. He walked or biked to most places in and around Bedford. The only luxury he allowed himself was the weekly Friday evening visits to the King's Arms.

One Friday evening, he had walked over to King's Arms alone and early. His regular Guinness-drinking companions, Janice Charlesworth and Carrington, were missing. The owner nodded, smiled and pointed towards his favourite corner as he entered. After the first sip, he persuaded another patron to play darts with him. They had been playing for an hour. Losing and about to throw a dart, Kalu was interrupted. He turned to look. It was Pardeep Kumar.

'Dr Badhan, sir, I need help.'

He took the teary-eyed young man to the corner table, ordered him a beer and said, 'Drop the sir and tell me what it is you need.'

'Sir, a young woman and me, we love each other. We plan to marry once I finish my BSc.'

'And what is the problem, Pardeep?'

'Sir, I'm ashamed to talk about our castes. I'm a Brahmin and she is a Chuhri.'

'And her family thinks you, a Brahmin, won't be doing them any honours marrying her?'

'Not only that, sir, my own parents are quite opposed to the match,' he said. 'And then a few days ago...' he continued, his body almost trembling.

'What?'

'Her brothers beat me up as I was walking to the college and then reported to police that I beat one of them.'

'Ah, quite the racket we've got going. Along with the caste shit, we seem to have imported this crazy practice too. Pretty soon the system is going to stop believing us altogether,' he said, paused for a moment and then continued, 'Sorry about the rant... If I know them I'll speak to them. I could approach them even if I don't know them, I suppose.'

Kalu had followed from afar the near deification of the untouchable icon Ambedkar in India, the rebellion and a welcome pride among the lower castes. But it had also turned some of them inward. Such a turn often made them reject any association with those born to the upper castes. Some in the lower castes deemed him a 'traitor' for embracing Simran and not hating Sureet or Amrit, even after the murder, while many in the upper castes considered him uppity. Although the publicity surrounding Simran's murder had raised his profile, people's attitude towards him was not always empathetic. It could be one of ridicule depending on where one stood on the question of caste.

Such was the state of caste in Bedford when Kalu walked over the Great Ouse Bridge to Ranga Ram's home. He had immigrated to England from Punjab several years after Kalu. Some years later, his wife and children joined him, among them Pardeep's love, Neetie, the only daughter, who was at college doing her BA in English. Neetie, Neetu Kumari, was a strong-willed twenty-one-year-old, not easily dissuaded from her chosen course, even by the threats, rebuke and ridicule she faced from the family.

Ranga's home was a few minutes past the Bromham Gurdwara. Had Kalu kept walking another couple of minutes he would have arrived at the Valmiki Gurdwara built by the Chuhra breakaways from Bromham's Ravidasia.

A short-haired brown man with a wrinkling face and grey stubble opened the door.

'I would like to see Ranga Ram,' said Kalu.

'I know you, the teacher Kahla, Udho Chamar's only child!' said the man, before shutting the door and taking Kalu to the front room.

'Please sit down. I'm Ranga. Will you take tea or beer? It's almost evening.'

'Oh nothing, really. I had tea before leaving home.'

'A beer then! Udho's son must have something at my home. Your father, he's a good man...single-handedly built the Bromham Gurdwara. And then us Chuhray broke away and built the Valmiki Gurdwara. The lower castes, the Dalits, mustn't fight each other. Tough enough fighting the upper caste bastards,' said Ranga as he went to get the beer.

Kalu noticed Ranga's use of the word Dalit. Clearly, he was up on the new terminology associated with the struggle of the lower castes for equality.

Ranga returned with two bottles of beer and a bottle opener. Sitting on sofas perpendicular to each other, both took a sip.

'I've come to speak to you about Neetie and a boy I know. His name is Pardeep.'

'That *kutti da putt Bahman*. It will come to no good. You know first hand what happens!'

'You wouldn't do what Amrit did! You must love Neetie.'

'Didn't your father-in-law love your wife? We all do what we have to. I won't be able to show my face to anyone. I'd be an outcaste. Dalits would stop associating with me or Neetie for fear of losing their kids to non-Dalits.'

Kalu took another sip from the bottle. It stuck in his throat like a lump of coal. He patted his chest with his left hand to relieve the suffocating feeling in his throat; he placed the bottle on the coffee table and took a deep breath.

'I too have his portrait,' he said gesturing towards the framed picture of Ambedkar, 'just like the one on the mantle. Quite a rational man, Dr Ambedkar. His second wife was a Brahmin.'

'The first was a Dalit though. And he didn't live in Bedford, work in a foundry and face taunts at a Valmiki temple,' said Ranga, his finger pointing at the portrait.

Kalu was soon back out on the street, retracing his steps home. He had left Ranga's house without meeting any other member of the family. Ranga probably didn't wish to pollute them with introductions to someone he must have thought of as an Uncle Tom himself. People like Ranga pursued the purity of the soul in temples and of caste in marriages, perpetrating a fraud upon both God and Ambedkar, Kalu reasoned.

The street lights shone on the wet pavement as Kalu walked back, umbrella overhead. His mind thought of home. But his feet took him to the King's Arms. He took off his coat, shook the water off and opened the brass-studded door. The creak of the door and some patrons' gazes welcomed him in. His favourite corner table had people at it. He walked to the table next to it and took the bench seat. His back rested against the wall as he waved to the bartender. The pint of Guinness arrived, its head still forming with bubbles rising to the top. He sipped it, watching the patrons laugh, talk and play darts. But then he spotted someone he thought he knew, and got up to walk over to her table, catching the bartender's eye to order another Guinness as he went.

'Hey Cathy, great to see you! Where had you disappeared to?'

'Oh Kahla, I just heard about Simran. I'm so sorry.'

'This beer is on me. Come join me unless you're with someone.'

'Thanks for the beer, all alone... Yes, I'd gone away to Glasgow with my boyfriend. Took me this long to discover he's a jerk.'

When he had last met Cathy, the tall, plump brunette, Simran's college confidante, they were together at King's Arms. The two of them had played darts as Simran watched before he was attacked by a roughneck. That seemed aeons ago. She was enrolled in teacher training but, madly in love with her boyfriend, had abandoned her studies and followed him around the country.

'I've come home. Half my life is wasted. So glad to bump into you though,' she said.

They talked and played darts. Cathy and Simran had been close. Simran had missed her. Meeting Cathy transported Kalu to his early days with Simran. The bout of nostalgia dispelled the disappointment Kalu had encountered with Ranga. He told her where he'd been earlier in the evening. As they spoke, he decided he was going to speak to Neetie. Cathy too thought he must.

'But before we part tonight, I want to say something to you. Janice told me you're reluctant to run for parliament. You've got to run, Kahla. We need politicians like you. I'm all in with Janice and others to help.'

She got up, gave Kalu a kiss on the cheek and left saying, 'Got to work in the morning. The life of the labourer!'

It took a little effort on Pardeep's part to persuade Neetie to see Kalu. They met in the college cafeteria, a safe place.

'Professor Badhan, I don't know how long I can last. I'm not allowed out of the home except to come to college. My brothers escort me here and back at the end of classes. The eldest has threatened to kill me if I ever see Pardeep again. I'm afraid they'll kill or hurt Pardeep too.'

'I won't tell you what to do but know that whatever decision you make, I'll be happy to help. You do know the obstacles you'd face marrying out of caste and without your parents' consent?'

'I've had a taste of it already. But I'm ready to marry Pardeep. I was raised here. I don't know caste. I don't give a damn about that shit, nor does Pardeep.'

Kalu shook her hand and patted her on the back. It was time for class. Pardeep, who'd been waiting outside the cafeteria, smiled at Kalu as he passed him by. He nodded and walked away.

Angad was eating peanut butter on toast with milk one afternoon when Kalu entered.

'Papa, a letter from Baba,' he said pointing to the telephone table. 'Papa, what's a Chamar?'

The unopened letter in hand, Kalu asked, 'Why do you ask?'

'During recess, I was playing in the gym and Gurinder pushed me, saying, "Get lost you Chamar."'

'Gurinder is a Jat boy from the neighbourhood,' said Banti, who had overheard the words Gurinder and Chamar.

Kalu sat down and explained as best he could to Angad India's caste and its British incarnations. Banjhan had transplanted itself in Bedford. The trek to Delhi and flight to London had all been an illusion. Kalu was exhausted. He craved caffeine.

'Bibi, a chai,' he said and collapsed on the sofa.

From the aerogramme the postmark 'Banjhan' stared at him. Banjhan was in pursuit of him. He tore the letter open. Udho had officially delegated the responsibility of managing the trust to the village panchayat—the trust that Master Hazara had threatened to set up and finally did, making Udho and Kalu its trustees. The final authority would of course vest in them. Udho had set up the hawala arrangements. And for the safety and security of the monies, Hazara, before his passing, had hooked Kirti up with the police.

Sipping the chai, letter atop his chest, Kalu dozed off on the sofa only to be awakened minutes later by the phone. Angad was doing homework at the eating table. The lights were on. Rubbing his eyes open, Kalu lifted the receiver and said, 'Hello...'

From the other end came a muffled hello.

'Speak louder,' said Kalu.

It was Udho. Kalu got the words police, Delhi and flight, but he couldn't get the gist of what Udho wanted to communicate.

'Are you okay, Bhapa?' said Kalu at the top of his voice.

'What is happening with your Bhapa?' yelled Banti, cooking in the kitchen.

'Okay...the police...see you soon,' Kalu heard Udho say.

'Send me a telegram... The bloody phone lines don't work,' said Kalu, the line going dead before he mentioned telegram.

'Bibi, Bhapa was speaking about the police. Hope everything is fine with him.'

'The food is ready,' said Banti, before asking what was wrong.

'Bibi, feed Angad. I'll eat a little later.'

He dialled the telegram office and arranged a telegram to India.

In the morning, Kalu and Angad walked out of the house together.

'Son, just wait. I'll be back in a minute,' said Kalu, running back in.

He reappeared wearing an overcoat.

'Papa, it's not cold and you are wearing an overcoat!'

'It's chilly and I want to look like I'm somebody when I meet your headmaster.'

'Papa, I don't want you to meet the headmaster. Kids will call me cry baby... I miss Baba. He always listens to me.'

In the blue school uniform jacket, shorn hair, the light-brown-skinned Angad with large black eyes kept his gaze focused on the pavement as he walked behind Kalu.

'Come on, walk a little faster. I miss Baba, too, but this caste nonsense...! Had enough of it already!' Kalu pulled him by the arm.

Soon, they stood at the school secretary's desk. Angad looked away.

'Dr Badhan, unfortunately the principal and the vice principal are both away today. Would you like to come back tomorrow morning?' said the secretary.

Angad hopped away without once looking back.

29

Kalu was asleep when he heard the telephone ring. Believing his ears were playing tricks on him or he was dreaming, he ignored it. But the phone continued to ring. He got up with a start when he realized it wasn't a dream, jumped out of bed and ran down the stairs.

'Hello.'

'Hello, Kalu, it's Kirti. Got your telegram. Udho should be at the airport on the BOAC flight tomorrow morning at 9:00...24 hours from now.'

'Yes, Kirti, but what happened? Bhapa sounded worried!'

'He will tell you.'

The phone line went dead. It was five in the morning. It was Saturday and therefore no college, and for once, no public or political commitments either. He had been planning to speak to Sergeant Abbott today about what, if anything, could be done to diffuse the tension in the Ranga household and between it and Pardeep and his family.

He made chai. With a mug full of it, he sat cross-legged on the sofa.

'Become a yogi, son?' Banti asked.

It was 7:00 am. On the sofa, still in shorts, his hair falling back over his head, beard flowing, not pressed and held in place as it normally was by the hair-fixer Kalu used, he did look like any of the countless god-men India had continued to produce. But he just sat there, ignoring Banti's jibe, surveying their life in England.

'Bibi, make me another chai. Your tea is godly.'

Kalu was one of the most integrated Indian immigrants in Britain. There weren't too many second-generation Indians yet in Britain. The first generationals, like Kalu, far outnumbered them. For him, it had taken thousands of hours of listening to BBC radio, reading and practising pronunciation to master English. The journey from Indian music and singers like Mukesh and Mohammed Rafi to The Beatles was longer and harder. But Kalu had persevered.

'I want to know and feel what makes an average Briton tick,' he had once said to Christine, his first girlfriend.

In Bedford, the past was threatening not only his future but also Angad's. It frightened him. The ghettos scared him. He had fled the ghetto of the Chamarli. But the chasm that separated Chamarli and Banjhan reproduced itself in the separate gurdwaras for different castes, the respective populations living close by, isolated from British society save the economic nexus. While they, the Badhans, lived in close proximity to many other Indian families, Kalu's work and activism ensured his immersion in the world beyond. The two opposing forces, centripetal everything Indian and centrifugal his college and politics, were in a constant tug of war. He and Pandit Karam Chand would have long debates about the desire to limit oneself to the familiar and the need to reach out and connect with strangers amid whom they had chosen to live. A few days ago, Karam had died of old age. Kalu grieved the loss of a Briton-Indian and pondered his own future.

Coming down the stairs and interrupting Kalu's meditation, Angad yelled, 'Papa, I need new shoes for gym, the old pair's soles have holes in them.'

Back to earth, Kalu said, 'Yes, son, I've got to do some preparation for college. In the afternoon we'll buy you sneakers and get some books from the library.'

'Baba took me to the library every Saturday. You've no time for me.'

'Well, Angad, he's coming back. I've got to leave early in the morning to pick him up. You want to come along?'

Angad nodded before running up the stairs to figure out which clothes he would wear to receive Udho at the airport. Udho always encouraged Angad to dress his best. His habit of dressing for erasure of caste worked to confuse people about class too, Udho had discovered.

After breakfast, Kalu perused the photocopied papers spread out on the table to prepare for his lecture on race, class and caste. His reading excursions took him far afield. This day before him lay excerpts from the works of Weber, Marx, Durkheim, Du Bois and Darwin. He had been reading for an hour and making notes when the phone rang. The loud ringtone sounded menacing in the quiet home.

'Hey Angad, you've turned the bloody volume up on this blessed thing?'

'Papa, I didn't touch it. It must be your ears. Age has its surprises,' said Angad, mature beyond his age, irritated at being taken to task for something he didn't do.

It was Raghbir. He had come across Neetie in Marks & Spencer where he had gone looking for a shirt. She had been crying. He had brought her home.

'Raghbir, bring her along. I'll meet you at the police station. Don't walk. Use your car.'

At the police station they met with the duty officer. He wanted to arrest Ranga, who Neetie said had assaulted her. Kalu persuaded him that charging Ranga would entail producing Neetie to testify in Bedford.

'Neetie, you should speak to Pardeep. You are adults. If you want to elope for safety, the police should help make it happen,' said Kalu.

It took the good part of the day for the police to arrange for Neetie and Pardeep to go away—to an unspecified large city. Kalu and Raghbir kept them company, but neither wished to know the details, in case Ranga ever came knocking.

The papers on the table stared at him when he returned. Atop them sat a note:

'Papa, again no sneakers and no library books. Wake me up to go to the airport. Love U, Papa.'

Remembering the sneakers from which his big toes protruded when he had spotted the Westfalia camper, he collapsed into the chair, his forehead on Angad's note on the table. Had Simran been alive, Angad would have had new shoes long ago, he told himself. But he didn't wish to wallow in self-pity. So he got up and made chai, filled a mug and tried to lose himself in the papers. Angad's note kept tugging at him though, like Angad would himself when he was awake. He walked about the ground floor for a while before going up the stairs to sneak a glance at the sound-asleep Angad.

'Puttar, wake up, time to drive to London,' he said, noticing the time on the bedside clock. He shook Angad awake.

Father and son, in three-piece suits, sat down to eat omelette with toast.

'Want more egg or toast, Angad beta?' asked Banti.

He shook his head.

'Give me more, Bibi,' said Kalu.

Soon Kalu was revving the car. He turned the headlights on and they were off to London.

The car had left the environs of Bedford behind when Angad asked, 'Papa, which Indian airport did you fly from in 1952?'

The question summoned up memories of the escape, vivid as ever. He had often looked back on those frantic couple of days, but it was the first time Angad heard of them: from Banjhan after Kalu had cracked the rapist Karam's skull with a lathi; later the same day from Hoshiarpur where he smashed the windshield and the rear window of the camper with the same lathi; the steel-tipped lathi consigned to the waters of the Satlej; the paranoia at Delhi Airport where any man in khaki felt like a potential threat.

'Papa, you could write a novel and call it "The Great Escape of 1952", like the *Great Train Robbery*,' Angad remarked to Kalu.

They had reached the outskirts of London. Kalu

switched off the headlights and said, 'Son, we're in London. You don't come here too often. Wake up. Look at the place.'

Soon, Angad was looking in all directions, taking in the sights, noises and traffic until they found a place to park near the terminal. A large crowd of people waited at the arrivals exit. Kalu stayed behind as Angad snuck over to the front of the crowd, looked back at Kalu and smiled. After that one look back, Angad's eyes remained fixed on the steady stream of strangers until he spotted Udho carrying his suitcase.

'Baba, here! Papa is behind me!' he jumped and said, breathlessly waving at Udho.

After hugs all around, Kalu took the suitcase. Soon they were riding back to Bedford, Angad shouting questions about India and Udho's trip.

'Baba, I wanted to go with you. Papa didn't let me go, saying not good to miss school. I'd have written a daily journal. It would have been fun.'

'Next time, Angad,' said Udho.

'Bhapa, everything okay in Banjhan?'

'Chacha Hazara was a big loss. I've asked the village panchayat to run the trust. I told them if they don't do it properly, we'd take the power back,' he said.

'But Bhapa, you'd called. You sounded worried... something about the police.'

'I set up everything for the hawala. That was fine. Karam's family bribed the police to revive his case. I was on the way to Delhi, when I called you. I thought they would get me. But our Kirti has become quite a big man. He got someone to call the dogs off... Anything new in Bedford?'

'Well, my college and other friends are pushing me for another run for Bedford's parliamentary seat. I don't know, with Angad and everything else. I need to spend more time at home.'

'Son, you should do it. Angad is big now. It would be

a great experience for him too. And you will leave him a good legacy.'

'Anyways...you know Ranga, right? Ranga Ram?' he asked, changing the subject.

'Of course.'

'I helped his daughter Neetie get away from Bedford. You know Pardeep? The BSc student? They wanted to marry. I was worried Ranga might do to her what Amrit did to Sim.'

'You shouldn't go around making enemies, son,' Udho said after a moment's silence, his voice barely hiding his dread. 'We already have enough.'

'All other enemies are nothing compared to caste enemies. They'll never go away.'

Kalu looked back. Angad was asleep. Udho too began to doze off. The police pursuit, the hassles of Banjhan and the sleepless hours of the long plane ride soon took their toll.

Within a few hours, the car was on the outskirts of Bedford. From the unfamiliarity of the motorway, he was about to enter the small but known world of their adopted home.

He wished to connect the small world of his home and college to the larger world of London and Britain. Every time he took a step towards that larger world, the smaller cast its shadow and pulled him back into its fold. At each step, parochialisms of different hues threatened to devour him. The turban and beard made him a Sikh in appearance. But they were little help negotiating the caste barrier that hemmed him in. Even the Labour Party seemed to have succumbed to an indifference to grotesque old-world schisms.

But Udho's hope that his son would leave behind a proud legacy for his grandchild had jolted him out of the sense of security he felt in his life of relative obscurity. The car had entered Bedford. It was on London Road. For a moment, he wondered how it might feel if he were elected and on the road to parliament in London. Home wasn't far, only a little further.

30

Several years passed by. A new election cycle was round the corner. It was a Monday. Kalu's first period was free. He walked over to Dean Symes's office. Janice Charlesworth was leaving the office as he entered it. They exchanged smiles. Janice and Robert were friends but he wasn't her dean. Kalu wondered about the early morning visit.

'Oh come, my friend Janice and I, we're plotting, you might say conspiring, to disrupt your life.'

'Born to weather disruptions...one such brings me here this morning.'

Kalu had earlier met the principal of Angad's secondary school, William Duncan. Duncan had received several other complaints besides his about the caste chatter among the students. It had been a long time since Angad had asked Kalu what a Chamar was after a classmate had insulted him for being one. The caste nonsense was as vehement and more pervasive in his school, because now there were more Indians in it.

'... But look, my friend, we've a hard time dealing with issues of poverty, class and racism. Caste we don't even understand.' Duncan had suggested Kalu come to discuss the issue at the Parent Teacher Advisory Committee meeting to which all parents had been invited. Kalu had come to advise Symes of his need to cancel the class for the evening.

'Kahla, I would've thought leaving the country would

leave caste behind! Anyway, I should tell you,' he continued, 'Janice and I were talking about the next general election. You must run. Come to think of it, it'd be a severe blow against caste and racism in Britain. We've formed a small group that includes Janice, Cathy, Carrington, some Labour activists and members of our faculty association. It'll expand as we go along. But for now, go deal with caste. We can cancel the evening class. Let's talk about the election some more, later.'

Kalu got back home late in the afternoon after a full day at college. Udho was busy with his hawala paraphernalia—a notebook and a pen which was permanently kept at one end of the formal dining table rarely used since Simran's murder. They had become used to eating at the table beside the kitchen in the large eating and sitting area. Angad, back from school, was doing his homework. He was an adolescent now, in the eighth standard.

'Papa, please don't go to the meeting tonight. Let Baba go. The whole school will know I complained. You'd tell the whole PTA meeting about it. Why can't we just let go of this caste thing?' said Angad, more conscious now of his reputation among his peers.

'Because it won't let go of Baba, Dadi, you and me—us. You tried, didn't you? It wasn't you who first raised it. Just as previously it was thrown at you, wasn't it? Just wishing won't kill it. You mustn't run away from difficult things, otherwise you'll be running your whole life.'

Angad ran upstairs. Kalu couldn't let his son face in Bedford what he had faced and fought in Banjhan. His right hand became a fist as his mind wandered to the punch he had thrown at the Brahmin boy in Banjhan who wouldn't allow him to sit with him on the only available seat in the class. He went upstairs to talk to Angad.

A few minutes later, he descended the stairs, wiping his own eyes and blowing his nose into a handkerchief.

'Papa, if you're going to go can I come with you?'

'No, son, the children aren't supposed to attend the meeting.'

He wouldn't have minded Angad going. It could have been great education in how the world worked but the school rules didn't allow it. Udho insisted on going with Kalu.

It was seven, time for the meeting to begin. But Kalu suggested they wait because some parents were still sauntering in.

'Hard to attend meetings in the evenings after working full days at the foundries and brickyards,' said Kalu.

The principal and the PTA executive nodded and waited for another few minutes before the meeting began. The secretary read the minutes of their previous meeting which were unanimously approved. The last item on the agenda read: Remarks by Dr Kahla Badhan and discussion. Soon it was called.

Kalu began by describing how his son learnt about the word caste from school and not at home, where he had lived with parents whose marriage was an anomaly in Bedford's Indian community for it was a union between two people of different castes. He explained the centuries of butchery visited upon the lower castes, them being considered beasts, not human beings. He drew a direct link between that and Simran's murder.

'As it is, in this country it's difficult to navigate racism, poverty and the stigma of class. Let's not add caste to the blight; another layer of oppression,' he concluded.

Duncan opened it up for discussion.

'Dr Badhan has raised a serious issue. I can vouch for the fact caste affects student life at school. Caste exists. Who would've thought it would be transplanted here?' someone said.

'My name is Dennis Brown. My son is at school here. I belong to the Ironworkers' Union and, by the way, I recognize Udho. I apprenticed at the foundry when he worked there. I'd heard the same shit about caste at the foundry then. Udho was kind. He ignored it. It's only got worse since. You can't ignore it. I say stop it. I know it's not the thing one should say but whosoever finds it impossible to stop has no business in this country. As the principal says, we've enough to do with poverty and racism without bloody caste.'

'Yes, yes,' said a few voices.

'You can't say that, we're British citizens,' yelled a brown man, without identifying himself.

'Oh yes, we can,' said a voice.

'My name is Helen Cunningham. My daughter goes here. As a citizen, you've rights but there are duties too. One of them is to not discriminate against others for reasons of colour, ethnic origin, nationality or caste—'

'Caste discrimination is up there with the worst,' shouted another and so did a few others, in support of the thrust of Dennis's, Helen's and Kalu's remarks.

'We've five minutes to go. I see no hands up nor hear any voices,' said Duncan. 'Perhaps...'

A man in a three-piece, black-striped suit with a matching tie stood up as he spoke.

'I am a trained engineer yet I work as a janitor, a job I wouldn't have touched in a thousand years in India. Britain robbed me of my professional dignity and my caste pride. It should at least do me the courtesy of the freedom to believe what I may about caste, mine and others', and treat them accordingly. I'm a Brahmin. My son goes to school here. He's a Brahmin and superior to the main speaker, the Chamar, and shall always remain so. Manmade laws can't change God's law of caste.'

A couple of boos disturbed the silence that followed. One was from Dennis.

'You see, that's why he needs to go back to where he came from. We're not perfect but he's deadly pollution; he thinks he can bring this caste shit and continue as if he never left India,' he said.

Duncan gestured the end of the meeting with his hands. The shock of the remarks by the 'engineer' had numbed him. Kalu was beyond numbing. He had lived it all his life.

'You see, son, again you have more enemies today than you had yesterday,' said Udho, as they walked out after thanking the committee, the principal, Helen and Dennis.

'I'll probably have more friends too than yesterday, Bhapa.'

Kalu opened the door and followed Udho in. Angad, doing homework at the eating table, jumped up from his chair, and asked, 'So what happened?'

'Beta, I didn't understand everything,' said Udho and looked towards Kalu.

'Angad, as I expected, there was a heated discussion. I won the room except this one man...'

'At school tomorrow I'll be picked on 'cause of what you did tonight. Sometimes I wish you knew less English, like Baba.'

'But son, without a fight I'm doomed to be derided as an untouchable. And what's more, you'll pay the price if I show my back to the fight.'

'But I'll definitely pay the price tomorrow at school.'

'Bibi, can you give your grandson some dinner? This feels like a Banjhan panchayat,' Kalu said, only half joking. 'I'm sure Bhapa is hungry too.'

'The meeting killed my appetite. I'll only have a little bit,' said Udho.

Banti, who was watching TV on silent for fear of distracting Angad from his homework, got up and served them food.

From the moment he put his head on the pillow until the alarm woke him up, Kalu slumbered through a night of fleeting dreams. He remembered only bits and pieces of them. Simran was there in one. She talked to him about how happy she was about Angad challenging him.

'I don't want him to grow up a timorous soul... And why won't you run for the damned parliamentary seat? You're the best Labour has!'

That woke him up. He jumped out of bed. Within an hour he was in his office at the college making calls to friends and supporters across the country, firming up support for his bid for the seat. Dean Symes called a large dinner meeting at his home. He had the dinner catered so he, his spouse and two adult children could participate in the deliberations without worrying about hospitality. It was official. A Committee to Support Badhan's Bid for Bedford headed by Dr Janice Charlesworth and Dean Symes was established. A press release to that effect was issued the next day. The battle lines were drawn and the bugle call reached all in Labour circles. The son of an untouchable skinner of dead cattle from Banjhan turned foundry-worker in Bedford was to be the standard bearer for the party that claimed to represent the working class of Britain.

31

The renewed bid for nomination took Kalu away from home more than before. Angad had come round to the idea of his father being around less and less. Udho and Banti were there, the human shock absorbers, to ensure Angad never lacked for affection and attention. The fact that they had always spoken Punjabi with him at home helped them communicate. As Udho's hawala business flourished, Angad helped him keep records. Whenever he got the chance, Kalu looked over the records Angad helped Udho keep, which always sat at a designated spot on the dining table. Udho would give Kirti instructions on the phone. They spoke to each other a couple of times a week. The money Udho earned, along with his pension, helped defray the costs of the household.

Late one evening, Kalu returned from a speaking engagement in Luton and slumped onto the sofa. Udho and Angad were updating the records.

'Bhapa, we're okay moneywise. The campaign committee pays for my travel expenses. Stop whenever you don't want to do it any more.'

'Son, it gives me something to do.'

'Let him carry on. It gets him out of the house. I get free time to see pictures on TV,' said Banti.

Listening to all this, Angad perked up and said, 'Papa, I like helping Baba with it. Let it be.'

Outnumbered and out argued, Kalu jumped up from the sofa and ran upstairs saying, 'Bhapa, Bibi, wake me up at five in case I sleep through the alarm.'

'Yes, puttar,' said Udho before Angad pulled his attention back to the notebook on the dining table.

Kalu did sleep through the alarm. Udho woke him up.

'Bhapa, I'm going to London. I will come back tomorrow.'

He got up and got to work immediately, reviewing the speech he was to deliver at the London School of Economics in the afternoon. Gulping down Banti's syrupy chai he left, dropping Angad at school on the way.

In the solitude of the drive to London, he went over what he had said to Udho about the hawala business. He didn't want his father to worry about finances in his old age. If they couldn't support the enlarged and renovated home, he was prepared to downsize. But he wanted his father to enjoy his years of retirement, bond with Angad and give company to Banti whose pain of separation from Udho for ten long years he still remembered as if it was yesterday. As well, he worried about hawala being illegal in India, and Kirti always requiring connections and police security to make deliveries. It was all too complicated. He cursed himself for not considering the political consequences of his father being involved in a questionable business, however risk-free it was in England. With Angad often assisting his Baba at the end of the dining table, the legal taint of the operation they were running concerned him even more. What message about ethics would it impart to his son?

There was no end to greed, he reasoned. Frugality must trump illegality. That he was on this long drive to London to speak on public and political ethics also played its part in helping him decide: Udho must stop the hawala.

After the speech, Kalu begged forgiveness of the London School of Economics professor he was supposed to spend the evening with and drove back. He went over his decision about Udho's business during the return drive. He worried about his father being upset over his insistence. But there seemed little room for changing his mind on the matter. He had no business addressing students on ethics with a hawala broker operating out of his home.

As he neared Bedford, the visibility on the road had diminished. The windshield became foggy on the inside. It was a drizzle outside, the finest drizzle he had ever experienced. He turned the wipers on but lowered the driver side window and thrust his right palm out to feel the particles of rain he couldn't see. The air felt moist but not wet. Yet it fell as rain on the windshield.

Reaching home, he parked the car on the street and entered through the front door. Angad walked to the entrance when he heard the noise.

Handing him his overcoat, Kalu asked, 'You up so late, no school tomorrow?'

Angad didn't answer as he hung the coat on the hooks of the mirrored console; Kalu walked to the papers spread atop the dining table.

'What's with the papers on the table?' asked Kalu before noticing Udho and Banti on the sofa watching the screen of the muted TV. Angad looked in the direction of his grandparents.

'Bhapa, why is everybody so quiet?' Then he noticed Banti's tears. 'Bibi, you never cry. What happened?'

No one said anything.

'Angad, son, at least you tell me if you know. What the hell happened?'

Angad narrated the story, as told by Udho to Banti, tearing up as he spoke.

In the afternoon, in his grey three-piece suit, Udho had gone to see Sohan Singh Gill. Gill had questions about the money he had sent through Udho to his relatives in India. When Udho got to the Gill home, five other people were present, one of them Daler Singh, the clean-shaven student and fan of Kalu and, like him, an immigrant. They had tea and samosas. Sohan asked whether Udho had checked with Kirti about the remittance. Udho had. The answer still was that Kirti had delivered Gill's money to his relatives. Gill's relatives had continued to insist the monies were never delivered to them. In the middle of the discussion, as everyone sat sipping tea and downing samosas, Sohan, with his protruding beer belly, moustache perched atop curled-up, fat lips, stood up.

'You Chamar, ugly bastard, you dare contradict my relatives. You dare say they're lying?' he shouted.

In a flash he walked over and slapped Udho before others could stop him.

'Stop acting like an animal, idiot,' Udho shouted and raised his fist. He pulled his hand back as others subdued the frothing Sohan, still shouting profanities. Udho left immediately and walked home.

Kalu's jaws clenched and heart raced. He wished he had Hazara's gun, the one that Udho had fired in Banjhan before Kalu had, with the steel-tipped lathi, floored Karam shouting vulgar insults about Banti. Udho sat on the sofa looking down. Banti watched him and wiped her tears. There were none in Angad's eyes any more, as if the telling had exorcised the hurt. For a few moments Kalu put his hands over his eyes, before walking over to the sofa. Sitting down next to Udho, he hugged him. Angad cuddled next to Banti who took him in her embrace. The muted TV played on.

For several minutes, their world stood silent. Then Kalu walked over to the dining table, gathered the papers and put them in an envelope.

'Bhapa, no more hawala. Better hungry than humiliated by the likes of Gill.'

It was quiet again. Kalu asked whether Daler had helped Udho.

'No, son. I think he was dumbstruck. Others intervened but he froze in his place. He's a young boy...probably got frightened.'

'Yup, recent immigrant, confused about all the caste shit in twentieth-century Bedford,' said Kalu. Grabbing at his stomach he said, 'I haven't eaten anything. I suspect you haven't either.'

No one said anything.

'Not eating isn't going to help. Bibi, I'll help you serve.'

Soon they were eating a late supper.

At 9:00 am the next day Kalu's car stopped in the parking lot of the police station.

'Okay, Bhapa, let's go,' said Kalu to Udho, who was refusing to get out.

'Complaining to the police won't do anything, Kalu. We'll just make more enemies.'

'Better off with the likes of Sohan as enemies,' said Kalu, holding open the passenger door.

Promoted sergeant, Sweeny greeted them, saying, 'Doctor, your friend Abbott has retired. You're stuck with yours truly.'

'Good to see you, though having to see you is always bad news.'

Sweeny wrote the complaint down and told them an investigation would be carried out.

'All right, then. We shall wait for your report of the completed investigation,' said Kalu before Udho and he took the last sips of coffee Sweeny had made for them and left.

And just like that, Udho closed the business down. No more papers at the dining table. They would have to tell Kirti about it, but that was the least of Kalu's concerns at the moment.

He spoke to Sweeny a few days later for an update on the investigation into Udho's complaint. It was ongoing, still incomplete, Sweeny informed him. But the next morning his phone rang again. No one present admitted the assault ever happened.

'You mean even Daler is unwilling to speak the truth. Jesus, what the heck is this world coming to?' Kalu said to Sweeny.

'Sorry, Doctor Badhan, there's nothing we can do.'

'I'm sorry, Sergeant. Thank you for your efforts,' was all Kalu said. But inside he wished he was a big shot in India and the incident had happened there. He would have loved to make Sohan confess. For all his rage, however, he would never want to import the bloody injustice he was familiar with back home.

He hung up, pushed against the sofa and spread his arms wing-like, as if trying to break free of something.

Done with his classes the next day at college, he went to the cafeteria, ordered a coffee and sat down in a corner. He wanted to write a piece on caste in a national daily in Britain and wanted to include in it the issue of honour killing, the kind Amrit had done to restore his honour in the eyes of the Goldington temple. Had Amrit resisted the taunts of the community about the 'dishonour' wrought by Simran, she would have been alive. Kalu had made extensive notes on the quadruple whammy of race, class, caste and honour killing. He was organizing his notes as Daler walked in.

'Dr Badhan, sir, may I speak to you?'

'Daler, please sit.'

'Sir, in the class you seemed a bit distant today. Perhaps you're cross with me. I owe you an apology and an explanation about your father and the assault.'

Kalu nodded.

'Sir, I'm new here in England, less than a year. I didn't see the assault coming. It was over in a flash. I should've said something, like demand an apology from Gill to your dad. But in the heat of the moment it didn't occur to me. My father was there. I've been told sons don't speak when fathers are present.'

'But despite being there, your father was absent. He could've insisted Gill apologize. He didn't. At least you could have told police the truth. But you lied.'

'Sir, my father told me he'd kill me if I cooperated with

the police because he'd be shunned by the Jats. I'm sorry, sir...please forgive me.'

Kalu sat in the corner for a long time after Daler left, thinking, writing and rewriting his piece. He felt his life and Angad's fate depended upon it.

32

The campaign for the Labour Party's nomination for the Bedford seat was in full swing. Kalu criss-crossed the constituency, meeting Labour members, activists and supporters. He hopped all over the country for the many speaking engagements that came his way. Dean Symes arranged it with the department so Kalu was free to travel, taking either Mondays or Fridays off to ensure ease of travel.

The same caste chatter and resistance as before began to emerge among the Indian-influenced Labour politicos responsible for deciding on the nominees. Dean Symes and the campaign committee, which now included Raghbir and Gurbat, who were all aware of caste, its impact in the moment and implications for the future of Britain, smothered Labour activists with telephone calls, letters and personal visits. The committee reported that the response to the campaign was better than the last time. Kalu saw the proof first hand when he attended a meeting at Cathy's place in Bedford. She had invited her neighbours to tea to meet Kalu.

'Last time I wasn't of a mind to support you. Call me racist but I didn't think a turbaned brown immigrant could win for Labour, not just in Bedford, but anywhere in the country. But you've changed me. You'd be a great candidate,' said the wrinkled old right-wing Labourite Agnes who lived next door.

Kalu arranged his family and financial affairs to protect the privacy of the three people at home. He wanted to ensure a degree of insulation for Angad in particular from the inevitable stream of invective directed at his father during the nomination—and if successful for it, the election campaign. He kept the family away from politics but couldn't shield himself from public scrutiny. Electioneering was nothing if not exposure. In the tumult of speeches, meetings, telephone calls and travel, his opponents spun fiction about Simran's death. Some implied he must have had a hand in the murder.

'The obstacles in an inter-caste couple's way soon tire them. The folly of the union dawns upon the couple and one or the other kills to end the nightmare,' went one argument.

In the midst of all this rumour mongering, Dean Symes called Kalu over to his office one day and pushed a folder in front of him. Kalu looked at the contents and said, 'Robert... F...ing bullshit,' pushing the folder back.

'Kahla, I know. But why?'

'Beats me, is all I can say. Gopal never spoke to me about any of this, before or after writing this shit.'

A balding Brahmin, the new head of the history department, Gopal Vashisht, PhD from the London School of Economics, had written a review of Kalu's teaching, as department heads were periodically required to and submit to the dean to ensure reasonable teaching standards and outcomes.

'Kalu, the faculty and the students think you're God. How in hell did he come up with this shit?'

'You speak to him about it.'

'I want you present when I speak to him.'

The folder in hand, Kalu went to the cafeteria, bought coffee, plunked the mug on the table, sank into the chair, and read and reread Vashisht's review. By the time he took the first sip from the mug, the coffee was cold. He gulped it down and bought a fresh one. Steam rising from the beverage, he sipped it, stared at the folder and pondered what could have earned him such criticism. The Vashishts were upper-caste Brahmins, deriving their name from the priest Vashishtha in the epic *Ramayana*. Lord Rama was one of his disciples. Gopal had not seen or heard Kalu teach. The latest student reviews had given him top scores. He battled with the thought that caste, his or Gopal's, had something to do with the review.

'Oh Professor Badhan, I was looking for you in your office,' said Daler, almost running to the table, distracting Kalu from his thoughts. 'I knew you had no class this hour and if you were at college, you'd be in the cafeteria.' Seeing the empty mug he said, 'How about another coffee?'

Kalu nodded. He had eventually come round to accepting the young man's apology and forgiven him for not helping prosecute Sohan Gill.

'Professorji, my dad...I've been talking to him. The other day he admitted to me we should've told police the truth. He sends his apology to you. But, er, right now I need your help with something else. I see you have this folder in front of you. If you're busy I can come some other time.'

'Thank your dad for the apology, it means a lot to me. What do you need?'

'All right, so...dad's friend, Pritam Singh Grewal has a daughter. A dropout from Mander. She works in a biscuit factory. Pritam has proposed her marriage with me. And dad likes it. Like me, she was eighteen when she came to England.'

'Wait a minute. Is her name Sarabjit Grewal?'

'Yes, Professorji. You know her?'

'Yes, she was in one of my classes. Between you and I, quite dumb!'

'But dad insists I must marry her. She knows our culture and language. It'd be easy on him and my mother, dad says. I told him I want to finish my doctorate and be like you. I'm not ready to marry yet and certainly not her. That's why I need help...'

'And what do you want me to do?'

'Talk to my dad.'

'You think he would listen to a Chamar?'

'No, Professorji. I told him I wanted to be like you. He said he'd listen to what you had to say about the proposal.'

'Daler, I'm not sure he'd listen, but I'm happy to help.'

Before going home, Kalu went to the office to review his schedule. Angad's principal Duncan wanted to meet with him. Tomorrow afternoon he could go there from college, see him and head home early to spend time with Angad. Meetings took up most of his evenings. The guilt of neglecting his son weighed on him.

He was partway home when he turned back to the college. He had left the review at the office. He wanted to read it again and write a response to place on the record in the administrations' files. Holding the raincoat and review he reached home. The muted TV was on. Angad was missing from his place at the eating table where he did his homework. Perhaps he had finished early and gone to bed.

'Bibi, so quiet around here. Where are Bhapa and Angad?'

'Angad is upset and your Bhapa is with him in the bedroom, trying to cheer him up. No one has eaten anything.'

Hearing Banti and Kalu, Udho came down.

'He won't listen to me,' he said throwing his hands up.

Kalu ran up the stairs and jumped onto the bed to lie beside Angad.

'Hey son, you don't want Baba and Dadi to stay hungry, do you?'

'I don't care. Everybody thinks they know you. Your politics makes people talk about us at school, about Mum,' said Angad.

Kalu took him in his embrace. His hand touched Angad's forehead. He felt the wet eyes and cheeks as he moved his fingers down, caressing his face.

'Son, what's the matter?'

'They say Mum wouldn't be dead if you hadn't married her. You killed her. Nana did it because you gave him no choice, they say.'

'They have nothing better to do,' Kalu said, wiping Angad's tears.

'If you didn't go make so many speeches, no one would know us. Then they wouldn't talk.'

'Yes, son, but the most important thing for me is what *you* think. You know the truth about your mum. She loved you so much. She wouldn't want you to not eat just because some idiot says something.'

It took some time, but Angad finally hugged him back.

'Look, Kalu's Bhapa. Look, they're coming down,' said Banti, jumping up from the sofa and walking to the kitchen to serve the evening meal.

Moments after they finished eating, the old grandfather clock struck the midnight chime.

'Goodnight, son. Sweet dreams,' said Kalu, tucking him in for the night.

'Love you, Papa.'

'Love you, too.'

Kalu picked up the review from the console and retreated to his bedroom. Time to wrestle the demons of academia, he thought. The review had undermined his faith in the nobility of academia, in the fairness of minds preoccupied by their search for the truth in their chosen fields. What Vashisht had written had no relationship to his teaching or the esteem in which he was held by his colleagues and students. Instinct told him the review was a hatchet job in the service of caste. It had happened because he was a Chamar running for a parliamentary seat. But he suspended judgement until after Symes and he met Gopal.

That night, in his dream, Simran and he made love. 'You're a good man with great instincts. Believe in your instinct,' she told him as they parted. He awoke face up in the exact spot he fell asleep in. Jumping up, he went directly to the phone and dialled Angad's principal.

'Bill, this is Kahla. Sorry to call you so early in the morning. Can we meet before school today?'

'Sure. How about 7:30?'

'See you then.'

Half an hour later he picked up the umbrella from the receptacle of the console and got into the car. Within a few minutes he was standing outside Bill Duncan's office speaking to his secretary when Duncan walked in. Kalu told him about Angad's complaint. Duncan knew about the insinuations regarding Simran's death.

'Dr Badhan, actually I wanted to alert you about the tension and pressure Angad might be experiencing. I've spoken to the erring student and his parents.'

'But the problems keep recurring, Bill. The teachers need to be educated about the stigma of caste just as they now understand racism.'

'We'll add a lecture on caste to the professional development events in the school. The problem would be to find a resource person. At the risk of pigeonholing you, may I ask you to talk to our teachers?'

'I don't particularly want to. But I'd do anything to help. Let me know the date well in advance.'

'Absolutely. You're a busy man, getting busier by the day. Oh, by the way, best wishes in pursuit of the nomination!'

A few minutes late for class, he was about to enter the lecture room when he spotted Gopal in the hallway.

'Oh Dr Badhan, Symes had suggested a meeting on Friday. Four pm. In his office.'

'Sure, I will see you then,' he said, walking into class.

Pacing the platform as he delivered the lecture that day, on class in history and the history of class in the Western European societies, several times he uttered the word caste instead of class.

'Remind me to talk about caste in history one day,' he told his students before exiting.

'Professor Sir, Professor Sir,' he heard Daler yell from behind and stopped.

'Sir, my dad would love it if you could come to our home for dinner Friday night. I know Gurbat is close to you. I've invited him too. Punjabi chicken curry, beer, Scotch... let me know if you need anything else!'

'No, that will do just fine, Daler. Friday, I think I might need Scotch. May I bring along my dad and son? I don't get to spend too much time with them.'

'Bring Banti aunty too, please. It'd be lovely to see her as well.'

'Oh thanks, but someone has to hold the fort.'

33

The wall clock above Symes's chair struck four. Kalu took his favourite chair opposite Symes, to his left. No political significance even though his politics was to the left of the Dean.

'Kahla, you ready?'

Kalu smiled.

'Why did he do this? Caste, you think?' asked Symes.

'I don't know, Robert, it would be unfair to ascribe motives without evidence.'

Gopal walked in. 'Hello, Dr Badhan, Dean Symes. Hope all's well. You called the meeting?'

'Please take a seat. No, all's not well. The review in Dr Badhan's case is totally off the mark, contrary to all the requisite indicia.'

'His attendance has been spotty and I spoke to students. They are dissatisfied with his teaching,' said Gopal.

'I didn't know we'd begun marking professors on how many lectures they miss. I thought only the quality of the final results mattered and in Dr Badhan's case they're excellent. And by the way, both President Cauldwell and I had preapproved his absences because of the special circumstances including at the time of the brutal and untimely loss of his spouse and now the nomination campaign. Then there's the question of his teaching. For years he's been rated the best in Mander College. Any other problems, Dr Vashisht?'

'No. Impossible, Dean, best professor. An...an...un... untouchable... I mean...that's not, uh... Sorry, I...'

They had never heard him stutter.

'I don't know what you're trying to say, Dr Vashisht. But seriously, withdraw the review in writing immediately or I shall go to the president and initiate the process of having you sacked!'

'Yes, yes, Dean, will do,' said Gopal and looked towards Kalu, who was now standing.

Gopal turned to the empty chair and then back to Kalu. Kalu shook Symes's hand and then extended it towards Gopal. The latter's hesitant hand limped into Kalu's. Gopal was still in his chair, staring at Symes when Kalu left.

Kalu didn't go to his office or the cafeteria. He walked home. As he opened the door Angad spotted him, his grin, and said, 'Papa, you look happy today.'

'Oh, that's because Bhapa and I are going to a party tonight. Would you like to come?'

'Oh, I don't know. Old Punjabi men sit there and talk about politics, India and gurdwaras. I'll stay with Dadi. She'll make me pranthas and kheer.'

'I'm going with you to a party?' yelled Udho from the sofa.

Kalu was quiet for a minute, wondering whether Udho would want to go to Daler's home. His humiliation in Daler's presence was still raw. For the lower-caste man, indignity was the very air he had breathed for centuries past. At the mere mention of Daler's invitation, the putridity of Banjhan's carcass pit, the stench from its piles of bones and rotten meat of skinned, dead cattle that forever lingered in his soul could waft back into Udho's nostrils.

'Bhapa,' Kalu said, preparing himself for Udho's reaction, 'I'm going to Daler's home. I'd told you his father had sent his apology for his silence at Sohan's home. He wants to see me and I want you to go with me.'

'That Mehar Singh Buttar sat there like Gautam Buddha. He didn't open his mouth. He could have at least said what Sohan did was horrible. He just sat there with his mouth shut. And you want me to go to a party at his house?'

The wrinkles on Udho's face had deepened.

'Bhapa, Mehar's sorry now. You're the one who keeps telling me to have fewer enemies.'

'I don't know anyone who forgives as easily as you. Simran disagreed with you when you forgave her father. And look what happened. My Angad lost his mother. I can't forgive. But if you insist, I'll go with you,' said Udho and sighed before getting up from the sofa and limping into the kitchen for a beer.

The limp looked more pronounced than it did in the three-piece, navy blue suit he had worn on the way to Hoshiarpur to make arrangements for him and Banti to travel to England. But maybe that was because at the time he must have been too preoccupied with escaping from Banjhan. Like ranch cattle, Banjhan had branded Udho, seared eternal humiliation into his body.

Lost in thought, Kalu walked upstairs to get ready for the evening.

Udho, wrinkled but clean shaven, Kalu, his face radiating youth dimmed only by a few greying hairs in the beard below his neatly tied turban—both men in blue three-piece suits were ready to leave for Daler's when the phone rang.

'Kahla, Daler asked me to pick you up. My better half is busy with her friends. Yours truly will party with you tonight. See you in ten.'

Soon, the three men dressed in three-piece suits, Raghbir wearing grey, were in the latter's car. A few minutes later, outside Daler's home, rubbing his hands to warm them up, Raghbir knocked on the door.

'Not that cold, Raghbir,' said Kalu.

'My friend Kahla...you're hot blooded and stubborn. No one else has the time to fight the battles you pick.'

'Some are thrust upon me,' said Kalu, as the door opened.

The gas fireplace was red hot. Gurbat was already there with his father. In the front room there were only males until Daler's sister, currently doing her 'A' Levels, poked her head into the room.

'Sat Sri Akal,' she said, leaning into the room from behind the door post.

The lighter skinned, petite nineteen-year-old looked more like forty-nine dressed in the traditional salwar kameez. Her braided, long hair fell to the front as she tried to hide behind the door post while extending the obligatory greeting. Unlike Daler, she wasn't allowed to party with boys, or even girls, on the weekends.

Kalu shook hands with everyone; Udho nodded a greeting and sat down.

'Professorji, we've bottles of Guinness. Shall we start with them?' asked Daler and brought out several opened bottles of beer.

'Puttar, I'll take a Scotch. Guinness is the beer of literate people. I've had it...but I was and still am an agootha chhaap,' said Udho.

'Would Johnnie Walker do?'

'*Haan!* I had taken one to India in 1952 when I brought Kahla and his Bibi here. We shared it in Banjhan.'

Kalu looked Udho's way and smiled. Udho's sunken eyes radiated through the wrinkles, grey eyebrows and invisible eyelashes. The others had had a few sips of beer and Udho of Scotch when Mehar said, 'Udho bhra, forgive me for remaining silent that day. I'm learning from Daler how bad we've been...and we've been bad. I'm sorry. I'm grateful you came tonight.'

'Uncleji, I'm sorry too. Sohan had no business raising his hand and hitting you,' said Daler.

Udho, who had been staring at his Scotch while others talked, looked up at the father and son.

'I thought we'd left all that behind in Banjhan but I was wrong. It's still with us. At least in Banjhan there were people like Chacha Hazara who fought this,' he said, placing his drink on the coffee table.

'Bhapa, even here we've people like Raghbir and Gurbat...and even Daler. They are fighting caste boundaries,' Kalu said.

'We'll see, son. I won't come between you and your friends and your hope. I wish you luck,' said Udho.

Kalu gave a slight nod, and decided it was best to talk about something else.

'I understand you wanted to talk to me,' he said, turning to Mehar.

Mehar told him about the marriage proposal from the Grewals and of his unhappiness at Daler's resistance. The portly Mehar was almost breathless by the time he finished the details of his friendship with the Grewals.

'Let the boy decide for himself. Kids need to make their own decisions. We're in Britain, not Banjhan, my friend,' said Udho.

Kalu took a deep breath and exhaled before saying, 'Thanks, Bhapa. Mehar Singh ji, you won't be surprised if I agree with Bhapa. Not because he is my Bhapa but because he's right. I don't know the father Grewal but I do know the daughter and I know Daler. I'd say it's a complete mismatch. Daler is bright, mature beyond his years and has the makings of a man who might do something for society, more than money, degrees or positions. He thinks of the world and the ways it needs changing, a thing larger than marriage and family. Let him pursue it.'

No one said anything; perhaps his frankness had left nothing to be said.

Piercing the silence he continued, 'Marrying her to him would be like hanging a tiny bell around the neck of a tall camel. My friend Daler is tall in intellect and wisdom.'

Mehar smiled, nodded, lifted his beer, said cheers and took a sip. Daler looked at Kalu and then Udho and nodded in a silent thank you. The food was ready. The men filled their plates and poured back into the front room. Daler's sister took hers and ate at the kitchen table.

A few minutes after the meal Kalu said, 'Raghbir, shall we?' as he got up to go.

'Brother Udho, thank you for coming. Your son makes us all proud.'

'Mehar, truth be told I was angry. I didn't want to come. I'm glad I came. In meeting there's healing.'

On the way home Raghbir told Kalu that he'd meet him the next week at the meeting of the nomination team. 'We're working long hours, burning the phone lines. It all looks good.'

The car sped. Like an honour guard, the lamp posts greeted it every few yards and lit the way.

34

Despite the calls made, letters written, meetings organized and addressed, the decision, due imminently was anyone's guess. The campaign committee was meeting in St Mary's Church, walking distance from Kalu's home. The granite exterior of the old church peered at him as he entered it as if trying to say, 'Welcome, boy from the hovel in Banjhan!'

He was late because Angad had needed help with his homework. He cleaned his fogged glasses with a handkerchief, placed the umbrella in a bulging receptacle and hung his raincoat on top of others on a peg. The door to the meeting room creaked open. All eyes turned, hands clapped and tongues cheered as if for a conquering war hero. The outcome of the battle was unknown and, according to Symes's sources, possibly some weeks away.

'In your absence we've had the meeting. You're only an aspiring nominee,' said Symes, well known for his playful sense of humour. His retirement from the deanship was some years away and the administration were so happy with him that they weren't going to castigate him for devoting some of his time to extracurricular matters such as a nomination or an election campaign for his able colleague from Mander. It only enhanced Mander's prestige. Being dean meant access to the faculty association, unlimited telephone calls and the standing that came with the office. And he was prepared to use it all. He needed Kalu to win; he had made it his own battle.

On the assembly line of grunt work, some folded the cyclostyled one-page letter—to Labour Party members and activists soliciting their support for Kalu—others licked and addressed the envelopes and yet others affixed the postage stamps. Kalu sat down on the empty chair between Janice and Cathy and began stuffing the envelopes. Helping Angad with homework had triggered memories of Simran. Seated between her two best friends, he imagined her in the church helping and cheering for his success. The phone on the wall rang. Being the nearest to it, Janice grabbed it. It was for Symes. His wife was on the phone. She spoke and he listened.

'The Party has made the decision. They were looking for me. My wife gave them the church number,' he said, hanging the receiver back on the mount.

In the din of speculation, conversations and anticipation in the room, the work of stuffing, licking and stamping resumed. Janice turned to Kalu and said, 'It's going to be fine, Kahla. I know you're worried.'

The eyes on her round face laser focused on Kalu, Cathy said, 'It'll be fine. No shame in losing...only in not even trying.'

The only child of two factory workers, Janice had been drawn to Simran and Cathy, one brown, the other working class. Fuelled by love of equality, her fealty to Labour had waned in the wake of Kalu's rejection as the nominee the last time he had campaigned for it. In reassuring Kalu, she was comforting herself. And so was Cathy, who too was invested in the outcome of the campaign. Remembering her bricklayer father, she looked at her hands, like her mother's, small and slim with long fingers.

Raghbir, Gurbat and other brown and black activists in the room saw themselves in Kalu. As for Symes and his wife, they had a special place for Kalu in their lives. Childless when they had first met him, they had come to see him as their own. He too gave them the respect ancient Indian culture extended to elders.

The man for whom all present had been hard at work for months, if not years, cast a glance at the room. In life he owed much, but his indebtedness to this roomful of people surpassed it all. The phone rang again. His moistened eyes looked towards it as Janice picked it up.

'Is Dr Badhan or Dr Symes there, please?' said the voice.

Janice gestured for Kalu to take it.

Kalu put it to his ear and said, 'Hello, Dr Badhan here.'

He listened to the voice and thanked it. Putting the receiver back in place, he waited for a split second, taking in the information, punched his clenched fists in the air and exclaimed, 'We...you've won the nomination.'

Despite the ensuing pandemonium, everyone noticed his moistened, smiling eyes. There were hugs all around.

Symes asked Gurbat and other young men to haul in the beer from the trunk of his car. Anticipating that the decision could come unexpectedly, as it in fact had, Symes had had it in the trunk for over a week. Beers in hand, the redundant nomination campaign committee reconstituted itself as the election campaign committee. The battle lines in the Bedford constituency had been drawn. Symes circulated his felt hat for the first donations to the campaign. From St Mary's Church, Kalu and company walked the few yards to the King's Arms. A smiling Symes stepped in through the creaking door followed by Kalu and the others. The owner and bartender nodded and smiled. The group talked and played darts over pints of beer late into the night. They had all had a few, Kalu the fewest. It was time to disperse. Janice and Gurbat wobbled behind the professor, the newly minted Labour nominee, up to his door.

Kalu heard birds chirp, the train come and go and the passengers board and disembark at St John's station. The candidacy barely hours old and the new campaign committee younger still, he had no campaign events for the day. With only an afternoon class to teach, the fatigue of months got the better of him. He lay face up in bed until the smell of skillet-fried pranthas from the kitchen wafted up the stairs and into the bedroom. He jumped out of bed, down the stairs and into the kitchen where he hugged Banti at the stove.

For the first time in years, he felt her hunched back. He had almost forgotten she had one though it had become more pronounced with age. She was good at concealing it.

'It doesn't hurt, I hope.'

'No, Kalu, only when I'm tired. I tell you all the time, Angad needs a mother. Even I'm going to need a daughter-in-law to take over the kitchen soon.'

Udho was already on the sofa sipping chai. Kalu poured himself a cup and began telling them about last night and the candidacy. As the story of the last evening advanced, he noticed Banti's hump straighten and Udho's wrinkles fade, at least a bit. Awakened by the noise, Angad was halfway down the stairs. Kalu saw him and asked, 'You okay, son? It's early, go back to bed. We'd wake you up.'

'Can't sleep with the noise you've been making. Did you say you are the candidate? Life at school is hard enough without it.'

'No, Puttar, good children don't say such things to parents,' said Udho.

Angad plunked himself next to Udho. Hugging Udho he said, 'Baba, I thought you're on my side. Papa's politics brings trouble.'

'Puttar, I'm proud of Kahla. My son's a big man now.'

'Still a Chamar who many Jats and Brahmins hate. I'm going to get ready for school. I've exams soon,' said Angad, and ran upstairs.

Part, Simran in stubbornness and Kalu in argumentativeness, Angad had been staying up late into the nights preparing for his 'O' Level exams. At his beck and call day and night, Udho and Banti kept him supplied with snacks and chai. Whenever he needed help with homework or preparations for the exams in Kalu's absence, all he had to do was to call Gurbat, Daler or Janice. Help was there for the asking and he did ask.

Kalu had forgotten that the papers of the next day's class awaited him for marking in the office. He got ready quickly. They ate a couple of pranthas each before Kalu drove Angad to school. Seated in the passenger seat, the boy spoke his mind.

'Papa, did you really have to do this political thing? What if someone decides to kill you?'

'No, puttar, it won't happen. We're going to be fine.'

'Really, Papa? The killed Mum.'

As he drove to college, Kalu couldn't shake off what Angad had said. He had never realized just how afraid his son was for him. How lonely it must've been for the child, he thought, until he revealed it a few minutes ago. How does one tell a child who lost his mother to murder, and that too at the hands of his grandfather, that everything will be fine?

At college, Kalu ran from the parking lot, up the stairs to his office and locked himself in to mark the papers. A red pen in hand, he sat down with the pile of papers in front of him. But he hadn't marked a single one even after the long hand of the office clock had gone one full circle. Angad's fear of the death of his remaining parent, his refuge, had frozen him. He imagined himself dead and Angad orphaned. Angad's imagined fate devastated him. But the fear of not marking the assignments too hung in the air. Marking was part of what earned him his salary. The salary brought everything into focus. Had death not been on his mind, the love of teaching alone would have been enough to begin marking the papers. But today, the mundane fact of earning his livelihood had to command him to do so.

He finished marking them well before his afternoon class and went looking for Robert Symes and Janice Charlesworth. Since being anointed candidate last evening, he hadn't spoken to anyone from his campaign committee. They might think him disinterested. They would be on the mark, too, for at least a few moments each day. In those moments he examined himself, his desires and fears. Often he felt he was obsessed with power, political power. He hated obsession, the opposite of rationality, a trait of his he approved of. He hadn't always been rational—cracking Karam's skull with the lathi; smashing the Westfalia camper's windshield. Perhaps his caste had made him hanker after others' approval to which being rational and well grounded seemed an easy path. Perhaps he was all an act. Right now, he was more than just disinterested.

The Dean was not in his office, so Kalu walked to Janice's office.

'Have you ever witnessed the fear of their only parent's death in the eyes of a child? I have, this morning, in Angad's eyes. Caste killed his mother. He thinks caste and politics may kill me,' he said to Janice, ignoring her updates about the campaign, which she had assumed was the reason for his visit. 'His fear terrifies me.'

'Kahla, why would anyone kill you?'

'For the same reason they killed Simran,' he replied, looking lost.

She took him by his arm and walked him to the cafeteria. The ordered coffees had not arrived when Robert came in.

'Aha, my office told me you were looking for me,' he said to Kalu.

'He's worried about the impact his political life's been having on Angad,' Janice said, summarizing the conversation they had had in her office.

'I saw Angad the other day...a grown, mature child. What's the problem?'

'Robert, Janice.' Kalu hesitated before saying, 'I don't think I should run. Angad needs me full time.'

'Less than twenty-four hours after the nomination...all the blood, sweat and tears...and you want to resign your candidacy? Go give your class an assignment and come back. We need to chat,' said Robert, and Janice nodded.

Kalu returned fifteen minutes later. After two more rounds of coffee and as many hours of discussion, Janice's promise that she would meet and speak to Angad once a week, and Robert's promise to have his wife Dianne do the same, getting up to go, Kalu said, 'You're right. I must deny the bastards the pleasure of seeing the back of me.'

35

In his world of classes and speeches, neighbourhood, public and private meetings, it was a thing of joy for Kalu to observe Angad, free from his 'O' Level exams, spend time with Udho and Banti. Together, they watched TV, Angad explaining the dialogues to them. On the weekends he and Udho went to the market and library. He hung around the kitchen more, to help the frail Banti. Janice Charlesworth and Dianne Symes, together and by themselves, visited him often, taking him out for coffee or lunch. It reinforced Kalu's determination to work even harder to win the parliamentary election. His victory would mean so much to the immigrants, progressives, people of colour and other minorities, he believed. It would also strike a blow against caste. His nomination had already dealt one: the so-called higher-caste lobby within Labour had failed to stop it.

Campaign tempo had accelerated. For several weeks, Kalu had been clocking nineteen-hour days, working and campaigning, running on adrenalin. Noticing him tired and cranky, Janice and Robert asked Kalu to take one day a week off.

'I can't rest until we win this bloody thing. There's more riding on it than I saw before... I see that now.'

'We all see it, Kahla, but you don't want to drop dead of exhaustion. The election is some months away. You've got to pace yourself.'

On his first day off two weeks later, he was resting on the sofa, reading the *Sunday Times*, when he noticed photocopies of two newspaper clippings on the table near the phone. One about news from the Canadian province of British Columbia, and the other closer to home, Bradford. The dates on them, written in hand, indicated they were not too old. He read them and reread them and then dropped them on his chest. Eyes closed, his clasped hands rested on them.

In British Columbia, a Sikh Jat father had hired a contract killer to send a kettle bomb as a wedding gift to his daughter and son-in-law. They had married against his wishes and 'below her station in life'. The kettle had blown up in the kitchen of the newlyweds, killing both of them. In the other clipping, a sixty-year-old divorced Sikh Jat from Bradford had married an untouchable woman, thirty years his junior, in India and brought her to England. Because of physical and emotional abuse at his hands, she had divorced him and made a life for herself. She was seeing an untouchable man whom she planned to marry.

'How dare she even dream of marrying a Chamar,' the man had been heard to say before his divorced wife disappeared without a trace. Apparently, he had killed her, cut her body up and stored it in his freezer.

Angad came down just then to make chai, the drink for the soul, as he had begun calling it. He had been reading Hazari's *Untouchable: The Autobiography of an Indian Outcaste*, which he found quite disturbing.

'Papa, were you crying in your sleep?' Angad saw tears streaming down Kalu's left temple.

Kalu sat up. Wiping his eyes with his shirt sleeve, he said, 'No, son, no. Did you put the clippings here?'

'Yes, Papa. I'd gone to the library. I thought you might like to know the conditions of lower castes and women are the same in Britain and Canada.'

Kalu stared at him.

'I'm making chai. Probably your soul is thirsting for it, too,' said Angad. They were joined by Udho as they talked and sipped the steaming chai.

'Hey, puttar, make another cup for each of us. Dadi is tired,' he said.

Angad obliged. It was time for a Hindustani show on TV that Banti never missed.

'Bibi, your hump and wrinkles...you should go for more walks. Angad, puttar, some days you should take Dadi along for a walk, not only Baba. She too knows stories of caste in Banjhan and Bharat. It's our past, yours and mine.'

'Not only past, Papa. It's our present, too,' Angad said, pointing to the clippings now back on the table.

'Papa, I've a question about your marriage to Mum,' Angad asked Kalu after a while, neither interested in the programme on TV.

'Ask.'

'I've been reading about caste... You know how everyone calls me Chamar? Both Jat and Chamar children do that actually. Mum was a Jat. Why am I a Chamar, not a Jat?'

'When a so-called upper caste marries down, neither is accepted in the upper caste. When Mum married me, I didn't go up. She came down. Therefore you're a Chamar. Jats will never accept you as one of them, except friends like Gurbat, Raghbir or Daler. And who knows, even they may shudder to imagine their children marrying you.'

'You knew all this when you married Mum?'

'Yes.'

'Then why did you marry and make her a Chamar?'

The question stumped Kalu. Why *did* he marry her? The question had occurred to him before, but he hadn't expected it from Angad. He wondered if the straightforward answer—love—would satisfy his precocious son. But Angad wasn't done.

'Did you marry her thinking your marriage might be exempt from the "marry down, go down" rule because of your education? And that it might lift you up and make you a Jat?'

Kalu remained quiet. Did he marry Simran to escape his caste? This increasingly felt like one of his internal monologues.

'Did you, Papa? Did you marry her to escape Chamarhood?'

'Angad, I didn't think about it at the time.'

'Or perhaps you did think, Papa. You thought it might make you a Jat.'

The TV screen showed an Indian interviewing another. About what, no one knew since Udho had turned off the volume to hear the discussion between Angad and Kalu. Kalu's eyes were focused on the screen.

'Okay, Papa, I've got to finish the last few pages of Hazari you had bought for me. It's quite interesting, even for a caste mongrel like me. Since I can't escape the past, I might as well learn about it. I'll speak more with Dadi and Baba too, but later,' said Angad, before running up the stairs.

Kalu resumed reading the *Sunday Times* which the clippings had distracted him from. Unable to resolve Angad's questions, nor able to make sense of what he was reading, he put the paper away. He dozed off after a while of blankly staring at the moving images on TV.

Banti was already in the kitchen cooking for the evening when he woke up.

'Bibi, please give me another chai,' Kalu said.

Udho limped into the kitchen to help Banti. Seeing Udho bring back his mug of chai, Kalu sat up. Angad joined them again just as he took his first sip. He had finished the book in the meantime.

'Papa, about caste and Sikhism...Sikhism rejects caste but Sikhs don't. So why wear a turban when it doesn't erase your caste? Baba is clean-shaven?'

Kalu knew his son to be a voracious reader, but this focus on caste was new.

'Angad, son, you're asking tough questions today. Save some for tomorrow.'

'I'm serious, Papa. For most Sikhs, the turban and unshorn hair don't make you their equal.'

Continuing to sip his chai, Kalu said, 'Just because others don't respect them one mustn't abandon the tools and symbols of equality. Giving them up and giving in is surrendering to evil.'

'I don't know, Papa. Symbols aren't equality. Equality has to be real. Among the Sikhs, it isn't,' said Angad.

He went back upstairs, not waiting for his chai. He clearly had something more interesting to do, Kalu thought. But he hoped he would stop haranguing his father. In the span of a few hours, he had twice sallied down the stairs from his bedroom, critiqued Kalu's and his life and retreated.

'Bhapa, would you like to join me for a Scotch?'

'Kahla, Scotch? How about a beer?'

'Bhapa, I'll take a Scotch and get you a beer. This boy...!'

'Yes!' Udho said, amused. 'You had no answers for his questions.'

With a glass of Scotch in his hand, Kalu nodded, extending a bottle of beer towards Udho. Father and son sat, Udho watching TV, Kalu staring at his own feet which once used to walk shoeless from the school to the Chamarli in the scorching dust of Banjhan's summer and the biting cold of Punjab's winter until Udho began sending money from England. He remembered the thing he liked about the turban. It protected his head from the summer sun and the freezing winter. But it did more. At the talkies in Mahilpur the turban allowed him any seat, not just at the rear in the untouchable row. Angad's words had rekindled those memories.

For the next few days, Kalu reflected on Angad's questions. They had sparked in him a searcher's zeal to look within. Peeling back layers of intellectual reasoning embedded inside him, about his beliefs, himself and the world, Kalu bared his soul to himself. Had he been on a mission to escape caste, bypassing it without confronting it? Was he, in fact, a coward? Teaching, campaigning and campaign committee meetings masked the turmoil within. But he persevered, abandoning neither the search fuelled by the inner turbulence nor the work of teaching and campaigning.

After the weekly campaign committee meeting on Monday evening at St Mary's Church, Kalu, Janice, Robert and Gurbat were downing a few beers at the King's Arms when Janice asked, 'Kahla, you look a bit lost. All okay?' Of the three at the table with him, Janice had known him and Simran the longest.

'Angad asked me recently whether I kept my turban and married Simran to escape Chamarhood. It's made me wonder.'

'Oh, Professor Badhan, stop thinking abouut the bloody castes. We've a campaign to run and win,' said the Jat Sikh Gurbat, looking up and scratching his shaved face.

'Untouchables can't stop thinking caste, Gurbat. We're constantly reminded of it. It dominates our existence!' said Kalu.

Robert and Janice looked into their beers and nodded.

'But don't worry, folks,' he said trying to lighten the mood. 'It won't affect the campaign. Role playing is my forte as an untouchable. From birth to death that's all we ever did for the upper-caste—' He held his tongue. It would have been un-parliamentary to say bloody upper-caste bastards.

Gurbat and Janice volunteered to walk him home. He declined the courtesy and set out alone.

36

The train had just made its midnight stop at St John's Station. Unable to sleep, Udho and Banti were watching the TV on mute, the sound being too much to bear for Udho's brain. Angad was pacing the hall between the kitchen and the sofas. He had called and left a message for Janice with her mother. He had called Robert too, but no one had picked up the phone.

The phone rang.

'Hello, Angad, you'd called.'

'Janice, Papa had gone to the campaign committee meeting. He hasn't come home. Do you know where he might be?'

'We all left King's Arms at the same time. He said he was walking home!'

Angad comforted Udho and Banti all night. He had just made the fourth chai of the night which Banti sat sipping while Angad wiped tears off her wrinkles. Udho didn't want more chai. So he poured him a Scotch instead. It sat there for an hour before Udho gulped it in one go. Udho and Banti kept snoozing on and off. Angad resumed his pacing and noticed a pile of papers on the dining table on the spot where he used to sit and help Udho run the hawala business. He recognized Kalu's handwriting. Kalu had scribbled and re-scribbled his name and its variations:

Kahla Singh
Dr Kahla Singh Badhan
Dr Kahla Badhan
Dr Kalu Singh
Dr Kalu Singh Badhan

There were mock ballots in the pile. Kalu had been working on how his name might appear on the parliamentary ballot. Angad heard the 7:00 am train pull into the station. He made another round of syrupy chai, the elixir for his soul, though today the soul's restlessness wasn't responding to it. Udho and Banti were up. He gave them another chai.

'Angad, puttar, save mine for Kahla. He'll be coming home soon,' Banti said, hiding her eyes behind the chunni.

Udho limped into the bathroom. Upon his return, he finished his chai, placed the mug near the phone and said, 'Where the hell is he?'

'Baba, I'm sure he'd be home soon. Want another chai?'

'No, Angad, can you phone Janice again? She might know now.'

'She might not, Baba, but I'll call soon, before she leaves for the college.'

Angad talked to the police, Janice, Robert and Raghbir. No one knew where Kalu had disappeared. The vigil on the ground floor of Kalu's home continued until, over twenty-four hours after leaving the King's Arms telling Janice and others he was going home, Kalu quietly unlocked the door of his home. Angad ran to the door and swung it open. Kalu stood before him without his turban, beard, brows and head hair.

'Papa, what happened?'

'You said the turban didn't erase caste. So I erased the turban.'

'But papa, what happened to the eyebrows?'

'Oh, but son, that was hair too, no? Go get me a chai, I'm famished. And Bibi, what happened to you?'

Udho and Banti had rushed to the door behind Angad. They had witnessed the exchange, the scene and the hairless Kalu. Wailing, Banti thrust her chunni into her eyes and collapsed on the floor. Kalu lifted her and put her on the sofa. Sitting beside her, he hugged and rocked her as she did him in childhood.

'What happened, son?' Udho asked. He hadn't believed a word of what Kalu had said to Angad.

'Bhapa, I'm all right. I'll tell you later. No need to worry.'

Telling them to sleep, he went to his bedroom. He spent the entire night looking at himself in the mirror, looking out of the window at the snow that fell but did not seem as white as before, and staring at the garlanded portraits of Ambedkar and Ravidas—the garlands appearing like nooses. In the morning he wiped his eyes dry, showered, put on a three-piece suit, descended the stairs and asked, 'Where is my chai, son?'

'Papa, coming,' said Angad putting his own mug down.

'Angad, make another round for me and Dadi too. You're such a good chai maker,' said Udho grinning ear to ear.

'Look, I'm fine. I'm going out for about an hour and will be back soon,' Kalu said to the family when they'd had their chais.

'No, Papa, I want to go with you.'

'No, I'm quite safe. I'll be back soon and tell you everything.'

Kalu borrowed Udho's gray felt hat to match his gray suite and walked to the front door. Before opening it, he turned and ran up the stairs. In front of the mirror on the dresser sat Simran's make-up accessories, untouched for years. With the black eyebrow pencil he drew his eyebrows before driving off. The car turned towards Mander College and stopped. He couldn't go to the college in the shape he was in. He turned the car around and sped on. In a few minutes, he stopped in the parking of the police station. He asked for Sergeant Sweeny. The Deputy Chief of Bedford Police was in, said the receptionist, and went inside to tell him someone was there to see him.

'What can I do for you?' Sweeny said, walking out to the front.

'Deputy Sweeny, Dr Kahla Badhan,' said Kalu, extending a hand to shake Sweeny's.

Sweeny shook his hand, examining him from head to toe.

'Ah, underneath you do look just like us. What happened to your turban and beard? The temples won't like you one bit now—if they ever did.'

'Chief, let's go into your office.'

The receptionist brought the two coffees Sweeny had requested. Kalu took the felt hat off. Sweeny noticed the pencilled eyebrows. Eyes wide and mouth open, he began writing down the events as described by Kalu. His head kept shaking as he asked, listened and wrote. He kept requesting more coffee for both of them. It took an hour and a half and eight mugs of coffee between the two of them to commit the detailed story to paper. Sweeny pushed the pad in front of Kalu to read and sign.

It read: 'On Monday night, as I walked from King's Arms towards my home, unidentified men—they spoke Punjabi, their voices I didn't recognize but I could tell there were three of them—ambushed and blindfolded me from behind. One of them stuck in my neck what he said was a gun. It felt it like one. I was pushed into what felt like a delivery van. They drove for about fifteen minutes before dragging me out in a place that was quiet except for the chirping of some birds. As I was being pushed through what felt like a door sill, I heard a motor vehicle go by. I was forced to lie down face up on the carpet. The wood floor under the carpet creaked as they or I moved.

'"We're going to shave your beard, hair and eyebrows off. We won't touch the rest of your dirty, polluting body, you bloody Chamar. First you married a Jat woman. She was killed but you were spared. You didn't learn anything because you had the audacity to compare Pritam Singh's daughter to a mere bell around the neck of a tall camel; that marrying her off to Daler would be like tying a bell around the camel's neck. How dare you, bastard Chamar?"

'I heard the buzz of an electric machine. Soon they were shaving my beard and head hair off. I realized the sound came from the electric shaver. One of them held my eyes closed with his hands as they shaved off my eyebrows. All the while the gun-like object was pushed against my body. They told me that being a Chamar, I was inherently dirty. Therefore, they would not shave my armpits or crotch. Once shaved, I was dragged and shut in a narrow place, like a closet. The place seemed empty but suddenly came alive with men's voices and the clanging of beer and liquor bottles. I suspected they were celebrating what they had done to me. I didn't recognize any voices. After several hours of partying, the same three men—I could tell from their voices—drove for over thirty minutes and dropped me on the side of the road. They told me not to move until I had counted to a thousand. I counted to two hundred and untied the blindfold. I was on the other side of the motorway from what looked like Kempston. The vehicle was long gone.'

'Dr Badhan, I'm so sorry. Obviously it's the Grewals who did this or had it done,' said Sweeny.

'Oh, by the way, I forgot to mention that there was a meeting some time ago, to which I had been invited to explain why I had insulted the Grewal girl by comparing her to a mini bell. I said I believed what I had said to be true in terms of her and Daler's intellectual capabilities. Sorry, I had missed that.'

'Excellent, I'll note it down in my report. We'll pursue it and will be in touch.'

'Thank you, Deputy Sweeny.'

He drove back home and invited Janice, Robert, Raghbir and Cathy to a meeting at his home in the evening. He then sat Angad, Banti and Udho down. Handing a copy of his written statement to Angad he explained to Banti and Udho what had happened.

'Papa, I feel like shooting these bastards,' said Angad.

'I feel the same, son, but it won't help end caste and hate.'

He hugged Angad and wiped his eyes dry with a handkerchief. Banti looked away. Kalu went and hugged her and wiped her tears too. Udho limped away to the kitchen, poured water in a glass and gulped it. Kalu asked Angad to make some chai. They sat for several hours, snacking and drinking chai, Kalu busting jokes—how he could now get an acting job in Hollywood replacing Yul Brynner, or at least Telly Savalas of bald Theo Kojak fame. He said he would prefer Yule Brynner's spot. He felt close to the famed actor for he was a Roma—whose ancestors were sub-continental Indians who had been brought as slaves out of India by different conquerors beginning with Mahmud of Ghazni.

The members of the campaign committee arrived at 7:30 pm. Kalu, still with pencilled eyebrows, wearing a three-piece suit, gave the copy of his written statement to them. They read in silence and shook their heads.

'Are you all right?' asked Janice.

'As good as I look. I have had to think a bit, I must admit. No, I'm not quitting. I'll show the bastards. But you'll have to hold the fort in public until my eyebrows are back, at least a shade. It might take a week or a bit longer. Until then, I can't teach. But for you all, I'm at the other end of the phone at home. Janice, please send me any reading or writing I need to do while waiting for the hair to come back. Odd for a Sikh, eh, waiting for the hair to grow?'

Udho joined them for some Scotch when the meeting was over. Angad grabbed a beer, the first of his life, and milled about. The party ended just before midnight.

The house became quiet. Alone in his bedroom, with his own thoughts, Kalu recalled something he hadn't told Sweeny and was glad for it. He had asked the taxi from Kempston to take a detour towards the Bedford City Centre and stop near the Great Ouse Bridge. He had stepped out of the taxi, walked to the top of the bridge and stood there thinking of the steel-tipped lathi he had dropped into the Great Satlej in Punjab on his way to Delhi. He imagined the lathi rising up from the Ouse into his hands. In his fancy, he found the abductors, beat their skulls to pulp and dropped the bloodied lathi back in the Ouse.

After lying awake in his bed for two hours and staring at the framed portraits of Ravidas and Ambedkar, he jumped up and ran down to the dining room. He grabbed the papers including the mock ballots on the dining table, and began working on them. By the morning he had the name as it would go on the ballot: Dr Kahla Chamar. He shared the decision with the committee. Janice asked why; Robert wondered whatever had gotten into him; Raghbir thought his spelling of the name Kumar as Chamar was a typing error. He had brought the truth of his Chamarhood into his name for all to see. Badhan was no longer needed to signify Chamarhood. Chamar itself would do. He was done fleeing, escaping or dressing up caste in surnames, unshorn hair or turban.

The campaign committee bent to his will.

The Prime Minister called the election. On election night, Kalu was declared the winner. In the morning, Angad went out and bought the Bedford daily paper. Kalu watched as Angad showed Udho and Banti a clean-shaven Kalu's photograph along with the headline on the front page: 'Dr Kalu Chamar Our New MP—The Change Has Come'.

Angad made chai. Between the sips of chai, the humpbacked Banti, the limping Udho, the hairless Kalu and the adolescent Angad danced. When Robert, Janice and Gurbat knocked on the door to congratulate him, Udho Chamar and his son, Kalu Chamar MP, were standing with raised glasses, about to down neat double Johnnie Walkers.

you'll have to hold the fort in public until my eyebrows are back, at least a shade. It might take a week or a bit longer. Until then, I can't teach. But for you all, I'm at the other end of the phone at home. Janice, please send me any reading or writing I need to do while waiting for the hair to come back. Odd for a Sikh, eh, waiting for the hair to grow?'

Udho joined them for some Scotch when the meeting was over. Angad grabbed a beer, the first of his life, and milled about. The party ended just before midnight.

The house became quiet. Alone in his bedroom, with his own thoughts, Kalu recalled something he hadn't told Sweeny and was glad for it. He had asked the taxi from Kempston to take a detour towards the Bedford City Centre and stop near the Great Ouse Bridge. He had stepped out of the taxi, walked to the top of the bridge and stood there, thinking of the steel-tipped lathi he had dropped into the Great Satlej in Punjab on his way to Delhi. He imagined the lathi rising up from the Ouse into his hands. In his fancy, he found the abductors, beat their skulls to pulp and dropped the bloodied lathi back in the Ouse.

After lying awake in his bed for two hours and staring at the framed portraits of Ravidas and Ambedkar, he jumped up and ran down to the dining room. He grabbed the papers including the mock ballots on the dining table, and began working on them. By the morning he had the name as it would go on the ballot: Dr Kalu Chamar. He shared the decision with the committee. Janice asked why; Robert wondered whatever had gotten into him; Raghbir thought his spelling of the name Kumar as Chamar was a typing error. He had brought the truth of his Chamarhood into his name for all to see. Badhan was no longer needed to signify Chamarhood. Chamar itself would do. He was done fleeing, escaping or dressing up caste in surnames, uniforms, hair or turban.